The Heartbreak Hotel

EMILY WRIGHT

THE HEARTBREAK HOTEL

For information contact:
Emily Wright
www.emilywrightwriter.co.uk
Purple Clouds Press
www.purplecloudspress.co.uk

Book and cover design by Diana L
Published by Purple Clouds Press
ISBN: 978-1-7395624-9-6

First Edition: March 2025

Subscribe to my newsletter to stay in touch and also receive a free sapphic novella!

www.emilywrightwriter.co.uk/contact

'Flowers grow back, even after the harshest winters. You will, too.'

— Jennae Cecilia

CHAPTER ONE

Ella

Ella had a habit of overreacting. She probably should've bitten her tongue when the old man took too long in the checkout queue, or when the teenager pulled out on her at the roundabout the other week. These things happened, she supposed. She could've exercised more patience, too, when the freckled barista dropped her steaming Arabica bean blend on the floor, speckling her expensive work heels with coffee.

But Ella was not overreacting now.

"You've got to be fucking kidding me," she snapped, catching the slight widening of Maeve's eyes.

Her boss cleared her throat, crossing one long leg over the other. Those piercing brown irises met Ella's again. "I'm not kidding, Ella. Starting one week today, you've been made redundant from Switch Studios." She held Ella's gaze coolly, despite the rage that was no doubt burning there.

Maeve was probably used to the anger. There'd been no shortage of arguments that year they'd dated. Particularly when Ella found out she'd been sleeping with the marketing company's receptionist as well. Annabelle was a slightly younger, slightly perkier version of Ella, except less confrontational and more flexible, too, if the constant posting about yoga on her social media was anything to go by.

Ella hadn't overreacted then, either. Deliberately overwatering all Maeve's office plants and throwing her belongings out of the office window barely scratched the surface. Of course, it would've been much more impressive if Maeve's belongings hadn't been just a sparingly used toothbrush and an old, oversized university T-shirt she slept in on the rare occasions she agreed to stay at Ella's place.

Maeve had always made it clear what she thought about Ella's smaller apartment.

Ella unclenched her jaw. "You can't be serious."

"I'm afraid so."

Ella shook her head, aggressively pacing the plush

carpet in Maeve's office. With a huff, she tucked her cherry-red hair behind her ears, only for it to spring straight back out again. It was in dire need of dyeing, the brown roots thick at her scalp, but this was far down on her list of things to do. She'd promised herself she'd book in with the hairdresser right after she'd finished with the McAndrews' file. Having to come up with catchy posts and hooks for a mind-numbingly boring garage-door company had zapped a lot of her brain power. Not that any of that mattered now.

"This is bullshit. Why me? What are you doing this for?" Ella stopped pacing and snorted, a habit her mother scolded her for whenever she got the chance. "Because of Annabelle?"

"No. It's got nothing to do with Annie."

Ella's insides boiled. She despised Maeve when she called Annabelle that. She'd never given her an affectionate nickname when they were dating.

"Bullshit."

"Ella. It doesn't have anything to do with her." Maeve's soft breath as she rose from her navy chaise-longue made Ella pause. "It's come from the higher powers. The directors say we're on a decline. We have to make cuts."

Ella dropped her head and pressed her lips together, trying to bite back a comment about Maeve's daddy dearest, one of the company directors. She'd always had a suspicion he didn't like her. Was this to do with her comments at the Christmas party? If he didn't want to get found out, he shouldn't have been letting his not-wife jingle his bells out in the open hallway.

I guess the apple doesn't fall far from the tree.

"I am genuinely sorry about this," Maeve continued. "I knew nothing about it."

Ella glanced up, inhaling at Maeve's sharp, triangular jawline, which was all too close to her. She followed the straight edges, admiring her pale cheekbones, before landing back on her eyes. A tingle ran from her sternum down into her stomach, and she cursed it. She cursed this woman for having any physical effect on her whatsoever. Her body had some nerve reacting that way.

Stupid heart.

She took a step back, brushing against one of the senselessly big ferns that crowded Maeve's office. She'd taken great joy in murdering one of those last year. This one would be next on her list.

"If there was anything I could do to keep you, I would," Maeve said, her gaze softening as it fell over Ella's form. "But it's out of my hands."

"Bullshit," Ella said again, but softer this time. The rare glimpse of the other side of Maeve, hidden deep beneath the business pantsuit and perfectly straight jet-black hair, was messing with her head. Her brain worked overtime to block certain memories of their relationship. The two of them snuggling together on a ski lift in La Plagne; fucking in Maeve's super-king-sized bed and then watching reruns of *Grey's Anatomy*; the adorable way

Maeve's nose scrunched when she really laughed. Ella wanted to bury these moments so deep they wouldn't resurface. It hurt too much to face them every day. Especially when it was all lies.

Nausea crept into her throat, and she swallowed it down. *How has it come to this?* Maeve knew the sexual power she possessed, and she wasn't afraid to use it. That was how she'd convinced Ella that workplace romances were the real deal two years ago. Look how well that turned out.

Not only had her boss stomped on her heart, but she'd also convinced her to keep working for her, to stay late, watching her ex and new girlfriend leave the office together, all while trying to go above and beyond… And for what?

A shitty end-of-year bonus and the rapidly fading potential of getting back together with Maeve?

At this point, Ella wasn't even second-best. She was fourth, fifth, *sixth*. The type that didn't win any rosettes for just the effort of participation.

Maeve gave Ella one of her signature half-smiles. The type that used to make her knees weak in the morning meetings. "You know how much I've loved working with you—"

"Let me stop you there." Ella exhaled, trying to regain her composure and push away any tingly feelings threatening to re-emerge. Getting laid had also been embarrassingly low on her list of priorities recently. "I don't wanna hear it, Maeve. I didn't believe you when you said you and Annabelle were a one-time thing, and I don't believe that you didn't know this was coming. How could you not? You've always been such a sickly little daddy's girl." Maeve narrowed her eyes, but Ella continued, the fire in her belly flaming again. "I've worked my arse off for this company. Stayed here when you asked me to, even with you parading Bendy Wendy in front of my face."

Her eyelids pricked, but she refused to cry in front of Maeve. Never again.

"Ella, don't be like that. It's nothing personal."

She scoffed. "Of course it's personal. You fucked me, then I pissed off your dad, so of course I'm the first one to go."

Maeve nibbled at her lip. "Blake is leaving too," she mumbled.

"Blake? You're seriously lumping me in the same category as Blake? The very definition of hopeless." The intern had only been at the company a few weeks, spending his first day going up and down in the lift, as he couldn't remember the correct floor. The rest of his time was consumed in a continuous loop of forgetting and resetting his computer password.

Putting them in the same box was ludicrous.

"It's not like that. You mean a lot to me, Ella. I promise you."

Realising she was clenching her fists, she relaxed them and met Maeve's gaze. Her boss had closed the distance between them, her perfume permeating Ella's senses, her tall frame towering over her in that dominating way that used to drive Ella crazy. But instead of arousal or anger at her boss trying to get the edge over her the only way she knew, a fuzzy sadness overrode her emotions.

"You *promise* me?" Ella sighed. "Remember when you promised you'd always love me? That you didn't want to be with anyone else? Some fat good that did me, eh." She pushed her hand against Maeve's chest, who fell a step backwards. "Goodbye, Maeve."

Ella turned to leave, catching the eye of one of her soon-to-be ex-colleagues noseying through the glass window. She briefly wondered how much the people in the office knew about their relationship. Or what they thought about her. Not that it mattered now.

"Ella, wait." Maeve's voice stopped her at the door. "Here." She handed Ella a white letter that had been sitting on her desk. "It's your official redundancy notice."

Ella looked at the piece of paper, then at the beautiful face of her ex-girlfriend/ex-boss. "You know where you can stick that."

And she opened the door, slamming it shut behind her before marching down the hallway. Tears threatened her eyelids again, but she clenched her jaw, meeting the eyes of anyone who dared look her way.

When she walked into work that morning, she'd never expected it would be for the last time. *What am I supposed to do now?* She stepped into the lift, blew out a breath at her dishevelled reflection in the glass, and pulled her phone from her pocket.

She knew exactly who to call.

***

"What a complete and utter cow!" Winnie slammed two more orange cocktails down on the table as she reclaimed the seat in front of Ella. Her long blonde hair was half-tucked inside her shirt like she'd got dressed in a hurry, but Winnie always had a habit of looking like she'd just rolled out of bed. "Just when I thought that lanky grasshopper couldn't get any worse."

"I know." Ella sucked hard on the straw, taking a few deep gulps. She could barely taste the alcohol over the fruit juice, but knowing Winnie, there'd be more than a generous helping. "What's in this one?"

"I'm not too sure, but I know it definitely has tequila." She offered Ella a toothy smile before nodding towards the bar. "It's something Calvin's been working on."

Tequila and emotionally unavailable bartenders were two of Winnie's favourite things. The friends-with-benefits arrangement Winnie had with the older, forty-something barman usually resulted in stronger—and cheaper—drinks for them both. Unless Calvin had found out about one of Winnie's rendezvous with the other staff. For a relationship that required a mutual understanding of low commitment, it was surprising how often the two ended up squabbling like an old married couple.

But Ella couldn't bring herself to ask about her best friend's latest bisexual love affairs. Her mind was stuck on that lanky, power suit-wearing, sex magnet of a grasshopper.

Normally, Winnie's nickname for Maeve made Ella laugh. Today, it made her belly churn in ways she didn't know how to articulate. It was much easier when she was angry, but now a few hours had passed, the anger, along with the threats to sue Maeve and her stupid Switch Studios, had trickled away, leaving these sickly sad feelings swirling in their absence.

Was this Ella's fault? Her motor mouth often ran up a bill without permission, like it had with Maeve's dad, and her lifestyle choices didn't exactly scream healthy living compared to Annabelle's… but multipacks of chocolate buttons and late nights in the office went hand in hand. Maybe she should've been more mindful; her metabolism wasn't what it used to be. Annabelle and her perfect white teeth were always munching something wholegrain when she manned the reception.

"Well." Winnie leaned back in her chair, raising her already half-empty glass to Ella's. "Now you don't have to see Maeve ever again."

Was that why Ella's stomach felt like a boat on a stormy sea? Not going into the office meant never seeing Maeve again. Ever. *Never again.*

The finality made her squeeze her glass tighter between her fingers.

"Is it me, Winn?" she asked, unable to look up from the ice in her cocktail. "Am I the problem?" Tears swelled before her eyelids, and she hated how small and pathetic her voice sounded.

Winnie pushed her glasses up her nose, studying Ella with large, angular eyes. Her gaze softened. "Listen. Maeve wouldn't know a good thing if it sat on her face, breaking those stupidly sharp cheekbones. That woman isn't good for you. She never appreciated how great you are at your job, even before she started taking her liberties. You deserve a million times better. A trillion. Quazril…whatever comes after that."

Ella sniffed. "I'm not sure."

Ella used to think what Winnie said was true. If the shoe were on the other foot, she'd be telling her best friend the same thing. But the two of them saw life differently. Winnie spent most of her time outside—as a professional dog-walker, she didn't have much choice—but Ella couldn't think of anything worse. Winnie was carefree, still living at her parents' house, enjoying life day-to-day, barman to barwoman, but Ella needed structure, purpose.

Without her job, something she'd invested four years of her time in, and something she was good at, what else did she have to do with her life? It's not like she had any childhood dreams to pursue—her brother Devin was the creative genius—or a significant other to distract her. She couldn't even remember the last time she'd come with a real-life person and not from her vibrator, and even that was gathering dust in her bedside table.

She'd been asked many times why she didn't leave her job after she and Maeve split, and Ella had always claimed that it was a pride thing. That she didn't want Maeve to 'win' the break-up. She felt stupid now. Not only had she lost most things in her life to Maeve, but she was also, rather embarrassingly, still hung up on her.

"Do you want me to key her Mercedes?" Winnie asked, raising an eyebrow. "I'm sure some of Calvin's rugby lads could rough her up too. Just say the word."

Ella gave her a small smile. It was tempting. But even if she did accept the offer, she doubted Winnie could be organised enough to orchestrate something like that. She'd probably key Maeve's dad's car by accident and get chased out of their estate by their three burly Dobermanns.

Winnie finished her drink and leaned forward, grasping Ella's hands. "I really hate seeing you like this."

"I'm sorry. I'll snap out of it soon."

"No, Ella, that's not what I mean." She sighed. "We said this was bound to happen at some point. It was only a matter of time."

Ella's eyes narrowed. "We? Who's we?"

"Me and Chezza."

"Fuck's sake, Winn." She huffed, shaking her head. "Can you please stop talking to my mum without me? It's so weird you have this secret little club."

"You could always join us." Winnie couldn't hide the smug smirk on her face. "It's not weird."

"It's a little weird. And her name isn't Chezza, it's Cheryl."

Winnie let go of Ella's hands and gave a playful shrug. Clearly, she and Cheryl wouldn't be cancelling their monthly salsa class any time soon. "Well, whatever. Me and Cheryl agreed that when this inevitably turned to shit—"

"Charming."

"—which it has…" Winnie gave her best attempt at a stern look, furrowing her dark brows in a way that was almost comical. "You should go to Sandy Springs."

Ella groaned. She didn't know what was worse. The fact that her best friend and her mum were still talking about her behind her back, or the fact that they were trying to maroon her on some lonely hearts' island for hippies.

"Not this again. I'm fine. I don't need to go sing Kumbaya round a campfire."

Winnie ducked under the table to rummage in the decade-old, tattered bag by her feet. Ella's stomach flopped when she slapped a white letter onto the table.

She didn't want to see any more white letters today.

"What is that?" she asked. She assumed her best friend wasn't going to give her a week's notice to terminate their friendship.

"You don't need to look so panicked." Winnie chuckled. "It's your Ella reset button."

When Ella didn't pick up the letter, Winnie unfolded it and read aloud in a deep and terrible American accent. "'Find yourself at a crossroads with nowhere to turn?'"

"Jesus Christ," Ella muttered, having a sip of her drink.

"'Dive into the transformative power of energy healing and mindfulness, immersing yourself in the natural beauty of the island of Sandy Springs, Portugal. Reset your life by—'"

"Alright, alright. That's enough."

Winnie looked up from the paper. "What do you think?"

"I don't need to reset my life." Even as Ella said it, she felt like a fraud. Yes, she had lost all sense of purpose and hope in the last twenty-four hours, but that didn't mean she needed this.

"It's already paid for," Winnie declared, folding the paper and placing it back on the table.

"What?"

"Chezza—erm, Cheryl—prepaid the course for you. All you need to do is choose your dates and pack your bags."

Ella stared at Winnie blankly, her brain struggling to compute what she'd just said. She shook her head. "Mum's been relentless ever since Devin got his new job, but I never thought you two would gang up on me like this."

Winnie sighed. "It's not like that. Your mum cares about you. She just worries." When Ella didn't reply, Winnie continued. "It's basically a free holiday. See it like that. Three weeks in the Portuguese sun, the sea at your doorstep. Cocktails." She lifted her eyebrows. "You deserve a holiday, to unwind a little. Then you can come back ready to boss life again."

"So, you and my mum have just been…waiting…for this to happen?"

Winnie gave her a sad smile. "Don't be like that. We just want the best for you."

Ella let out a humourless laugh. "And you really think that would be me, on this mindreading-power island thing?"

"If you come back able to read minds, I think that will be pretty useful."

Ella took a long pull from her straw, savouring the fruity flavour. She didn't want to be ungrateful. She just hated taking handouts from her parents; she'd worked hard to establish her own life, without their help or money. Clearly her mother still thought her choices were disappointing, but not everyone could be a superstar doctor like her brother Devin.

However, she supposed the trip *was* already paid for… and cocktails on the beach sure did sound nice. The last time she went away was years ago, when she went skiing with Maeve.

Don't think about that lanky grasshopper.

"Thank you," Ella said, forcing herself to smile. "I really do appreciate you looking out for me."

"Always." Winnie placed her hand on hers and squeezed. "Does that mean you're going to go?"

Ella finished her drink, finally tasting the sting of the tequila resting in the bottom. "Fine, I'll go. It's not as if I have anything better to do."

She really hoped she wasn't going to regret it.

CHAPTER TWO

Ella

Ella pushed her sopping hair back from her face, flinging water droplets through the air like bullets. She could hardly breathe through the rain pouring from the skies. She couldn't recall the last time she'd done so much exercise either, never mind while lugging two giant suitcases and battling the elements.

Where are the staff?

Since Duarte had dropped her and Pauline by the dock what felt like a lifetime ago, she'd not seen another soul. The Portuguese captain had barely spoken a word of English, as demonstrated by his misunderstanding of the words "slow down" as he careened over the choppy waves. Not only did Ella's undercooked plane panini threaten to resurface, but she'd also lost her favourite wide-brimmed summer hat to the North Atlantic ocean.

Duarte's manic laughter had temporarily drowned out the sound of Pauline, though; the fifty-something brunette had been crying non-stop since they boarded the flight in Manchester. Ella had the pleasure of being Pauline's confidante, learning all about the woman's recent divorce.

What a treat.

The wail of Pauline's sobs faded as Ella stomped ahead, flip-flops slapping against the wooden slats. Surely they couldn't be far now? Her feet ached, blisters forming between her toes as she forced herself up the incline. Had she known she'd be hiking up this hill soaked to the bone—dragging not only her hefty suitcase behind but Pauline's, too, after the woman had struggled to carry it— she would've thrown herself overboard with her beautiful hat.

Maeve had said she looked like a young Audrey Hepburn in that hat.

Anger spiked up her spine. *Fucking Maeve. This is all her fault.*

Sandy Springs looked nothing like the pictures on the website, though Ella was struggling to see through the rain pelting her in the face. Dark, thick clouds blocked the light from the sky, making the air muggy.

Isn't Portugal supposed to be sunny? What gives?

Her muscles burned as the walkway evened out, revealing a handful of wooden cabins through the fog and a giant "Welcome to Sandy Springs" sign hanging from two towering trees.

"Thank you, baby Jesus," she whispered, stopping for a second to pluck her wet shirt from her skin. She couldn't wait to sit down and neck a cocktail or six to wash this shitty day off her.

Hearing Pauline's heavy Darth Vader breathing draw closer, Ella forced her aching feet to move and her arms to drag their cases. She'd hoped that carrying her luggage would help the woman keep up. As annoying as Pauline's sobs were, she didn't want her falling behind. She had shared her salt and vinegar Pringles with Ella on the plane, after all.

Ella gritted her teeth against the pain. *Nearly there. Tequila sunrises await.*

Her suitcase caught on a raised wooden slat, slipping out of her hand and off the path. "No!" she shouted, lunging after it and tumbling down the grassy verge headfirst, with Pauline's suitcase falling after her. Bushes and stones scraped at her skin, poking her ribs and tangling in her hair. When she stopped rolling, landing at the bottom in a heap with Pauline's mammoth suitcase on top of her, she screamed. She spat sand from her mouth, wiped her tongue on her arm, and spat out even more sand, then screamed again, frustration echoing through the rain and trees. Everything hurt.

She screamed at Maeve, at losing her job, at Winnie and her mother for convincing her to come on this stupid trip. She thrust a fist into the sand next to her, connecting against a rock instead.

"Fuck's sake!" She nursed her hand between her knees, her chest aching from all the exertion.

She didn't care anymore. She was just going to lie here in the sand until bears came to eat her. *Do they even have bears in Portugal?* Knowing her luck, probably not. She'd have a slow and painful exit from Earth listening to Pauline's whining.

"Golly. Is my suitcase alright?" Pauline asked, appearing over her, mascara dripping down her pale white cheeks. "That was quite a little tumble, Ellie."

Ella clenched her jaw, gritting more sand beneath her teeth. "I told you, it's Ella."

"God, I'm sorry. My mind's been a sieve ever since the divorce with Albert."

You don't say. Ella wanted to cry. This wasn't worth a lifetime's supply of Pringles.

"Is everything alright?" a perky voice asked. "I heard screaming."

Ella looked up to find a woman standing there, cast in shadow. "Do I look alright?" she barked. She couldn't make out the colour of the woman's hair in the darkness, but it fell in loose beachy waves far past her shoulders.

The woman carried on, undeterred by the venom in Ella's tone. "Here, let me help you up." Warm hands gripped her arms, lifting her easily to her feet. "You both picked a brilliant night to arrive. Let me guess—you're from England?"

"Yes, we are," Pauline jumped in.

"Ah, that explains the downpour then."

Ella couldn't place the accent. It sounded English but with small energetic inflections hinting at someplace else. She attempted to dust herself off, but it was useless. The water and sand had clumped together, sticking between every crack and crevice.

The woman laughed, and Ella's head snapped round to the sound. How could this person be laughing? She could make out her profile now, her face lit by the moonlight that had appeared from behind the clouds and was glancing through the canopy.

"We wondered where you'd both gotten to," the woman said. "Romeo was supposed to meet you at the docks, but I'm guessing something else happened."

"I'll tell you what happened," Ella breathed, anger seeping into her chest. "I had the flight from hell, boarded a boat with a madman for a captain, lost my favourite hat, got caught in a torrential downpour, rubbed my feet red raw, then fell down a cliff. What part of this is supposed to be a holiday?"

Her words rang out into the night. The pitter-patter of rain against the wooden slats filled the silence that followed. At least it was slowing now.

"What was wrong with the flight?" Pauline asked.

"And a cliff is a bit of a stretch." The woman studied

Ella's face, her eyes a dark, stormy sea. "Have you hurt yourself?"

Her feet hurt, her arms stung like she'd lost a fight with a street cat, and her entire body was cold and uncomfortable, with so much sand in her pants, she was gonna have the smoothest shave down there in years, but all she could do was sigh. The last thing she wanted was to spend hours in some wooden cabin being checked over by someone whose first-aid qualification had been purchased online. She needed a drink. A Winnie-strength extra tequila-type drink.

"I'll survive," she said. Her focus fell on the name badge pinned to the woman's vest. Riley.

"There you go. Oh, here." Riley leaned closer. "You've something in your hair." With a gentle tug, she untangled a twig and discarded it. "Shall we get going? This is amazin'." She plucked up their suitcases like they were made of candy floss and indicated for the two of them to walk.

Ella assumed she worked here and wasn't just some nutjob roaming the island about to steal all of her underwear, so she followed her through the trees.

"How is this amazing?" she asked once they were back on the path.

"I've never heard of a more obvious selection of signs. Your familiar spirit is leading you."

She snorted. "My familiar spirit? You're kidding, right?"

If Ella had a familiar, it must be a dysfunctional

drunk living in its parents' basement, eating Coco Pops out of the box.

"I'm not kidding, Ella. It's exciting. Discovering your guide is a life-changing experience."

"Right. Of course. Silly me." She shook her head. "Wait. How'd you know my name?"

Riley turned to her with a grin. "Your guide. They told me."

A little shiver ran up Ella's neck. "Really?"

She lifted up Ella's suitcase. "No. Your name is written on here." She grinned wider, and Ella's neck tingled.

Must be the cold seeping into her bones.

"I'm Riley, by the way," she said, with far too much joy. "Normally we wouldn't meet until tomorrow, but…you know, Romeo, he often gets lost."

Sounded like he and Blake from the office would be two peas in a pod.

Ugh. Ella didn't want to think about her job or lack thereof. She tried to respond, but it came out as a sort of grunt. It'd been a long day.

When they walked under the giant welcome sign, and Ella saw other indications of human life, she released a chesty sigh. Soft torch lights guided the pathways, and her eyes roamed over the white wooden beach huts as the rain slid off the slanted roofs.

"How you doin' back there?" Riley jogged back to check on Pauline.

Ella strode in front, hoping they'd hurry up, but when

another wail echoed behind her, she knew Pauline had snagged the poor woman in her web. For god's sake.

"Are we nearly there?" she asked through gritted teeth, as they passed several more huts without stopping. She'd take a flea-bitten hammock at this point, anything to stop walking.

"Actually, yes."

Thank the lord.

"Pauline, you're right up here." Riley guided her up the path, unlocked the door, and then stopped to chat with her on the doorstep. Ella couldn't make out their conversation from her point on the path, but it wouldn't take a genius to guess it was about Albert, Pauline's ex-husband.

She gritted her teeth. *Why is this taking so long? Fucking Pauline.* She spun to glare at the two of them. Riley's sleeveless vest was soaked through, rippling with every movement and showing off her lean arm muscles. How she could still be smiling *and* talking to Pauline at the same time boggled her. And why wasn't she wearing a coat? Ella decided she must be on drugs.

Finally, Pauline was gone, and Riley rejoined her.

"So, which cabin is mine?" Ella asked.

"Yours is just a little further up this hill."

Ella groaned, seriously contemplating throwing herself down the cliff again just so she wouldn't have to walk any more.

"Nearly there. I promise."

"Define nearly there."

"See that tree with the creepy fingers? It's right next to it."

"Fantastic. Creepy fingers cabin."

Riley let out a breath of laughter and, uninvited, the edges of Ella's mouth curled.

True to Riley's word, they reached the cabin in only twenty-eight extra steps. Ella knew because her feet throbbed in time with each one. They paused outside, the smell of rain mixing with the colourful flowers planted by the doorstep.

"Here you are, Ella." Riley placed her suitcase down and slipped a key out of her pocket to unlock the door. "Your journey begins."

"Is all that stuff really necessary? I can't wait for the journey to be bloody over at this point." She slipped off her shoes, letting out a moan at how good the cool stone floor felt against her sore feet.

"The real voyage of discovery consists not in seeking new landscapes but in having new eyes."

Ella glanced at the woman, ready to tell her where to shove her voyage of discovery, but when they locked eyes, the words caught in her throat. Riley was studying her carefully, her irises a lighter blue now that Ella could really see them. Her skin was bronzed by the sun, but the freckles coating her nose, cheeks and arms pointed to an otherwise fair complexion.

She's actually pretty cute.

Oh, no.

Riley's lips pulled into a smile. "Can I get you

anything?"

Ella's mind gutter-dived for a moment, thinking about Riley's strong arms and how they might feel wrapped around her.

"I…uh…" Her hand instinctively shot to the top of her head, but any attempt to smooth her damp, bramble-filled hair into something acceptable was useless. She tore her eyes away, making a show of looking around her pristine white room. *Get it together, Ella. Don't be so desperate.* "I don't think so. Just point me in the direction of the nearest alcohol."

"That would be approximately 600km that way," Riley said, pointing back towards the ocean. "On the mainland."

"What?!"

"Sandy Springs is an alcohol-free experience."

"You have got to be kidding me."

"I'm afraid not."

Images of herself sunbathing on the beach, sipping piña coladas as beautiful women fanned her, dissolved in front of Ella's eyes. "What about locals? I bet they have alcohol." She sounded a little unhinged now, but she couldn't tame the shrill pitch of her voice.

Riley didn't comment but just gave a soft shake of her head.

"For god's sake, what is this hellhole?"

To Ella's surprise, Riley grinned, bringing out two dimples in her cheeks. Ella's eyes were drawn to them as she squashed her mouth into an amused line.

"Senhor Arenoso strongly believes in the detox of alcohol to bring about great change, but you'll learn more about the course tomorrow. I suggest you get some sleep. You've had quite an eventful day…so I'm told." She beamed, mischief glinting in her gaze.

"Eventful is putting it lightly," Ella grumbled, feeling her lips twitch at the corners.

"*Boa noite*, Ella," Riley said, ducking her head in a slight bow before disappearing down the path. The way her accent curled around the words made heat flush up Ella's neck, lingering long after she'd closed the door and collapsed onto her bed.

***

"And your sex drive? What's that like?"

Ella fought back a yawn, covering her mouth with her hand. "Excuse me?"

The man clicked his pen, bushy eyebrows furrowing slightly. "Do you often feel lethargic?"

Her first session with Marco Marcos, her assigned guidance counsellor for her time here, was going splendidly. He'd already highlighted her family strains, anger issues, and resistance to change. Now, he was trying to come for her love life.

"I have absolutely no issues in the bedroom department, Marco. Don't worry about that."

It was true she'd been a little out of practice recently,

but she'd be fine once she got back in the saddle.

The older man nodded, scribbling away in his notepad. She swore his cheeks reddened underneath the dark facial hair. He pushed his dark-rimmed square glasses up his nose and clicked his pen again, drawing her attention to his hairy fingers. "I've noticed you seem tired. Would you like to talk about that?"

Ella huffed, peering at the clock ticking away on the opposite wall. As soon as this was over, she had free time for the rest of the day. She couldn't wait to set her bikini free and get to the beach. It'd been too long since she'd taken a dip in the sea. "I didn't get enough sleep," she said, hearing the annoyed lilt in her voice. "A cockerel woke me up—"

"That'd be Bernardo."

"Uh, Bernardo, sure. Well, anyway, he woke me up at four, then just when I got back to sleep, some idiot rang that giant bloody bell in the courtyard."

Marco sighed, scratching at his beard. The man really was the hairiest person Ella had ever seen, even despite his shiny black head, which was reflecting the bright lights overhead. "Romeo was supposed to wait until seven for you new starters today," he said. "He's always getting confused."

You don't say.

"So, to summarise, big day, little rest. I'm sleepy."

"Mm-hmm. And do you usually feel tired when you're at home? Or do you feel well rested?"

What is this guy's problem?

"I'm mostly fine."

"Mostly? Would you like to expand on that?"

Not really, Marco Marcos, no.

She clicked her tongue. "Life is tiring, isn't it? Sometimes we just need a break."

His mouth pursed, and he continued scribbling. "Interesting. Yes."

All in all, her first day hadn't been too shabby. Some extra hours' sleep wouldn't have gone amiss—*damn you, Romeo*—but Ella's attempts to stay in bed and miss the introduction were denied by her rumbling tummy. Ultimately, she was glad she hadn't missed the breakfast, because it was top tier. Steaming coffee, fresh fruit, warm bread, pastries and jams, and ice-cold juice. She'd skipped the granola in favour of more pastries, and had been seated on the other side of the room from Pauline, too— *winner*—barely having to make small talk with the floppy-haired man seated next to her, as the course leaders did most of the talking.

The course creator and leader, Senhor Arenoso, had opened the day with a speech that would've been more profound if Ella hadn't been so focused on the flakey golden pastries melting in her mouth. Despite the heat, he was dressed decadently in a long burnt-orange kaftan, with a mix of gold and silver jewellery decorating his fingers and neckline. She'd caught the main gist of his opening lecture—*reset your life, love yourself, rediscover peace and transform into a freer, better you…* yadda, yadda, yadda.

The rest of the leaders had politely introduced themselves, but smiley Riley was nowhere to be seen.

Ella wasn't sure if she'd imagined the woman as a post-traumatic stress response, but then she'd seen her name on the schedule. Yoga and surfing. That explained the strong physique, then.

Schedules were filled from six to twelve in the morning, with yoga, meditation, energy-healing workshops and various other things with names Ella couldn't pronounce, and ended with a session with the guidance counsellor every two to three days. Afternoons offered the choice of additional activities or free time at the beach. No prizes for Ella's preference.

Thankfully, the session with Marco Marcos drew to a close, and Ella stepped out into the hot Portuguese sun.

The sea was calling her.

She followed the grainy trail down to the beach, wincing at the blisters between her toes. The ocean was crashing, getting louder and louder, the smell of salt guiding the way to the sandy shores. Once the path ended, she removed her flip-flops and pushed her toes into the sand.

Fuck, that's hot!

She did a little hop, skip and a jump, her thighs jiggling as she rushed past two leathery brown bodies soaking up the heat. She powerwalked towards the sea, sweat trickling down the back of her neck. The tumbling waves promised to soothe her. It'd been too long. She needed to feel the water on her skin. Ella loved the water, and a big smile took over her face as soon as she was within reach.

She dumped her bag on the sand and removed her flowery kimono, freeing her red bikini. Winnie had promised it complemented her curves instead of covering them, unlike the swimsuit Ella had originally picked out. Her rounder body shape had followed her into her thirties and still took some getting used to in the mirror. As with this trip, Ella had decided to trust her best friend, perhaps against her better judgement.

But it wasn't as if her own decision-making had been stellar lately.

Memories of Maeve swirled around her, all long legs and sharp cheekbones: the steely glint in her eyes rooting Ella like she'd been slapped, her perfume swimming through her veins, blurring the images of their last few years together.

"You are *so* funny." The memory of Maeve's silky voice echoed in her ears as she perched on Ella's desk, bearing down on her with curious brown eyes.

Ella had melted under the string of compliments in those early days. Ever since Maeve had got a promotion at work and moved to their floor, she'd spent an increasing amount of time at Ella's desk. Ella felt special. Especially when drawing the curious eyes of jealous coworkers nearby.

"What are you doing tonight?" Maeve had asked, her fingertips deliberately teasing the button of her silk blouse. "I've got a special project that I'd love to get your opinion on if you don't mind staying late."

"I'd love to," Ella had jumped in, all too quickly for the cat-and-mouse game Maeve loved to play.

"Fantastic." Maeve's voice lowered, dropping to that husky rasp that made Ella want to curl up on her lap and purr. "I'll make it worth your time. I promise you."

The image merged with their latest encounter, hitting Ella hard in the stomach. *"You mean a lot to me, Ella. I promise you."*

"No swimming today," a young, gangly boy called from the top of the wooden lifeguard chair, pulling her from her memories. "The current is too strong."

Ella looked him up and down, then turned back to the waves frothing and crashing against the shore, feeling a little flustered. "It looks fine to me."

"After-effects of all the rain yesterday. Big waves. Strong current."

She squinted under the light. The boy's spidery legs were too long for his body, the giant structure making him look like an oversized baby in a highchair. *Is this Romeo?*

She glanced up and down the shoreline, spotting a stretch of white sand beyond some jagged rocks. Sheltered from view, she'd be fine to take a little dip. She really needed to clear her head. She wouldn't go in far.

"Thank you, sir," she said, flashing him a wink. She caught his cheeks flushing before she dashed down the beach.

At the other side of the rocks, she dumped her bag again, sweat now dotting her upper lip and eyebrows.

With a child-like squeal, she strode into the shallow waves, the water embracing her hot skin like a cooling balm.

Yes. This is more like it.

She sank backwards, letting the sea buoy her. One with the water, everything relaxed. She let out a guttural sigh, squinting up against the sunshine. Then a crash of water slapped her across the face, and she spluttered, swallowing most of it as it knocked her sideways.

She scrambled, righting herself, before another wave dunked her again. Her chest tightened, struggling for breath as she tried to breach the surface. But she could no longer touch the floor. How had she ended up so far out?

Shit.

Flapping like a penguin, she fought against the current, but a strong tug sent her in the opposite direction, pulling her further down into the salty depths.

CHAPTER THREE

Riley

A soft sea breeze fluttered Riley's hair around her face, obscuring her vision. She sighed, setting down her paintbrush to scrape her wild mane into a bun on top of her head before plucking up the brush again, dipping it into the blue paint, and swirling it across the canvas.

Her strokes were purposeful, aggressive, mind and hand blurring as one to blend the colours into something powerful. Heat pricked the back of her neck, sweat beading her forehead, but she couldn't stop. The waves on the canvas stood taller and more destructive than the ones in front of her eyes, but they matched the tumultuous feeling deep in her chest.

Sensing her pulse racing, Riley closed her eyes to focus on her breathing. Sleep had eluded her last night; it always did around this time of year. Senhor Arenoso had encouraged her to take some days off, but the last thing she needed was time alone. They'd agreed for her at least to miss the morning introductions so she could prepare for the weeks ahead.

The crashing of the waves against the shore lulled her. Fresh salty air filled her lungs. *In and out.* She exhaled through her mouth. The cries of petrels and shearwaters cut through the sloshing sound of the ocean as they ferried back and forth from their nests in the cliffs. She flew with them in her mind, dipping and diving over the sea until all she felt was the wind on her face and the sun on her skin.

She smiled. She often sat out here on the beach cliffs or on her hammock in her garden, watching the birds. How elegant and nimble they were as they flew, returning year after year after migrating north. Riley found them fascinating. How they could navigate using the earth's magnetic fields, using the sun and stars to guide them. Like humans used to before the world got too complicated.

Her breathing settled into a calm, steady rhythm, and she tilted her head skywards, letting the orange sun paint her eyelids. She used to hope her familiar would be a bird.

Her connection to them was so strong, she was sure that if she had wings, she'd be able to tune into the earth's vibrations, too, zip and soar through the sky without any worries. But she trusted Senhor Arenoso's judgement.

Opening her eyes, she squinted under the bright light, feeling much more grounded. That feeling was what so many people came here searching for, and she had the privilege of experiencing it all year round. She was wholeheartedly grateful to Senhor Arenoso for that. He'd no doubt saved Riley's life four years ago.

She exhaled, rolling her neck and stretching side to side. She wasn't sure how long she'd been out here, but judging from the sun's arc in the sky, it'd been hours.

Her eyes combed the canvas. The rough marks of blues and whites collided with purples and reds, in a fashion Marco Marcos had deemed "deeply emotional". She lifted her gaze beyond the painting to the line where the sea and horizon met. There wasn't a cloud in the sky. The sun glinted off the surface of the water, until the waves broke through, spitting froth up onto the rocks. It was a shame the sea was so violent today. An afternoon surf would have been perfect.

A flash of something red in the water caught Riley's eye.

What is that?

She looked closer, following the object as it swirled through the water. *Oh shit. That's a person.* Adrenaline spiked up her spine, and she clambered down the rocks leading to the beach. Hot stones burned her feet, but she barely felt it, tearing off her vest and shorts to reveal her blue bikini underneath.

She sprinted across the sand. Keeping an eye on the bundle of red and white, she dived into the sea. She worked her arm muscles as fast as she could, cutting through the water. The waves pulled and pushed against her, but the fire flowing through her veins propelled her forward. As she got closer, she realised the person was a woman. Her lifeless body bobbing along the waves forced Riley's burning muscles to work faster. *Nearly there.*

She reached for the woman and, remembering her lifeguard training, tilted her chin up and swam backwards to keep her airways out of the water.

The sea threatened to upheave them, but Riley shielded the woman with her body, breaking the waves away from her. Her heart raced, fighting with everything she had to pull her out of the water and onto the sandy shore.

She called for help, although she knew this area of the beach was unguarded. She called again anyway, her own lungs fighting for breath, before laying the woman on her back and brushing her tangled red hair from her face.

Riley inhaled. It was the woman from last night, Ella. What was she doing swimming in the sea with the warnings out?

"Ella! Ella, can you hear me?" Riley shook her, leaning over to check her breathing.

Oh shit. Oh shit.

She couldn't tell if Ella was still breathing, but she needed to act quickly. She was going to have to give her mouth-to-mouth and then start chest compressions. With one hand, she tipped Ella's chin backwards, using the other to pinch her nose, then closed her mouth over hers, blowing into her airway.

When Ella shot up, spluttering into Riley's mouth, she fell backwards, hitting the sand hard. She scrambled up, supporting Ella's shoulders.

"Ella, thank Jesus. Are you alright?" She rubbed her back as she bent over.

Ella coughed and spluttered, water dribbling down her chin—but she was breathing. Riley's chest loosened, and she allowed herself to relax a little. Ella's cheeks were flushed, her red hair slicked against her back, but her brown eyes were present.

Riley brushed her shoulder. "I should probably put you in the recovery position."

"No," Ella whispered between coughs. "I need to sit up."

Riley debated doing it anyway, but she supposed Ella was conscious enough to know best for herself. Then again, she'd ended up in this mess in the first place, so maybe not. She took a seat beside her in the sand and worked on calming her own thundering heartbeat, while keeping a keen eye on the woman next to her. She rubbed her amethyst necklace between her fingers, channelling the calming energy into her own body.

Eventually, Ella's coughing subsided, and she tilted

her head back to the sky. "Fuck's sake."

Riley shook her head and let out a chuckle of disbelief. Ella nearly drowned, and that was her first response? She quickly swallowed her laughter; what Ella had done was really dangerous. "How are you feeling?" she asked.

Ella glanced at her, eyes red and squinting. "Like I've been inside a washing machine and then drunk a gallon of bleach."

"I'm not surprised. What were you doing out here? The warnings are out. It's not safe to swim."

"You don't say."

"Ella, I'm serious. You could've died."

Ella turned to her then, her eyes flicking over Riley's face. "Yeah, you're right. I'm sorry." She groaned, hanging her head forward. "This island is trying to kill me."

Riley couldn't deny the redhead had a habit of finding herself in peculiar situations. "Do you feel sick? Light-headed?"

"A little."

"Come on. I'll take you to medical."

She flapped her hands. "No. No, please, don't do that. I'm fine."

"Ella, you need to be checked by a professional—"

"I'm fine. I'm fine. Look!" She got to her feet and started doing a weird jig back and forth, waving her arms.

What the...? Riley bit back a grin. "Yes, that's some wonderful dancing, grand, but you might have swallowed a lot of water or have a concussion or something."

"Hey. This is just how I dance."

Riley laughed. "You know what I mean. Who knows how long you were under the water for? It's dangerous."

"It wasn't long." She stopped dancing, her mouth falling into a flat line. "Please, Riley, don't make me go. I've had such a horrendous few days. The last thing I want is to spend the rest of the day cooped up with a stranger poking and prodding me."

Riley sighed, unable to hold the woman's soft brown gaze. She knew how much she hated anything to do with hospitals herself. How easily they brought back memories. But she should follow protocol. Though Ella seemed fine now, she might not be later. Even if Leonor from Medical was about as useful as a solar-powered flashlight. "I'm sorry. Come on, it's not far."

"I just want to get some fresh air outside, that's all. I promise I won't wander off. Please, Riley."

Riley chewed her lip. "You shouldn't be on your own in case somethin' happens."

"Stay with me, then."

As Ella locked eyes with her, a flutter spread through Riley's chest. She couldn't help it; Ella was pretty—even after being tumbled around the North Atlantic with spit down her bikini top. "What?"

"You're a first aider, right? I assume so, judging by your impressive life-saving skills. Thank you for that, by the way. Top job." Ella's mouth lifted at the edges, and Riley's focus fell onto her plump lips before bouncing back to her eyes.

She cleared her throat and returned the smile. "You're welcome."

"Is that a yes?"

Riley shouldn't really spend time with clients outside of the course. After the António triplet scandal a few years ago, Senhor Arenoso had drilled the importance of separation into the staff. When it came out that the handsome guidance counsellor had impregnated three sisters, they'd almost had to close the course completely. The locals were furious, tabloids ruined business, and fighting off the lawsuits had exhausted Senhor Arenoso. It took years to rebuild the trust. The course couldn't afford any more bad press. This wasn't Portuguese *Love Island*.

But Ella shouldn't be left on her own. Riley wouldn't be able to forgive herself if something happened. She *had* had a rough few days… and it wasn't as if Riley had anything else to do today. She could keep an eye on her until she was sure she was safe. She knew the signs to look out for.

"Okay," she agreed. "We should get you a drink, though."

Ella's eyes lit up.

"Not that kind of drink."

Ella huffed. "Party pooper."

Riley nodded to Ella's bag sitting on the sand. "Do you have some water in there?"

"No." When Riley raised her eyebrows, Ella said,

"What?"

"It's thirty-two degrees, and you haven't got any liquids with you?"

Ella brushed her wet hair back over her shoulders with a slopping sound and shrugged. "I really wanted to go for a swim."

"With the warnings out and the waves like this? You'd have been safer taking a dip in the volcano over there," Riley teased before pressing her lips together; she needed to be more professional. She blamed it on the adrenaline.

But a loud laugh erupted from Ella's throat, and Riley felt her own smile take over her face.

"You're right," Ella said. "I'm a disaster. I guess that's why I'm here, though, right?" She opened her arms and spun in a lazy circle, before her gaze snared Riley's, twinkling with mischief. "Help. I need to find my familiar sharpish before something else tries to kill me."

She's teasing me. Riley had met many naysayers before; it was all part of the job. People had different beliefs, different levels of openness and spirituality. That was to be expected with a race as varied and diverse as humans. It didn't matter to her what people said; she'd found stability and peace in her life—at least, the closest thing to it. There were still days when she couldn't get out of bed. Nights where she woke up in a hot sweat from the nightmares. But life couldn't be perfect; she'd accepted that. She was doing fine, all things considered.

Ella shrieked suddenly, arms out mid-spin, looking

at her red bikini, which had a generous helping of sloppy white bird excrement dripping down it.

Riley chuckled, peering up at the escaping perpetrator as it soared over the ocean waves. "Balearic shearwater."

Ella turned to her with wide eyes. "A what now?"

"It's a type of bird."

She scraped off as much poop as she could and washed her hands in the shallow of the sea.

"It's lucky, you know," Riley commented, as Ella bent down to splash water across her chest. She couldn't help but admire her curves as they jiggled with the movement. It was hard to tear her eyes from Ella's shapely white thighs, soft stomach, and full breasts.

Remember António and the triplets.

She forced her gaze back over the sea and the cries of the birds calling to her. Perhaps Ella's familiar could be a bird. It might explain this. "It could be another indication from your guide. Another sign," she said.

"A sign I should pack up and go home, maybe." Ella stood up, fresh water droplets dripping down her cleavage, and Riley redirected her eyes to hers. "How's that look?" Ella asked.

"Perfect." When surprise flashed across Ella's features, Riley stammered. "Er—you know, perfectly fine."

Be professional, Riley. Jesus. It's like you've never been around a pretty woman before.

"I've got some water in my bag," she went on, her

mouth running to try to distract from her earlier comment. She started leading the way, then turned back to Ella, almost colliding into her. "Do you feel okay to walk? My things are at the top of those rocks."

"Ah, I'm not sure." Ella bit her lip. "You might have to carry me."

Carry her? Riley was strong, but even she would struggle to lift someone up the unsteady cliff face.

"Joking." Ella burst into a grin, and she poked Riley in the side. "You were actually considering it, though. That's cute."

Riley's cheeks flushed, and she turned to hide them. She hadn't been called cute in a long time, not since she'd stopped entertaining the idea of a relationship on the mainland. It was too much effort, and honestly, she just wasn't up to it. But it wasn't like she came to Sandy Springs for the gay scene. Good job, too, as the population was in its hundreds, and calling it slim pickings would be overreaching.

She didn't even know if Ella was queer—not that it made a difference.

They strolled back along the sand towards the cliff, the sun bathing them in warm light. Riley bent to collect her discarded clothing on the way, feeling a flash of adrenaline as the moment saving Ella replayed in her mind. It had all happened so quickly; it felt like a dream still clinging to her eyelids. She watched Ella in her peripheral vision, amazed by how unfazed she seemed about the ordeal.

"Do you need any assistance?" she asked, when they reached the boulders that led up to the top of the cliff. The climb wasn't difficult, but Ella had almost drowned earlier, and anyway, she didn't want to make assumptions about someone's physical capabilities.

"I think I can manage."

"I should go behind you."

Ella raised an eyebrow, and a teasing smile played on her lips.

"In case you fall," she added.

"Right."

They ascended slowly, Riley guiding Ella up and telling her the best footholds to use. She tried her best not to stare at the woman's round bum, but it was difficult when it was shaking in her face—and when her red bikini fit her body shape so well. She focused on the climb instead, and soon, they were at the top.

The wind picked up, a welcoming coolness against Riley's hot skin. She hurried to her canvas, which was standing on a large stone, and covered it with a sheet before Ella could see it. Some tubes of paint had rolled away across the rocks, so she plucked them up and dropped them into her bag. As much as she loved the birds, they were thieving little shites.

"You paint?" Ella asked, circling the covered easel, intrigued.

"Sometimes." She dug around until she found a bottle of water in her bag and handed it to her.

"Thank you." Ella took long gulps, and Riley

followed the movement down her delicate throat, watching the muscles in her neck shift. Her skin prickled, and she looked away, tidying up the rest of her equipment.

"What do you paint?" Ella asked.

"Erm, mostly landscapes, occasionally some abstract stuff."

"Cool. Can I see?"

She scratched at her neck. "I–uh–don't really… No, I…erm."

Ella sensed her unease and stepped away from the painting, dropping her hand from the sheet. Riley let out a breath. She'd only shown Marco Marcos because he'd suggested there might be underlying messages that could hold the key to curing her nightmares.

So far, unsuccessful.

"You should sit down for a bit," she suggested. "Here." She handed Ella her round meditation cushion.

Ella ran her fingers over the blue and white patterns zigzagging over the handwoven fabric. "This is beautiful. And it's so soft."

"Thanks. Gloriana made it herself. You'll see her at the markets in the week."

Ella placed it carefully on the rock, glancing at Riley as she hovered over it.

"It won't bite, I swear."

"I just don't wanna ruin it with a giant imprint of my arse."

Riley's mouth quirked, and she bit back a laugh. Ella sat down with a happy sigh, and she took a seat beside her on the hard rock surface, feeling the heat transfer through her skin. She closed her eyes, letting her energies settle.

"I feel bad," Ella murmured, causing Riley to peek at her. "You're on the ground."

"I honestly don't mind."

A comfortable silence settled between them. Riley let her eyes shut again, tuning into the different sensations. Among the calls of the birds and the heat on her face, she sensed something new and strong pulsing around her. She opened her eyes to find Ella staring. Her pulse skipped a little faster, wondering what she was thinking.

Luckily, Ella blurted it out a second later. "I like your dolphin tattoo."

"Ah, thank you," she said, caught a little off-guard. She traced over the black marking that rested between her shoulder blades. Had Ella been checking her out too? The thought of that excited her much more than it should have, and she looked away.

"What does it mean?"

"It's my familiar."

"A dolphin?" Ella lifted her eyebrows, but they weren't taunting. They were encouraging. She wanted to know more.

"Dolphins represent harmony and balance," Riley continued. "They're considered intelligent, a symbol of protection and resurrection in many cultures, but they keep their playful nature. They're a good mix of strengths, I suppose." She exhaled. In truth, she'd struggled to accept her guide wholeheartedly. She wasn't sure what strength and harmony Senhor Arenoso saw in her. She wanted to be like the dolphins but didn't quite believe it; the idea of balance made her laugh. Plus, why did she long to be so like the birds?

"That makes sense. I can see that about you."

Riley swallowed, taking in the softness on Ella's face. Her brown eyes shone in the sunlight, radiating warmth that heated Riley's cheeks and neck. It felt like all the air around them had squeezed and swirled, pulling them closer together.

Riley believed in energies. And right now, Ella's were vibrant and pulsing out from all around her. Either that, or there was an earthquake about to happen.

"Do you?" she managed. "I'm not always so sure I see it."

"I do. Plus, you literally just saved my life. That's pretty dolphin protector-esque."

"I suppose you're right." Riley smiled, the heat slipping lower down her sternum and into her belly. She forced herself back on the rocks to look up into the blue sky, needing distraction. They needed distance.

Riley wasn't doing anything wrong. She was making sure Ella was alright after her earlier incident, and then she was going to escort her home. That was it. She focused on the swirls of white now floating across the vast blue sky. Would it feel freer to be a cloud or a bird?

"That one looks like an ocean wave," Ella said as she sat on the hard surface next to Riley, following her gaze.

"Fuck. That's hot." She jumped back up, brushing her hands over her bum, then dug a pretty kimono out of her bag, laying it down before rejoining her.

They both looked up at the sky, laying side by side, close enough that if Riley reached out her arm, she could brush against Ella's. But Riley wasn't thinking about that.

"That one looks a bit like Kylie Minogue."

Riley laughed, low in her throat. "How?"

Ella leaned closer, directing Riley's sight with the point of her finger. Her sweet scent mingled with something fruity, making her inhale sharply. "There are her eyes, and that's her mouth. See?"

Riley had no idea how the wispy clouds could possibly resemble Kylie Minogue, but she nodded anyway. "Cirrus clouds are my favourite."

"Of course *you* have a favourite type of cloud."

Riley turned her head to look at her. "You don't?"

"Can't say that I've ever given it much thought." Her eyes crinkled at the edges, her gaze moving over Riley's face.

Riley's heart quickened, thumping away in her chest. Surely, if Ella was straight, she wouldn't look at her like that? She needed to put a stop to it—whatever it was—for the sake of her job.

She cleared her throat, casting her eyes away. "So, are you feeling any better?"

"Yeah. You know, I actually feel good. Got the sun on my skin and nothing to do. I just wish I had a margarita in my hand."

Riley turned her head, allowing her gaze to fall over the woman next to her. Neat, arched eyebrows framed her eyes, with a straight nose that had an adorable little point at the tip. Her eyes were closed, and she beamed, oozing an infectious stream of happiness for the first time since Riley had met her.

Thank the guides I missed the morning introductions to come and paint. She didn't want to even consider the other outcome if she hadn't seen Ella tumbling around in the sea. She allowed herself to look for just a few seconds more, the warmth emanating from Ella coating her own skin, before forcing her gaze elsewhere.

Then, realising she hadn't replied to Ella's comment, she cleared her throat. "Well, Senhor Arenoso does say that contentment is having everything you need but not everything you want."

Ella hummed, running a hand over her stained bikini top, discoloured from the bird. "Yeah, maybe you're right. I have a feeling…like my luck might be about to change."

A caw from up above caught Riley's attention, and she turned just in time to watch the white poop fall from the sky like an atomic bomb, for the second time today, landing straight in Ella's hair with a slop.

Maybe her luck isn't changing just quite yet.

CHAPTER FOUR

Ella's morning routine of bustling city life, strong coffee, and frantically ironing a pencil skirt seemed a distant memory. She used to practically punch her phone to stop her alarm in the morning, but for the second day in a row, she'd been startled to life by Bernardo the cockerel, and she couldn't exactly punch him.

Or could she?

Considering how her first days had gone, Bernardo would no doubt have the upper hand, leaving Ella to be rescued by a rather tall, handsome, bronzed woman with muscular arms.

Which might not be such a bad thing.

Since walking her back to her cabin yesterday, Riley had continued to pop into Ella's mind uninvited. Not only had she saved her life, but she'd also been kind to her, without the expectation of something in return.

It is her job, though, her inner pessimist chided.

Okay, maybe the devil on her shoulder had a point, but still, Riley had chosen to spend the rest of the afternoon with Ella instead of shipping her off to the medical hut. Was that usual?

God, I sound desperate.

Ella grunted, phone in hand, as she stretched her arm higher, parading around the stone floor on her tippy-toes. There had to be signal somewhere in this place. The man at reception had already cheerily informed her there was no Wi-Fi at the resort, his enthusiasm matching that of a children's TV presenter. Senhor Arenoso believed that the discovery of your 'soul key' couldn't be found in the pixels of your phone screen.

Well, Ella believed that Senhor Arenoso was a fun sponge.

There was no harm in seeing what her friends had been up to. Winnie loved a funny meme or a cat video. It wasn't like she was going to stalk Maeve's girlfriend and mock her yoga posts while drinking wine straight from the bottle... Ella never did that—hardly—but it wasn't fair that Annabelle received free makeup and clothes and tickets to local events just for bending over. *What gives?* If she'd known filming herself twisting her body into a pretty pretzel came with such good benefits, she'd have done it too.

A thought struck Ella like a stone. What if she became better at yoga than Annabelle? Three weeks should be more than enough time to get a head start. Combine that with a hot tan, some new clothes, and some flashy social media posts, and Maeve would soon remember what she was missing. Maybe she already had, and Ella hadn't received the message yet.

She needed some signal on this damn island. Stat.

Getting no luck with her arm waving, she climbed onto the window ledge, resting against the wardrobe to get more height. Her phone's signal bar flickered to one, and she let out a little squeal. When nothing came through immediately, she frowned. *I need more height.*

As she swivelled, the tree with the creepy fingers caught her eye, its branches pointing and mocking her. That certainly would be high enough. She dashed outside, still wearing her pink strappy pyjama vest and shorts, the early morning air already warm against her skin. Tucking her phone into her waistband, she gripped the branch and lifted herself up. *Oof.* Her arms trembled, and she pushed her toes into the rough bark, climbing higher, until she found a good spot to sit. With a grunt, she retrieved her phone from her shorts to check the signal. *Three bars. Hallelujah.* She smirked, and her phone vibrated.

Three texts from her mobile phone provider. The

smile dropped from her face. The phone vibrated again. A twenty percent discount from her local pizza place.

Well, damn.

Embarrassment chased the disappointment blooming in her stomach. Of course Maeve hadn't texted her. But she could change that. Maybe this course was the perfect opportunity to win her back and prove everyone wrong.

Her phone buzzed to life, leaping from her hand. Adrenaline spiked up her spine as she scrambled to catch it, managing to grip it between her thumb and forefinger before it tumbled from her place in the canopy. She pushed up from the branch, frowning at her mother's white face peering back at her. The picture flashed as it continued to ring, then she sighed and answered, making sure to switch off her camera.

"Hello, darling!" Her mother's face greeted her, more tanned and weathered by wrinkles since the picture on Ella's phone was taken.

"Hi, Mum." Ella squinted as the pixelated image of her mother jumped across the screen. The blue background was unfamiliar. "What're you doing calling me so early?"

"It's evening in Hawaii. Your father and I are on a cruise."

Of course. Why wouldn't they be? "Are you having fun?"

"Why can't I see you? Give me an update. How's things with you?"

Ella suppressed a snort, brushing moss off her hands,

as the last few days flashed behind her eyelids. Better not mention the near-death experience. Or her newly hatched plan to win back her ex-girlfriend. "The signal isn't great, and it's only my first proper day today. Not much to report."

"Have you met anyone nice?"

Riley's dimpled grin jumped into her mind, and she hesitated. "A couple of people."

Her mother latched onto the delay, her voice bearing an accusatory tone. "Remember this holiday is for you, darling. Not for romance—"

"Mum. Come on. I've been single for ages."

"All the more reason for you to try and climb the first woman you see."

Ella was thankful her camera was off so her mother wouldn't see her scowl. She spoke about her like she'd the sexual aggression of a puma and not as though she'd spent the last year pining over her long-legged ex-girlfriend.

"I'm not going to...*climb*...the first woman I see." She huffed, inhaling the deep, leathery scent of the bark and branches. At least her mum couldn't accuse her of not being in touch with nature too.

"Winnie warned me about this."

"My god." Ella rolled her eyes so hard, she thrust her head back into the tree trunk with a thump. "Can you please stop having this weird relationship with my friend?"

"Nonsense. You could always join us. You still

haven't replied to our murder mystery dinner party." A clatter in the background made her mother swivel her head. Ella's eye caught on her expensive necklace and a suspicious-looking purple mark, before she focused back on her. *Jesus. Is that a hickey?* Even her parents had a better sex life than she did. That was soul-crushingly depressing. "And I do miss you, you know," her mother continued. "Don't think I haven't noticed you missed the last two family barbecues."

Ella sighed. "Sorry… I've just been working a lot."

Guilt sunk like a stone into her stomach, along with an itchy feeling creeping up her neck that she couldn't escape. Had she been inadvertently shooting warning flares? Were her whole family in on the creepy tag-team of mother and best friend enrolling her in the fix-your-shitty-life course? The Maeve complications aside, Ella used to love her job. She brought her knees to her chest, feeling her mother's words weave around her. What could everyone see that she couldn't?

"I worry about you, darling. I just want the best for you." Her mum peered into the camera, almost like she could sense Ella's thoughts derailing. Then she perked up, her back straightening into perfect posture. "Did you hear about Clarice?"

Flawless timing for the mention of her brother Devin's pearly-toothed doctor fiancée. Ella hadn't spent much time with her—but Clarice hadn't found her Hannibal Lector impression funny, and that told her all she needed to know.

Distant voices and the crunch of footsteps caused Ella to raise her head. The ugly green uniform the staff wore caught her eye. She leaned forward to get a better look at the faces and spotted a woman with long, wavy hair. *Shit. It's Riley.*

And Ella was sitting in a tree in her skimpy pajamas like she'd escaped from a zoo.

Her mother continued talking. "Clarice has been offered a promotion. And your brother is in line for one too. We should have a get-together once you're back and celebrate. What do you say?"

What do I say to my perfect brother and his perfect fiancée, parading their perfect lives down my throat? Yippee do.

Ever since she'd had to sit through her younger brother's endless violin concerts and endure the mention of his *musical marvel* or *unique genius*, she'd always taken a backseat. Nothing she did ever came close. Even if Devin abandoned his career and family to live in the woods and become a professional yo-yo master, she could never imagine her mother sending him to Sandy Springs. They'd probably pay for a front-page write-up in the local paper.

Riley's voice carried on the wind, getting closer. The woman walking beside her laughed. Who was she?

"Sorry, Mum," Ella hissed. "I have to go. Yoga starts soon. I'll speak to you later."

"Why are you whispering—?"

But Ella ended the call, pivoted her body

horizontally, and got a face full of tree bark. *God. I hope she doesn't see me.* She'd already made a royal arse of herself in front of Riley. She didn't want to do that again quite so soon. She should be focusing on Maeve anyway, not other distractions.

'*This holiday is for you. Not for romance.*' Her mother's voice echoed in her head.

She rolled her eyes again. Ella hated how she knew. She didn't like being predictable.

"Honestly, I'm doing good. I promise you," Riley's voice cut through the leaves. Ella held her breath, angling her body to match the tree branch. "Senhor Arenoso's already been checking up on me."

I'm one with the tree.

The bark scratched against her cheek as she inhaled, slow and steady, the air humid against her neck.

"We should hang out soon," the woman said, her brown ponytail swaying with every step. "It's been a while since we've been on a hike. Let's do something." Ella recognised her from the welcome meeting. Jane was another one of the yoga instructors on the course.

"I'm sorry I've been distant," Riley said. Ella caught a whiff of coconut and sea salt as she passed. "I don't want you to think…"

Her voice faded as she disappeared over the hill and down towards the courtyard. Ella waited a few moments before fully relaxing and pushing up into a sitting position. Her gaze followed them, wondering if she and Jane were just friends.

A twinge of jealousy pinged through her stomach, which was so absurd, she had to laugh. Yes, Riley had been giving off the *queer vibes* yesterday with those inquisitive eyes, adorable dimples and lovely, big hands, but Ella's body had no right to behave in such a way. Aside from the fact she painted, liked clouds and swam like a sexy dolphin, Ella hardly knew her.

Panic bolted up her spine as another buzz startled her, and she almost dropped her phone. It was a picture message from Winnie. Ella opened it, shaking her head at the sight of her best friend sprawled in a bed, her blonde hair fanned around her head like a lion's mane, her naked chest visible as she pointed to the sleeping woman next to her.

Miss you, bestie!! it read. *Tell you about this one soon… Don't do anything I wouldn't do.*

That didn't leave much. Ella grinned, sent off a quick reply, then stuffed her phone back into her waistband. She needed to get ready for her first official day and her first class with Riley. She wasn't sure what to expect, but putting on a bit of makeup and her favourite push-up bra couldn't hurt. She had to be camera-ready for her Instagram. Even if climbing up this tree every time she needed to post wasn't exactly ideal.

She glanced down, and her belly plummeted. The ground was further away than she expected. Her vision swayed, and she gripped the branch beneath her. *Shit.*

She thought about calling for help, then imagined the look on Riley's face when she had to rescue her from the tree like a helpless cat. No. Ella had gotten herself into this mess and she could get herself out of it. She peered over the side, and her stomach lurched again.

Where's my monkey-familiar guide thing when I need it?

With a deep breath, she shuffled backwards, keeping a firm grip on the tree. A step at a time, she lowered herself, until the branches stopped, and she needed to drop. Hanging by the tips of her fingers, legs swaying unceremoniously, she let go, landing on her bare feet. *Yes!* She beamed, feeling like she'd just landed a triple backflip at the Olympics.

Applause rang out from behind her, and her face fell. She slowly turned.

"Wow! That was incredible," Pauline cooed. She was dressed in a purple chiffon dress that didn't really go with her oversized pink hat with white feathers. She glanced up at the tree, eyes widening. "Did you sleep up there?"

Ella snorted. "Yeah. Oops. You caught me."

Pauline shifted uncertainly, looking back at the branches. "Well…uh… Are you ready for our first yoga session?"

Ella glanced down at her pink pyjamas. "Not quite."

"I'll wait for you, and then we can walk down together." Pauline flashed a thumbs-up, her cheeks lifting and bunching the bags under her eyes.

Guilt washed over Ella as she scrambled for an excuse, but she needed to be on her A-game. "It might take me a while to get ready."

"I don't mind." Pauline adjusted her hat, tucking dark brown hair behind her ears. "I've always wanted to try yoga. My husband, Albert, never wanted me to—well, ex-husband." Her lips wilted, and she sniffed.

"Okay!" Ella jumped in, eager to stop her train of thought pulling into doomed-divorcee station. She let out a sigh and forced a smile. "Erm…would you like to come in and wait?"

"Groovy." Pauline linked her arm with Ella's, and the woman's flowery perfume assaulted her nostrils. "I just knew we were gonna become the best of friends. I had a feeling."

Oh, no… What have I done?

Pauline tugged her towards her door, and Ella inwardly cursed, sending prayers to any potential guides listening up in the clouds to come and save her.

CHAPTER FIVE

Ella

The morning sun shone brightly, warming the back of Ella's neck and legs. She and the other ten people from her group were facing the front, awaiting Riley's arrival. Their yoga mats lay on their left, and the grey stone courtyard stretched ahead of them before disappearing into a beautiful view of the ocean. Green vines snaked up the wooden beams on either side, their pink and yellow flowers overhanging the pathways to the breakfast hall and reception building. At the front, a round fountain shot water up into the sky.

Everybody was silent, even Pauline next to Ella—though she was probably all cried out from earlier. Despite Ella's best attempts, the woman had depleted Ella's tissues and rubbed snot all over her favourite pyjama top. The rest of the group were women, except for a tall, skinny man called Rick and a balding guy who was dressed like it was winter instead of the hot Portuguese summer. Ella's gaze roamed over his multicoloured wool jumper before settling back at the front. She dreaded to think what he smelt like under there.

Waves crashed in the distance, mingling with the tinkling of wind chimes. Ella was more than ready to learn some new poses to make Maeve's girlfriend eat her free designer hats—and then some. How hard could it be?

A gong sounded, the deep hum echoing through the air. Riley appeared from underneath the canopy of flowers, dressed in her smart green uniform, and took her place in front of the fountain.

Ella's belly tingled against her best efforts. Riley's long blonde hair was pulled up into a bun on top of her head, two strands framing either side of her face, drawing attention to her strong jaw.

"Good morning, everyone." She brought her hands together and flashed a practised smile at the group. When her gaze avoided Ella's, the tingles in her stomach dropped like falling knives. "I'm Riley, and I'll be taking your yoga sessions for these three weeks. Every morning, we'll convene here, join together for breathing exercises, and start the day by tuning into the earth's natural energies."

Breathing? Ella's disappointment sunk even lower, curdling around her insides. That was hardly the tricky headstand-bendy-legs pose Annabelle constantly bragged about.

Riley took a few steps, her bare feet graceful on the stone. "I know some of you are probably thinking *'Breathing? What does breathing have to do with anything?'* but it is the very core of our being. There's nothing more natural and universal than breathing. We do it all the time without thinking about it at all, and by making this a conscious effort, we can strengthen the connection with our minds and bodies."

Her attention drifted over the group again, passing over Ella like she didn't even recognise her.

Ella hadn't known what to expect seeing her today, but the lack of acknowledgement stung like a wet fish to the face. She'd hoped their afternoon spent cloud-gazing and talking had meant something, and had proved she still had those qualities Maeve once fell in love with. But the message was loud and clear: Ella was still at the top of the loser pile. Riley had just been doing her job, after all.

Of course that's all it was. She was so desperate to be wanted, she'd misread her kindness as attraction. *You idiot, Ella.*

"Many of you might think the most important part of yoga is the poses," Riley continued, "but in fact, it's our breath. How many of you feel stressed in your day-to-day life?"

Everyone raised their hands, but Ella watched on, squashing her mouth into a hard line to stop it wobbling.

"Part of your time at Sandy Springs is reminding yourselves about the simpler things in life that are often overlooked or forgotten. Something as simple as a few minutes focusing on your breathing can have many positive effects, like relieving stress and anxiety, improving sleep, and lowering blood pressure. The best thing?" She grinned, and Ella could see the dimples in her cheeks, even from metres away. "Anyone can do it."

Riley guided the group through some breathing techniques as the sun arched higher. Even with the peaceful atmosphere and the lulling waves of the sea, Ella's temple throbbed. She relaxed her jaw and tried to focus on inhaling and exhaling, but it looked stupid—she knew. She'd been peeking at everyone else sitting cross-legged on their mats.

The fact that Pauline kept trumping out of time with the windchimes didn't help matters, either.

She didn't want to look stupid. She'd spent her whole life trying to fit in. To be as talented as Devin or as thin as Winnie. To be pretty enough for Maeve, and smart enough for her family. But it was never good enough. Ella always fucked it up somehow. Even trying to help Pauline, she ended up falling down the cliff and acting like a deranged ape in front of Riley.

No wonder she isn't interested.

She scrunched her eyes tighter, trying to focus, but

her mind drifted to Maeve's long legs. Her mother's cheerful holiday face. Her brother, his perfect fiancée, their perfect twins and their three show-quality Ragdoll cats. And here Ella was, sitting with a bunch of life's rejects, with no job prospects, barely clinging onto her own self-worth. Even getting rejected by Riley hurt, and she'd only known her for two minutes. Maybe Riley would prefer Annabelle over Ella, too.

God, what am I talking about? I am pathetic.

She clenched and relaxed her hands in her lap, the soft skin a little sore from her tree-climbing expedition earlier. Her breaths came hard and fast, air pushing through her nostrils like a steam train. That definitely wasn't the group's objective. Great. Now she couldn't even get breathing right. She was the queen reject of life's rejects. What was—

"Ella." Riley's soft voice made her jump, and she snapped her eyes open, finding her calm blues gazing back at her. Riley placed her hands on her shoulders as they heaved up and down. "Breathe with me. In through the nose. Out through the mouth."

Ella did as she was told, spellbound by her swirling irises and the shape of her lips.

"Breathe slow and deep. One…two…three…four." Ella breathed with her, looking deep into her eyes. The mix of blue and turquoise steadied her, but the longer she looked, the more variations she noted. A neat hazel ring around Riley's pupil. A smaller cobalt one, too. She observed a particularly nice fleck of green as it glinted in the sunlight, the colours seeming to liquify and shimmer. Her heart finally settled into a steady rhythm, and the corners of Riley's mouth quirked, her eyes taking on a new look that made Ella's belly tingle.

"Good. Now, I want you to try something with me." She took a seat beside Ella on the stone floor and easily crossed her legs.

Very flexible, Ella noted.

"Close your eyes again," Riley said, waiting until Ella had shut them before continuing. "Stay with the same breathing cycle, but this time, imagine a bubble forming around you. In, hold, then release, all for four counts. Every time your mind tries to take you somewhere else, acknowledge it, but then focus back on your breathing and building your bubble."

Ella tried, but she was conscious of the others watching her. Riley too. She didn't want to look more of an idiot than she already had.

She opened an eye, shooting a glance at Riley. Her eyes were closed, hands relaxed on the bend of her knees, chest rising and falling in a perfect rhythm. Ella could count the freckles across her cheeks.

"No peeking." Riley's lips curved into a smile.

Ella's cheeks flushed. *How did she know?*

She clamped her eyes shut again and sighed. *I can do this. It's as easy as... well, breathing.* She relaxed her hands, trying to mirror Riley, and counted to four. In through the nose, out through the mouth. Her mind protested at first, but then she visualised her breath forming a protective bubble around her.

Inhale… The bubble glowed, its pale blue hue radiating light.

Exhale… The protective circle stretched, growing stronger with every breath.

Inhale…

When Riley's voice announced it was the end of class, Ella could hardly believe it. A light weightlessness cradled her body, and the floating sensation lifted her to her toes. She squinted against the bright light as Riley brought the session to an end.

The group bowed as a collective, and Ella flinched, pain spreading up her back. Was that from her tumble down the cliff or her near drowning? Who knew.

She stretched, feeling a warm tug in her muscles, keeping her eye on Riley as she spoke with Rick by the fountain. His hands moved wildly as they chatted, like he'd just seen a UFO battle with sky sharks and not spent the last hour practising steady breathing.

Pauline popped into view, lifting her arms up to the sky. "Wowsies! Wasn't that fantastic? I feel s–o–o–o relaxed." She plopped the pink hat back on top of her head, almost knocking it into Ella's forehead. "Who do you have for your energy alignment class, bestie?"

Ella took a step backwards. "Senhor Arenoso." The official fun sponge himself.

"Ooh, you lucky kitten. I hear he's the best."

Ella snorted. Lucky wasn't a word she would choose to describe herself. Instead, she had to be on her best behaviour. She couldn't exactly skip the sessions to practise her candid photo shots. The last thing she needed was the course leader on her back too.

"Are you going on the hike to the ruins this afternoon?" Pauline asked, tucking her hair behind her ears. "I hear they're stunning, and you get the best view of the whole island from up there. But we can only go when the tide is out."

"No, thanks. I think I'll pass." All of Ella's earlier lightness was already seeping away. That was the trouble with this sort of thing; it never lasted. The bubble always burst. "I'm gonna hang around the docks, see if I can bribe someone to fetch me alcohol from somewhere."

Pauline laughed uncertainly, unsure if Ella was joking. Ella wasn't sure either. But it sure beat an afternoon drowning in the sea.

"Do you want to walk to breakfast together?" Pauline asked.

Sensing there was no use in resisting their budding friendship, Ella accepted. She rolled up her yoga mat, tucking it into one of the cubbies at the side of the reception building, before making her way to the front. Pauline trotted behind her.

Riley looked up as they approached and gave them a small smile. "Hi. How did you find your first class?"

Ella searched her gaze for any flicker of playfulness, but Riley's stance exuded formality. "It was…fine, thanks."

"I loved it!" Pauline squealed next to her, the sound

echoing through the courtyard.

"I'm glad you enjoyed our first session, Pauline. I look forward to seeing you both tomorrow."

And that was that.

After breakfast, Ella and Pauline went their separate ways for their first energy alignment sessions. With a happy bellyful of fresh fruit and pastries, Ella took the stone steps down to Senhor Arenoso's hut. Grass coated the clifftops, small yellow flowers sprouting from the cracks. The humid summer air carried the fresh blend of earth, salt, and pollen, and she inhaled deeply as she passed some derelict cabins with crumbling roofs, wondering what was inside. Compared to the rest of Sandy Springs, they were an eyesore. She'd have to have a peek inside another time.

She descended the steps further, carefully stepping over a colony of ants as they carried what looked like flakes of pastry across the path, and then another hut came into view before her. Nestled in the edge of the cliff, its huge round window looked out across the ocean, and moss and wildflowers sprouted from the roof and clay walls. The wooden bifold doors hung open, a gentle breeze tousling Senhor Arenoso's shoulder-length dark hair as he sat cross-legged in the centre of the room.

Ella approached him quietly, unsure whether to alert him to her presence or not. Was it against conduct to disturb someone meditating? Were they like sleepwalkers, and waking him could result in a startled fight and end with her broken body at the bottom of the cliffs?

She waited outside the doors for a moment, admiring his rich copper skin and thick, black moustache. He was dressed in a simple red kaftan embroidered with gold markings, very casual compared to his decadent dress for the introductions yesterday.

Just when Ella was about to leave, he blew out a loud breath and turned to face her.

"Ella. *Bem-vinda*. Welcome. Please take a seat."

She stepped inside, the strong aroma of incense tickling her nose. Dark wooden slats coated the interior, with colourful artwork adorning the walls. A tall bookcase lined the back, with leafy plants hanging from the ceilings in cream macramé baskets. Ella glanced at the long table centred in the middle of the room and opted to sit in a rickety-looking chair in the corner.

"*Interessante*," Senhor Arenoso commented in his thick accent, tilting his chin towards her. "Why did you choose to sit there?"

"Erm…" Ella scanned the room, noticing several comfier chairs behind the table that she'd missed. "Sorry. I, uh, didn't think it mattered."

"Everything matters. Even the teeniest, tiniest of things." He stood, the breeze wafting his kaftan as he crossed to the other side of the room. *I hope he's wearing underwear under there.* "Can I offer you a drink? Water? Tea, perhaps?"

"Tea sounds great, thank you." Ella swallowed, picking at the skin of her thumb. Was that a trick question too?

"What flavour would you like?"

He opened a creaky cupboard, revealing far too many variations of tea. Ella just wanted Yorkshire Tea from back home. *That many flavours is just ridiculous.* "I'm happy with any," she lied.

No doubt I failed that secret test too.

"Very well." He plucked two bags from his collection, flipped on the kettle, and spun to face her. "Ella, just by looking at you, I can tell you're deeply troubled."

Her mouth dropped open before she could mask it. *Talk about brutal honesty.* His directness almost made her miss her mother's not-so-subtle 'your brother is the best' digs.

"Most people are troubled," he continued. "Modern-day living takes a toll on our minds and bodies, trapping us in a vicious cycle of disrepair. But being alive is a gift. The greatest gift of all. We can't treat ourselves like we're expendable. There is and only will be one of you, Ella Cargill. Ever."

Her skin pricked at the mention of her full name. She resisted the urge to roll her eyes.

"Being at Sandy Springs, you'll become more sensitive to the sensations happening in your body. The energies around you, and how everything on Earth is connected. We're part of one whole—we're the earth, and the earth is us." The kettle hissed, and Senhor Arenoso filled the cups with boiling water, handing her a mug with a cockerel on it. "Our energies are the difference between living a stressed life and a contented one. And do you know who holds the key to unlocking these secrets?"

"Erm…you?"

He beamed, his teeth blindingly white against his sun-kissed skin. "You, Ella. You hold the keys to your own life."

That explains all the fuck-ups, then.

He sipped at his tea, even though steam billowed from his mug. "I sense your resistance. You're not the first person to step onto this island with scepticism, you know. But I assure you, if you surrender to the process, your life will never be the same again."

Surrender to the process? What is this place, a cult?

He closed his eyes and inhaled deeply, looking out across the ocean. Ella followed his gaze, watching the waves lift up and kiss the rocks where she and Riley had been yesterday.

Heat prickled her neck remembering their encounter, and she sipped at her tea for distraction. The water scalded her tongue, and she hissed. Then the taste registered, and a mix of conflicting spices assaulted her senses. She scrunched her nose. *What in Satan's mistress is this poison?*

Oh, god. Is it some sort of hallucinogenic to unlock my inner and deepest thoughts?

Ella didn't want that. She'd spent the entirety of her adult life trying to do the opposite of unlocking her thoughts. Life got depressing far too fast when she realised how far away she was from achieving her dreams—or from admitting that her dreams up and left her the moment her ex-girlfriend did.

Senhor Arenoso handed her a glass of water, and she gulped it readily. "Thank you."

His dark eyes studied her for a moment, and she shifted in her seat. "What your time here aims to do is give you the tools to help build your life the way you want. Everything is intertwined, Ella. Every creature and every element is a thread of pure connection, harnessing energy and contributing to the earth's heartbeat. You are part of a complex energy system. Amid the grind of daily life, people forget that, and their chakras become blocked, disrupting their emotions and keeping them trapped."

Nerves gathered in Ella's belly, tightening at the thought of what *unblocking* her chakras might entail. She imagined it wouldn't be a quick-fix over-the-counter laxative.

"Ultimately, what you get out of this is up to you," he continued, caressing a plant leaf between his finger and thumb. "You have your own free will. The staff here, along with the spirits, cannot fix your problems for you, but they can help guide you as you form your path. The question is: are you ready to take the first step?" He turned to face her, his regal essence flowing off him in waves.

He'd make a killing as a door-to-door salesman.

"Yes," Ella said, her response sounding more like a question than a definitive answer.

Senhor Arenoso smiled, though it didn't quite touch his eyes. "*Está bem.* Let's get to work."

***

When Ella left Senhor Arenoso's hut, her brain ached like it'd been drummed by a hormonal woodpecker. She couldn't handle any more talk about energies or chakras. She was up to her eyeballs with hippie chitchat.

She'd be lying if she said that some of the things didn't resonate. The principle that all things on Earth and beyond were connected did give her a swell of purpose, but he was right, she was resisting. Why, though, she couldn't quite put her finger on. She just wished things were simpler.

"Surrender to the process."

The only thing Ella wanted to surrender to was a soft, cool bed or alternatively, with the same compelling urge, a strong, beautiful woman. But to her surprise, it wasn't Maeve's long legs filling her fantasy. It was the smiley yoga instructor.

What is it about the Portuguese sun that makes me so damn horny all of a sudden?

She padded along the sand in her bare feet, taking note of the green lifeguard flags this time. Causing a scene wasn't on her agenda today, even if it might mean Riley gave her some attention.

"Is that what your life has come to, Ella?" she chided herself, crunching a broken shell beneath her foot. "Throwing your body to the sea with hopes of getting fondled by the attractive yoga instructor?" She laughed out loud at the ridiculousness of it. She wished she could call Winnie and tell her.

The thought caused her lips to shrivel as she imagined also telling her about her plan to win back Maeve. She knew exactly what she'd say: what a terrible idea. Deep down, she knew she was right. Both ploys reeked of such desperation, Ella wondered if her best friend could sense it across the Atlantic. She groaned, wishing she could just call her. It was difficult to know what she should do. Loneliness enveloped her like a blanket.

Most of the group had gone on the hike to see the ruins on the island, which meant they'd be gone for hours, and she had most of the beach to herself. The last thing she needed was Pauline chirping in her ear while she tried to unwind, but as she padded through the sand alone, Ella realised that the woman's company might not be such a bad thing. She was nice, and that was more than most people.

God. She rolled her eyes at herself. *Now I'm missing England's divorcee of the year, too?*

She dipped her toes into the sea, letting out a sigh as the water lapped at her ankles. The large rocks came into view, secluding the beach from the main stretch, and she tilted her head back, catching the birds ferrying between the cliffs. Being in nature settled her, and she continued to paddle, breathing in the salty air.

A particularly round bird darted overhead, and she tracked its path towards the crags, catching sight of someone standing at the top. Riley. *Again? You've gotta be shitting me.* Ella stopped walking. She didn't want the woman to think she was following her. That would be weird.

But she didn't want to hide, either. She could be normal. Maybe.

She pressed forwards, splashing the water around her calves. Senhor Arenoso said she needed to form her own path and follow the earth's energies. *No matter what Riley or Maeve are doing.* Ella needed to try, and she wouldn't let any beautiful women get in her way.

CHAPTER SIX

Riley

Riley swung gently side to side, her body cradled by the hammock. Aside from the faint fairy lights hanging over her cabin door at the top of the path, darkness enveloped her. Her gaze passed over the speckled stars in the sky, and she let out a heavy breath, disturbing her cat Ziggy, who was lying on her chest. He meowed, stretching out his legs and scratching his nails up Riley's stomach.

"Sorry, Zigs," she whispered, running her fingers through his soft orange fur. Gentle purrs rumbled in his throat, and he rolled over. The hammock was a Ziggy magnet.

The sweet aroma of the strawberry tree caught on the breeze, and with a deep breath, Riley turned her attention back to the night sky. An iridescent crescent moon made the hue a deep, intense black, the moonlight reflecting on the ocean waves.

Sleep had eluded her again. It always did this time of year, but normally, stargazing and meditating helped. Caught in a stare with the tar-like sky, her mind buzzed as though the nearby crickets had crawled right inside her skull. Cuddling Ziggy eased it a little but didn't quite calm the storm weathering in her chest. The nightmares had come thick and fast tonight, forcing her up and out of her bed.

The screeching of tyres, Elodie's high-pitched scream, the crunching and cracking of metal. The boy's crying. She didn't have to close her eyes to see the damage. It cast itself onto the sky above her like a projector, morphing the constellations to reenact her dreams. The blood, the debris, the flashing sirens. The memories still made Riley's stomach sick.

She knew it would pass eventually, and patience was key to bringing her mind back to balance. But Riley was tired; tonight, she just wanted it to stop.

Squeezing her eyes shut, she focused on her breathing, trying to take her attention away from the intrusive thoughts. *"Observe them, and then let them pass. Focus on your breathing."* Senhor Arenoso's voice echoed through her brain. *"You'll be okay."*

But the images still burned behind her eyelids.

A swirl of red hair joined the mix, a lifeless body rolling through the waves. Saving Ella had flared up some old memories, blurring the lines between past and present. She opened her eyes, but Ella's face remained, floating above her in the starry sky.

She couldn't think about Ella now as well. Clearly, immersing herself in nature wasn't working.

She scooped Ziggy up into her arms, breathing in his comforting scent, and carried him up the path to her cabin. Once inside, she laid him on the blue bedspread, and he flopped onto his back, exposing his white fluffy tummy. Riley half-smiled, giving the soft fur a tickle, before turning her attention to the bookshelf beside the bed.

Her chest tightened when her eyes locked on one particular album. She hesitated, but the urge compelling her forced her feet to move. The album's thick spine was worn and creased by time, but Riley couldn't look away. She'd been fighting the impulse for days.

She pulled it out and thumbed through the pages. Elodie's pale face smiled back at her, posing on their bed, selfies of the two of them kissing in Barcelona and Madrid, Elodie's dark hair caressed by the wind. Each happy photo of them together twisted her guts tighter and tighter into a ball.

What am I doing?

Recounting a painful trip down memory lane wasn't going to help her. Marco Marcos would have a fit if he knew. Falling into these bad habits went against a lot of philosophies she held close. She'd tell the clients in the course that they needed to break the cycle, not to dwell on what they knew caused them pain, not to give up on the breathing techniques she'd practised with Ella yesterday.

But Riley was a hypocrite.

Her gaze combed over cinema tickets and faded receipts, blurry Polaroid pictures from their trips to Amsterdam and Paris. Riley never cared much for the city breaks and drinking, but somehow, she didn't mind when it came to Elodie.

But Elodie would roll her eyes if she could see her now. She'd never understood the need to keep "pointless junk" and would question the reasons for Riley taking random mementos from their dates—but this just proved Riley's point. Without this album—without all of these things—it would be as though the two of them never even occupied the same space. As if Elodie wasn't the love of her life.

It had been years since she'd seen or even heard from her, but that didn't stop the fresh, familiar pain from sliding into her chest and squeezing around her heart, like it always did this time of year. How quickly they'd gone from soulmates to strangers was something no amount of time could help her understand. Her new thoughts about Ella only seemed to exacerbate the guilt.

She and Elodie had been together for most of their twenties, until that night coming back from Elodie's parents' house changed everything.

One minute, they had their whole future ahead of them. The next, their lives were never the same.

The car accident was the catalyst but not the figurative nail in their coffin. Their relationship couldn't withstand all the aftermath. The media, the court-case, how Elodie turned to the bottle instead of her for support…. Riley couldn't save someone who wasn't willing to help themselves. She knew this—she saw it proven day after day at work—but still, she couldn't help but feel responsible for how things had ended between them. Ultimately, she wasn't enough.

Would it be the same with Ella?

Her head spun, Elodie and Ella tumbling together in a tangled mess. She slammed the photo album shut, kicked it away with her foot, and dragged herself to the kitchen cupboard. She rummaged around, yanking out half-empty bottles of vegetable oil and condiments until she found the bottle she needed at the back and pulled it out.

She poured the whisky into a glass, swirling it before taking a sip. The rich, smoky taste coated her tongue, and she winced. Riley hated the stuff. It reminded her too much of her Irish father.

But needs must.

She took a bigger gulp, eyes watering as a splutter caught in her throat. "Jesus." She could hear the sharp twang of her father's tone in her ears, almost see his thick head of grey hair as he sat at the bar in the living room with some of his poker buddies. She tried to mask her own accent the best she could—any reminders of her childhood just brought on uncomfortable conversations—but some other habits were harder to erase.

A montage of memories bombarded her, images of picking up a drunken Elodie from the bathroom tiles, sick in her hair. Then an angry father, trashing her house, slurring his words like missiles. She drained the glass then poured out another, cradling it to her chest as she strolled across the wooden floor. Drinking only made her feel worse, but tonight, she couldn't stop.

A meow made her pause and turn. Ziggy lay twisted into a shape that couldn't possibly be comfy, but his green eyes were trained on her.

"You're not judging me, are you, Zigs?"

He blinked, then decided to clean himself. *I'll take that as a no.*

She approached her canvas. The black hole at the centre swirled outwards in aggressive swipes, curling in swift movements towards the edges.

She took another swig from her glass, relishing the warmth in her belly, and picked up her brush. Her thoughts filtered into the strokes, hard straight lines, blues and reds and purple. She drank again and painted more, until her heart hammered against her ribcage, and she took a step back to admire her work. The whirlpool had taken shape, the layers of colours adding depth and highlights, but her eye was drawn to the small faceless person, tiptoeing around the edge, about to fall into the hole.

How poetic.

She finished her drink with a gasp, leaning forward as the sensation rushed to her head.

You're just as bad as Elodie.

Her thoughts tried to overwhelm her, but the booze provided a velvety barrier. Yes, her breathing was ragged, and her behaviour was questionable, but as Riley straightened to take in the painting before her, pride swelled in her chest. Seeing the inner turmoil on the canvas gave her a boost.

"Marco Marcos can't say I'm not being proactive," she murmured, adding touches of white to the waves.

"*Shame you'll do nothing with ye life,*" her dad's voice echoed, hand on the bottle, swaying in the doorway. "*Just runnin' away like ye mam.*"

"Oh, shut it, Da." Riley laughed at the slur in her voice. If only she could say those words to him now. She could imagine the way his lip would quiver and his eyes would darken, but she wouldn't be scared. She'd just say it again, louder.

Okay, that's enough whisky tonight.

Guilt swam into her stomach. Senhor Arenoso would be disappointed if he knew. Riley had a feeling the guru already suspected she wasn't doing as well as she said she was. He had a talent for such things and had already checked on her twice this week. Jane had, too.

Riley sighed. She'd blown Jane off a few times, not up to having company, but she needed to be better. She would be happy-go-lucky Riley in the morning. She just needed to sleep off this alcohol and let the sun warm her bare skin. She just needed the anniversary to pass. Then she'd be fine again, just like she always was.

And being fine was better than the alternative. Riley had seen the other side, and she wouldn't follow in Elodie's footsteps. Or her dad's.

Tonight hadn't been great, but she'd get back up and try again. She just needed to refocus and recentre. Clear her head of Elodie- and Ella-related things.

She sighed again, allowing her mind to wander. Ella's teasing smile popped into her mind, followed by the cackle of her laughter, and the funny dance she did after being pulled from the water. It was true, the redhead was cute, but she was also unpredictable. Ella would invite chaos into Riley's life—look at everything that had happened so far. That was the opposite of what Riley wanted. She needed balance. Peace. Quiet.

Her job and life here gave her that. She couldn't jeopardise them, especially when she was already teetering around the edge of a whirlpool, trying not to fall in. Who was she kidding? She was in no place to pursue anything—even if she was, any sort of relationship with a client was seriously off-limits. If she lost her job, she didn't know what she'd do.

It wasn't as if she could go back to Ireland.

Riley needed to keep her distance. No matter how attractive the curvy redhead might be, or how intriguing her fiery personality seemed, appearances could be deceiving. She had to remember that.

She couldn't let a silly crush get in the way of her progress.

CHAPTER SEVEN

Ella

Ella sipped from her glass of water even though she wasn't thirsty. The throbbing in her temples wouldn't ease. The cool liquid slid down her throat, and she took another drink before glancing back at Marco Marcos. He spun a pen between his fingertips, his inquisitive brown eyes not leaving hers.

They'd quickly shifted from the polite niceties of "how are you finding your time here?" to the more serious, making-you-reconsider-every-decision-leading-to-this-moment questions.

When Ella set her glass down but still didn't say anything, he raised his wild brows, glasses bouncing on the bridge of his nose.

She sighed and looked away at the framed picture of a crab on the back wall. Even its beady eyes were judging her. "I don't know how to answer that."

"Honestly."

She met his unwavering gaze again. "How am I supposed to know if I'm a disappointment? You can call my mother if you like."

He clicked his pen twice before twirling it between his hairy fingers. "That wasn't the question, Ella, but it's interesting that you connected those two elements together. Why do you think your mother is disappointed in you?"

Ah, shit.

While their mum accompanied Devin to each of his violin practices, their dad got lumped with ferrying Ella to the various extracurricular activities her parents had signed her up for, hoping she'd find her calling. Swimming, dance class, tennis, and a painful martial-arts taster, where Ella took a beating from a girl four years younger than her, splitting her eyebrow. The trip to A and E didn't deter them, and the cool touch of her mother's comfort grazed up Ella's forearm. *"We'll find you something that makes you happy, darling."*

Ella had settled for netball. Her parents loved coming

to watch the matches—Dad calling encouragement from the sideline, Mum in her Barbour jacket, scarf wrapped tight around her neck, and Devin sitting cross-legged on the floor, head deep in a science book.

But Ella didn't feel the passion playing the way Devin did. She found hers perfecting the details of a project, finding the perfect font, and seeing the growth of her clients on her computer screen. Concrete proof that she was doing something that mattered.

But now she was useless again. No wonder her parents wanted to intervene.

She chewed at her lip, feeling it wobble. She didn't want to open that can of worms. She looked down at the printed A4 resting on her lap, where a stick figure flailed its limbs helplessly, its top half attached to balloons and its lower to weights holding it in place. Words were placed inside. *Disappointment. Lonely. Worthless. Shame. Guilt. Pain.*

A delectable word cocktail. Ella was spoilt for choice. After yet another confusing yoga class this morning, with Riley blowing hot and cold and Pauline gushing about how amazing and life-altering the ruins were, Ella felt a connection with all of the words at once. Exploring her feelings about her mother and living constantly in Devin's shadow would only make her feel worse. *No thanks.*

She readjusted her bikini strap under her top, moving it off her sunburnt skin. Falling asleep on the beach yesterday had come with the nasty price of a sore nose, chin, shoulders, and chest, too. Under Marco Marcos's stare, it seared even more.

Without saying a word, he scribbled in his pad, eyebrows twitching like caterpillars crawling across his face. Then he flipped to a new page and leaned back in his cream chair with a creak.

"Often, when we feel stuck, identifying the root of these feelings can help us understand those emotions and navigate a way forward. There's so much pressure in day-to-day life, Ella. Most of the time, these pressures are ones we needlessly put on ourselves. I can help you. I *want* to help you. But if you're not honest with me, that makes it difficult."

Ella clicked her tongue. All this talk was prickling her nerves extra hard today. She was trying. In her own way. It wasn't her fault everyone else was better.

"You seem annoyed," he commented. "Would you like to expand on that?"

No alcohol. No phones. No Maeve. No Riley. Every time Ella went to the beach, it tried to bloody kill her. Everything she said was monitored and picked apart. The way she moved and *breathed*, for Christ's sake.

This place sucks. Worst. Holiday. Ever.

She imagined the giant crab crawling out from behind the painting and seizing Marco's bald head in its shiny, red pincers.

"I'm fine," she said, with a sigh.

His stare flitted over her face. Then he clicked his pen and started scribbling.

Get me out of here.

***

When the session finally drew to a close, Ella stomped out into the afternoon sun, her head still aching and her skin feeling like she'd been rolling around in nettles. A visit to the beach was out of the question. She didn't want to see anyone, and she certainly didn't want to see Riley.

Actually, the more she thought about it, the more appealing it sounded to get on the first boat she could see and return to the mainland. What were Winnie and her mum thinking, sending her here? She needed to hear her best friend's voice and tell her how stupid this all was.

Goats, grazing on the hillside in their pens, bleated at her as she passed, while a bored-looking teenager sat on the crumbling stone wall offered a bob of his head. More people greeted her on the way, but Ella marched forwards, until she spotted the tree with the creepy fingers swaying at the top of the path.

She dumped her bag at the tree's base and retrieved her phone from inside. After a quick glance around, she heaved herself onto the branch, wincing as her sore skin brushed against the bark. She gritted her teeth and kept climbing, letting out pained grunts until she reached the same place as the other morning. Her signal bar jumped up, and she switched her data on. Her phone immediately vibrated with notifications, and the corners of her mouth lifted.

See, you're not a complete lonely loser.

But then her eyes scanned the words on her screen,

and her blood ran cold.

No. She read it again. Then she clicked the notification, bringing up a picture of Maeve and Annabelle, beaming and holding Annabelle's newly engaged hand up to the camera.

Ella's gaze fixed on their perfect smiles, and tears pricked her eyelids. She homed in on the gigantic, beautiful rock on Annabelle's finger. They were engaged? Maeve and Annabelle…engaged? Her mind couldn't comprehend it, but there it was, right in front of her, in perfect filtered pixels.

A surge of emotion overpowered her, and she let out a sob. This wasn't right. Maeve wasn't supposed to marry Annabelle. It wasn't supposed to be like this.

She brushed stray tears across the back of her hand, reading through the comments with blurry eyes. All the congratulations from her old coworkers, Maeve's dickhead dad, Maeve's friends that Ella had once considered her own friends too.

Truly, worst holiday *ever*.

She was never going to be good enough, no matter what she did.

She leaned back, letting the sadness consume her. Memories of their relationship played in front of her eyelids, the sinking feeling spreading into her chest like sludge and weighing her down, until it was all she could feel. All the words from Marco Marcos's sheet swirled around her at once. Ella stopped squashing down the emotion and let it all out. She didn't care anymore.

Too late to react, her phone slipped out of her hand. It clunked as it hit multiple branches on the way down, then landed on the hard ground with a smash.

"No! No, no, no!" She slammed her fist into the hard bark, instantly regretting it as pain shot up her forearm. With a heavy body, she lowered herself down to the ground, dropping clumsily onto her arse. She scrambled to her phone, pain throbbing up her back, and flipped it over. The black screen was shattered, and despite her pleas for it to work, it remained unresponsive.

How was she supposed to call Winnie? She was officially stuck here now. Permanently.

God. What a way to hit rock bottom. Arse first, falling out of a tree.

So she sat, cradling her smashed phone, and let the tears fall. She felt crushed. By all of this. Not even a bathtub of margaritas would help. And now she couldn't even speak to Winnie about it. Another sob broke from her throat, and a shadow passed over her.

"Ellie, what's wrong?" A tall man was approaching. She recognised him as Rick from her course. Those pale calves were bright enough to blind someone. "Are you alright?"

She sniffed, not having the energy to correct him on her name. She truly did not care. "I'm fine." When he hovered, glancing around for some assistance, she added, with a little more bite than she intended, "Rick, please leave me alone."

He took a step backwards. "Uh, sure." He gave her

an awkward salute and shuffled off.

Ella waited for his floppy head of hair to disappear down the hillside before groaning. She didn't mean to be rude, but she only wanted to speak to Winnie. She always knew the right thing to say to pick her back up again.

But that wasn't going to happen; she was on her own. And unless she wanted to follow in Pauline's footsteps, she couldn't just stay curled up in a ball and cry. Maeve had moved on. Ella needed to, too. She just needed to get up off the ground.

"Get it together, woman," she muttered to herself.

With a heavy sigh, she forced her limbs to move and wiped her face, but the tears wouldn't stop. Her mind was running in circles around her, and she pressed her palms into her eyes, overwhelmed.

"Ella?" another voice called behind her.

Ella didn't have to turn to know it was Riley. *Great.* She didn't need her adding to the mix as well. But Ella felt the woman stand next to her and lay a gentle hand on her shoulder.

"Are you hurt?" she asked.

Ella didn't know how to respond. Truthfully, everything hurt. She didn't know where to start.

"Ella, please. Talk to me. I'm worried."

Ella didn't want to open her eyes and see the sympathy no doubt showing on Riley's face. Maybe if she squeezed her eyes tightly enough, she could rewind time and pretend none of this had happened. But she was done pretending. It didn't get her anywhere.

"I swear everything I touch turns to shit or tries to kill me," she started. "I was only trying to call my friend, and now…I can't even do that. I'm just stuck here…"

Riley rubbed her back, and Ella just wanted the ground to open up and swallow her whole. Any minute chance she'd had of scoring with the beautiful blonde had officially leaped off a cliff to die forever. Just like her last pathetic attempt with Maeve.

"Come on," Riley urged, trying to guide Ella towards her. "It's going to be okay. I promise."

Ella didn't like promises. Maeve had promised her too many things that had fallen apart. Their own home. Being co-partners of Switch Studios. A whole life together. But there was something about Riley's voice that made Ella drop her hands and open her eyes. When the kaleidoscopes focused, Riley's steady blues looked back at her, and a cool balm spread across Ella's chest.

Riley gave her a small smile, indicating behind her with the lift of her chin. "Come on. I have a phone you can use. You can call whoever you need to."

Ella's lungs heaved as an involuntary sob escaped. The idea of speaking to Winnie relieved some of the pressure in her head. "Thank you." She sighed, her words coming out in a soft whisper.

"Just don't tell Senhor Arenoso," Riley joked, her mouth pulling up at the corners. She led Ella away from the tree and towards some stone stairs leading further up the hillside. Ella's mind was too overrun with everything to speak, so she just focused on Riley's back.

Riley held back the overgrown branches covering the path, and Ella thanked her as she hurried past. The steps opened up into a small, lush garden. A blue, striped hammock hung between two large strawberry trees at the bottom, with more steps leading up to another cabin, pink oleander shrubs blooming on either side. Ella's eyes darted at all the colour around her, and she breathed in the sweet, fresh scent, trying to calm her sniffles.

When she hesitated, Riley led the way, encouraging her like someone trying to round up a stray dog.

The wind tousled Ella's hair as she reached the last step, and she turned around to take in the sight. *Wow.* She'd thought the view from the courtyard was impressive, but this was something else entirely. The elevated height gave a god-like view over Sandy Springs. The white slats of the cabin roofs disappeared into the green canopy, and she could just make out the tiny people gathering in the courtyard. The endless, unruly ocean stretched beyond them to the blue sky, sunlight glinting off the waves. She could see for miles. Her gaze followed the land as it curved, spotting the dock at the bottom. *Is this where Riley saw us on that first night?*

She cringed at the memory, then cringed even more at the state Riley had found her in just ten minutes ago. *Fuck's sake.*

She glanced back at Riley, standing tall in the doorway. Now that her initial panic had passed, the reality of the situation was starting to sink in.

This was Riley's cabin. Her own personal cabin.

Ella's eyes were drawn to the large wooden dreamcatcher hanging over Riley's bed. The soft blue duvet and decorative pillows, including an adorable "bee happy" one. She tried not to let thoughts about Riley and her bed spiral into anything else. She cleared her throat, not knowing where to look.

"The phone is in here," Riley said, holding the door open for her. "It's a landline, plugged in behind the sofa there. Call whoever you need to. I'll give you some privacy." She smiled, dimples forming in both her cheeks, then ducked back out the door, leaving Ella alone in her cabin.

Ella couldn't shake the feeling that this wasn't normal procedure for Riley—but then, what did she know? Riley was probably just being nice. *It's her job, Ella.* She shouldn't read into it.

Although…

Riley's space sucked Ella in as her gaze roamed over her belongings. Embroidered artwork brightened up the wooden walls, along with a variety of paintings that Ella wondered if she'd created. A covered canvas rested on an easel, with pots of paint gathered underneath. Large wooden shelves overflowed with books of all colours, and every corner or shelf had another green plant soaking up the sunlight that was pouring through the windows.

Ella briefly thought of the plants in Maeve's office before pushing the thought away. She didn't want to cry about Maeve ever again. Or think about her here. Riley and Maeve were nothing alike.

She ducked behind the yellow sofa and picked up the landline phone. Luckily, she'd known Winnie's number by heart since they were teenagers. She dialled it and took a seat on the sofa, sinking into the soft cushion.

Winnie didn't answer. Ella sighed and called again, holding the phone to her ear with her shoulder.

She answered on the fifth ring. "Uh, hello?"

"Hey, Winn. It's me."

"Ella! Hey… How's it going?" There was a muffled sound on the other end, and a deep voice mumbled in the background. "I'm sorry, Cal, but this might be important."

Winnie's heavy breathing was suspicious. "Am I interrupting anything?" Ella asked.

"Nah. It's fine… Oh, Calvin, grow up." Winnie blew out a breath. "Men. And they like to say that women are the dramatic ones."

Ella bit her lip, shaking her head. "Were you…?"

"Yeah, but it's fine. A break in the middle will just make it last a bit longer." She laughed. "But enough about me. How are you? What phone are you calling me on?"

"I'm… Winn." Ella swallowed. "I… It's…so difficult here."

"Have you given it a chance?"

Her accusatory tone made Ella sit upright. "Yes, of course—"

"Ella, you can't bullshit me. You need to listen to what they're saying. Focus on you for a change."

Ella rolled her eyes. "God, you sound just like Senhor Arenoso."

"Just call me 'wise one' from now on."

She snorted. "You're stupid." Then she remembered about Maeve and Annabelle. Her smile quickly soured. She told Winnie.

"Ah, fuck. Ella, I'm so sorry. That's never nice to see. But you deserve better. You know that. You do."

Ella let the words roll around her mind before responding. She unpicked other memories she'd shoved into the recesses of her brain. How Maeve turned her nose up at her for reading fantasy novels and watching romcoms. Their polarising moral views and how Ella was banned from discussing politics with Maeve's family. How, when Ella put on a few pounds, Maeve offered to pay for a gym membership, which just made Ella feel worse.

She knew on a logical level that she and Maeve weren't right for each other, but there was something about that door being slammed so firmly in her face that unsettled her.

"Let me hear you say it," Winnie said, with all the enthusiasm of a cheerleader. "I deserve better."

"I'm not saying that."

"Come on. You know I won't stop until you do."

"Fine." Ella huffed, but her mouth pulled at the corners. She could always count on Winnie. "I deserve better."

"Louder!"

"I deserve better!"

Winnie cheered, and she laughed. "So, whose phone

are you calling me on?"

"It's Riley's, she's—"

Winnie wolf-whistled down the line, and Ella pulled the phone away from her ear. "No. It's not like that. She just works here."

"Mmm. I don't buy it. I have an Ella bullshit detector that's currently flashing red and whirring like an air-raid siren."

"Winnie." Ella rubbed her hand over her face before continuing. "Fine. But it's not what you're thinking. I don't think she's into me at all."

"How could she not be? Look at you!"

Ella smiled at her best friend's enthusiasm before the feeling fell away. "I don't think so. She works here, and I just keep being so stupid around her."

"Isn't that the Ella sign that you're into someone?"

"Hey!"

"You know what I mean."

Ella could see the nonchalant wave of Winnie's hand in her mind's eye. She missed her. She could almost see her sipping cocktails in their favourite spot, too, complete with a grumpy Calvin tending the bar.

"I don't want you to be chasing this girl instead of focusing on you," Winnie went on, "but I'm not gonna tell you to be a nun, either. A good shag might just set you right."

Ella blushed, and she looked for Riley, even though she knew she couldn't hear her. "Oh my god, Winn."

"I mean it, Ella. I want you to do things for you. Find

your groove again. If sleeping with a hot woman helps you do that, I'm all for it."

Ella laughed, tracing a circle on the cushion with her finger. "How do you even know she's hot?"

"Well, is she?"

Riley's prominent cheekbones, blue eyes, and strong physique flashed before her eyelids. Her toned arms and dimples. But she was more than that. The kindness she'd shown Ella stirred a warm feeling in her belly. "Yeah, but—"

"Knew it." Winnie's voice took on a serious tone. "Look, I know it's not exactly what you thought you'd be doing at this point of your life, but life is unpredictable. Roll with it. Seize every moment. Take advantage of this course. Don't regret it."

"Sounds like you could get a job here, Winn," Ella grumbled.

"That's 'oh wise one' to you."

The sun streamed through the tall, open windows, warming Ella's skin. She looked out, wondering where Riley was, but could only see the ocean from here. It did seem like she was stuck here for the foreseeable. She might as well make the most of it.

"So," Winnie said. "Tell me more about this Riley."

CHAPTER EIGHT

Riley

Riley sat on the bottom step, looking out over the ocean as the sun beat down on her, but her mind kept replaying the same thought. *What are you doing?*

She'd done the complete opposite of staying away from Ella, and now the redhead was in her cabin. Her cabin! What if she went through her things? What if someone saw them together?

Riley, what are you doing?

Her heart thumped hard in her ribcage, and she plucked the amethyst necklace hanging past her sternum to rub it between her fingers. Sucking in a deep breath, she imagined the air reaching the ends of her fingers and the tips of her toes. Panic pushed back, and she closed her eyes, trying to bring her heartrate down.

She couldn't help it. Seeing Ella upset triggered a protective urge in her. She just wanted to help; that was all. She'd sprinted over after spotting her with hands covering her face and soft sobs leaving her lips. The absence of her bubbly personality and fierce laughter had caught Riley off-guard. The vulnerability she'd shown her—intentionally or not—made all her reservations take a back seat. She didn't know why the reaction was so strong, but now Ella was in her home... What was she supposed to do?

Ella's voice cut through the cries of the birds, followed by laughter, and she grinned. *She's feeling better.*

Okay, so that worked. As soon as Ella finished her phone call, she'd leave, and everything would be fine. There was no need to panic. Nobody needed to know.

Riley couldn't help but wonder who Ella wanted to call. An ex? A friend? She chided herself; it was none of her business. She shouldn't care—she didn't.

The murmur of Ella's voice faded away, but when she didn't appear, the fear flared up in Riley's stomach again. What if she looked at her paintings? The photo album of her and Elodie? *Oh god. My sex toys under the bed?*

She hopped up the steps, dodging a fuzzy bee as it

flew across her path, and hovered outside the cabin, straining to hear any conversation. Hearing nothing, she lightly tapped on the wooden door and entered.

Ella lay awkwardly across the yellow sofa, her legs bent at an unnatural angle. A soft bundle of fluff curled up in her lap, her fingers combing through Ziggy's fur. She looked up when Riley appeared, her eyes wide.

"I was afraid to move," she said in a hushed tone, as though Ziggy were a sleeping infant. "I didn't want to disturb him."

Thick, gooey warmth spread through Riley's belly. She tried to mask it, but the feeling amplified when Ziggy purred, and Ella shot her a delighted grin.

"Oh my god," she whispered. "I think he likes me."

Riley took a seat on the arm of the sofa, peering at her traitorous little baby in Ella's arms. She couldn't find herself to be annoyed that Ziggy's loyalty had jumped at the first pretty woman to walk in here, but she couldn't get used to the happy feeling swelling in her chest, either.

She glanced down at the floorboards instead. "So, uh, everything go alright? With your phone calls?"

"Yes. Thank you." Ella spoke so softly, Riley struggled to hear her. "Thank you so much for letting me use your phone."

Riley chuckled. "You're welcome, but you really don't need to be quiet around him. He'll sleep through anythin'. Even Bernardo's crows."

"Ugh! I hate that cockerel." Ella's vehement grunt, combined with the whispering tone, made Riley laugh more.

"Really. Ziggy'll be fine. You don't need to whisper."

"Ziggy," Ella cooed, threading her fingers through his ginger hair. "That name suits you perfectly, doesn't it?" She gazed at him, batting her thick black lashes.

Okay, now I am a little bit jealous.

"He's so gorgeous. Is he yours?" she asked.

"He is, but don't let that pretty face fool you. He's smashed his share of plant pots when he gets late-night zoomies, and he thinks my surfboard is his personal scratching-post. Not to mention my childhood teddy bear that he did unspeakable things to. I've never been able to look at Mr Buttons the same again."

"Mr Buttons?" Ella cackled, and eliciting that response coated Riley head-to-toe like sunshine.

"You seem to be feeling better," she noted.

Ella dampened at that, breaking eye contact. She circled Ziggy's belly a few times before she spoke. "Yeah…thank you for being so kind to me. I'm sorry you had to see that before."

"You don't need to apologise for anything."

She met Riley's eyes then looked away again. "That's sweet of you to say, but I don't want to be a burden. I'm sure you're busy."

Riley frowned. "Ella, you're not a burden. No one is perfect all the time."

"I bet you are." Her words hung in the air between them. Her hand stilled on Ziggy's tummy, her cheeks reddening to match her hair. "But I should go. I just…" She glanced at Ziggy and smirked. "…Can't move."

Riley's mind hitched on Ella's words. Perfect? Memories of her drunken stupor the other night flashed before her eyes. Riley was far from perfect; Ziggy would attest to that if he could speak. After he'd demanded he be fed, of course. "You want me to take him?" she asked.

When Ella nodded, Riley scooped the fluffball into her arms and carried him to the bed. Lazy green eyes blinked back at her before he rolled onto his back with a stretch of his legs.

"Your place is really cool," Ella said. "I guess your favourite colour is blue, huh?"

Riley turned back to face her, surprised to see she'd taken a few steps and was now standing inside her "bedroom". Riley adored the open-plan design of her cabin, but now that Ella could see everything in her space, she wished she could close the doors and hide some of it away.

"Erm…yeah." She scratched at her neck. "Thank you." She followed Ella's gaze to the paintings hanging on the walls, hoping she wouldn't ask about them.

"Did you paint these?"

"Some."

When she didn't offer anything else, Ella turned to her, raising an eyebrow. "Are you not going to tell me which ones?"

Heat tickled the back of Riley's neck, and she scratched at it again. "I don't really share my work with people."

Perhaps sensing her unease, Ella let it go. Her attention wandered over the frames and canvases, lingering on a watercolour of the olive trees that Riley had painted in her first month on the island.

"Well, whoever painted these is really talented." Ella threw a smile over her shoulder.

The compliment landed right in the centre of Riley's chest, and she couldn't stop the feeling from spreading into her heart. Maybe Ella was just being polite, but the way she continued to admire the small details on the canvas made the compliment resonate even more.

Her focus drifted over Ella's body, her wide hips and round bum, thick thighs hugged tight in her denim shorts. Someone like Ella was probably never short of dates. Riley's love life was laughable in comparison.

But there was no harm in just looking, right?

Ella's voice made Riley's eyes snap upwards.

"I guess I should get going, but thank you again for letting me use your phone…and pet your cat." Ella lifted her shoulders, exhaled, and then leaned down to give Ziggy's belly a tickle. He chirped, and she jumped back, startled.

God. She's cute.

Riley tucked her hands into her pockets, biting back a grin. "You're welcome."

They held eye contact until little tingles rippled along Riley's arms, making the hair stand on end. Ella's irises swirled like golden honey in the sunlight, and the way they bore into Riley, confident and alluring, set her heart racing.

Her focus dropped to Ella's full lips as she wet them with a flick of her tongue, sending a ping of arousal between Riley's legs. *Jesus.* She shuffled her bare feet against the cool flooring, looking anywhere but at Ella's gorgeous pillowy mouth.

How long had it been since she last kissed a woman? She could hardly count the mouth-to-mouth with Ella on the beach. Her spluttering into Riley's mouth was hardly the stuff of romance novels.

She breathed in Ella's sweet perfume, mixed with an air of cocoa body butter.

How long had it been since Riley had even held another woman? She'd given up on the idea of relationships a long time ago. They were too fragile, too easily broken. All she could do was focus on the present; the future held no promises and offered no certainties. She couldn't think about it at all. Her memories of Elodie tried to pull at her, but she couldn't let them.

She blinked, coming face to face with Ella once again. Ella readjusted the straps of her top, revealing sore red skin underneath.

"Are you sunburnt?" Riley reached for her but thought better of it, her hand hovering awkwardly then dropping by her side.

"It's nothing." Ella tried to cover herself but winced in the process.

"Here. Let me help." Riley moved to root in the

kitchen drawer, pulled out some scissors, then snipped a stem off the aloe vera plant sitting on the counter. She split it open with her hands, and the cool juice glistened under the light pouring through the windows.

Ella eyed her warily. "I'm not eating that."

Riley laughed and shook her head. "I don't want you to eat it. Rub it on your skin, and it helps ease the pain. Nature's own anti-inflammatory."

"Really?" She didn't seem convinced, but when Riley nodded, she shrugged. "Go on then. It can't make it worse."

She turned her back and scooped her hair into a bun on top of her head, exposing her delicate neck, then hooked her fingers under the straps of her top and bra and lowered it off her shoulders.

Riley swallowed. Ella wanted *her* to apply it? Before her brain jumped in and made her say something stupid and refuse, she gently squeezed the gel out of the stem and onto Ella's skin.

Ella hissed at the contact, and Riley's stomach rolled. She shouldn't be getting turned on by this…but she couldn't find it in her to stop. Easing out more aloe vera juice, she let her fingers rub soft circles across Ella's shoulders, taking extra care on the sore spot on her neck.

"It feels nice," Ella said in a breathy whisper.

Heat pooled between Riley's thighs. Ella's voice triggered an instinct inside her that she hadn't felt for a long time, and she started to pulse. Her hands longed to explore the contours of Ella's body, to hear more of her breathless tone and see what other responses she could pull from her lovely mouth. She swallowed, realising her fingers had stilled on Ella's shoulders, and continued her massage. When Ella's red skin was completely coated, silky and smooth, she blew out an unsteady breath.

"Okay. That's all done." The words came out softer than she'd intended. Where had her voice gone?

Ella turned to face her slowly, and Riley's eyes were drawn to her bare chest. White bikini lines hooped around her neck, leaving the rest of her skin tender and pink.

"What about the front?" Ella asked, her voice low in her throat.

Jesus. Riley's neck flushed, creeping up and into her cheeks. She didn't know where to look. Not at Ella's thick lips, which were just inches away from hers—and definitely not at her full cleavage, which was hovering gloriously below Riley's face.

"I…uh–I think you should do those–er, that part." She managed to meet Ella's gaze briefly before glancing away.

"I don't want to get my hands all slimy. Please…if you don't mind."

Riley cleared her throat, trying not to focus on the desire pooling in her underwear or the way her whole body hummed at the feel of Ella's body underneath her fingertips. "Alright."

Carefully, she squeezed the plant, biting her lip as the gel coated Ella's chest.

Good god, Jesus almighty.

Her fingers worked in slow circles as the sound of their breathing filled the room. She took extra care at the base of Ella's neck and across her clavicles, feeling her gaze on her. The air thickened, pushing them closer together. Riley tried her best not to look down Ella's top, but the very thought of caressing her breasts and pushing her onto her bed spread a deep ache through her pelvis.

With an awkward pat, she finished rubbing in the gel and took a step back. "There you go."

Ella looked up, locking Riley with those big eyes. "Thanks."

Riley glanced away. "I'll, er, cut some more for you to take with you." She forced herself to move, her head and heart warring over how this was simultaneously stupid and brilliant. Her unsteady fingers snipped another stem from the aloe plant, and she handed it to Ella. "Just apply it whenever you need it."

Ella nodded but looked like she wanted to say something else. Then she gave her a small, genuine smile. "Really, Riley, thank you."

Her heart fluttered. "No problem."

Ella glanced around the room, lingering on Ziggy. "Anyway, I'll head off. I imagine you have a busy afternoon."

Riley checked her watch. "I actually have a surfing class soon, so I should make my way to the beach."

They watched each other for a moment, and Riley's heart thundered louder with each passing beat. Ella's attention dropped to Riley's mouth, and for a few agonising seconds, she begged that she'd kiss her.

Riley, what are you doing?

"Do you want to walk down together?" Ella asked.

Riley couldn't think of a reason not to. She could hardly get in trouble for walking with a client. *Massaging their chest and shoulders, perhaps.* "Alright. Sure." When Ella didn't move, Riley indicated behind her. "I, uh, just need to get changed."

"Oh, yeah, of course. I'll just—" Ella hurried out the door, taking her bag with her, leaving Riley breathing heavily in her bedroom.

This was fine, wasn't it? The adrenaline firing through her veins, combined with the wet sensation between her legs, made it hard to tell. She'd bent more than broken the rules at this point, but at least there was no chance of getting Ella pregnant and creating a scandal, right?

Ugh. Stop making excuses.

She changed out of her bra and damp boxer briefs and swapped them for her swimming costume. She preferred the tight fit to a bikini when surfing. She had small breasts and found bikinis that suited her tall and lean frame hard to come by—less chance of accidental nipple slips while surfing, too.

After giving Ziggy some love and a kiss on his head, she grabbed her surfboard and joined Ella outside. The hot sun warmed her skin immediately, and she slipped on her shades before leading them down the path. Their footsteps slapped against the stone.

"You really do have a beautiful place here," Ella said from behind her.

"Thank you." Riley spun, almost knocking Ella's head with the end of her surfboard. Luckily, she ducked out of the way.

"Seriously, am I cursed?" Ella tightened the scrunchie holding her hair in place. "Maybe Duarte put a spell on me when I boarded his boat. Or Pauline."

They laughed, and Riley gestured for Ella to walk in front. Her voice had vanished, her body still throbbing in inappropriate areas.

"Have you lived here a long time?" Ella asked, as they joined the dusty path leading down the hillside.

"Four years."

"Wow." She held back the bush branches to let Riley past, then slipped back in front of her. "Do you think you'll stay forever?"

That question hit her square in the face. She hadn't really thought much about it. Thoughts of the future didn't come easy to her, not when her previous plans had been ripped away so easily. All she could do was focus on the present moment and take it day by day.

She adjusted her board under her arm. "I'm not sure, to be honest."

"Would you go back home?"

Riley couldn't stop the snort from leaving her lips. "No."

They reached the bottom of the path and started walking side by side to Ella's cabin, even though it was in the opposite direction to where Riley needed to go.

"How come?" Ella asked, holding up her hand to shield her eyes from the overhead sun.

"Ireland isn't my home." It sounded harsh, but it was true. Ireland hadn't been her home for a long time.

Her mind dwelt on the wooden plaque that used to hang above their front door, reading '*Home is where the waves are*' in slanted script. Riley never understood it when she was a kid. How could anyone live in the sea? Wouldn't the water be cold and unwelcoming? Wouldn't the dark be frightening?

It wasn't until she was twelve, coming home to find her dad's eyes vacant and glazed, still tapping ashes into an overflowing tray, that she really understood. Being outside and riding the ocean waves, feeling their energy wrap her in their protective arms for a while, felt much safer than the four walls of their house.

Riley wasn't used to having so much focus on her; it was normally the other way around, with her tending to clients' needs and questions, so she shifted the conversation, feeling more in control now her clit had stopped aching. "What about you?" she asked. "Have you thought more about your path?"

Ella let out a soft laugh, kicking a loose stone with her sandal. "Yeah… I guess I'm still finding my way or whatever."

"Beautifully put," she teased.

Ella glanced at her, and Riley grinned, her pulse quickening again at the look in her eyes. Teasing Ella came naturally to her, despite Senhor Arenoso's rules, which should've kept those parts of Riley tucked away. She couldn't help it.

"I thought I heard traces of an accent," Ella said, a curious lilt to her voice.

A little ball of dread lodged in Riley's throat. She didn't want to talk about her family. Or lack thereof. Thankfully, they'd just arrived at Ella's cabin.

"You ever tried surfing?" she asked instead, pretty sure she knew the answer.

Ella shook her head as someone on a bike rang their bell, and they hurried off the path. The bike peddled past, pulling a cart full of oranges, and a teenage boy called out "*Obrigado*", a "thank you" in Portuguese.

"You should try it sometime," Riley said. "Surfing." She wanted to blame her invitation on her reluctance to talk about herself, but it wasn't entirely true. She wanted to see more of Ella, but as soon as the words were out, she wanted them back.

She shouldn't entertain this. She knew that. But the excited feeling swirling in her stomach overrode her brain's sensibilities.

Ella eyed her, the corners of her mouth curling in a way that made her lips utterly kissable. "Mmm. I'm not sure," she said. "I'd hate to have to be rescued again."

"I wouldn't mind." Riley's face warmed, but she held Ella's gaze. The afternoon sunshine illuminated the gloss across her collarbone, neck, and chest. A fire blazed inside Riley, remembering the feel of Ella's skin beneath her fingertips. The tree with the creepy fingers seemed to lean towards them, eager to eavesdrop on their conversation. Bustling voices carried up from the courtyard below.

"That's good to know." Ella's attention dropped to Riley's mouth before bouncing back to her eyes. "But for now, *sesta* is calling me."

"Alright." Riley swallowed. It was definitely hot out here today, and her dry throat had nothing to do with the fiery stare and the attractive woman wielding it. "*Boa noite*, Ella."

Something flashed over Ella's features, and she lingered a moment too long before uttering an adorably clumsy "*tchau*" and disappearing into her cabin.

Ella's absence pulled a plug, sucking all the energy from around Riley. She missed her as soon as the door closed.

She pressed her forehead against her board and blew out a breath. *Boy, am I in trouble.*

CHAPTER NINE

Ella

Ella woke from her nap covered in sweat. The AC was blowing cold air through the room, but her mind couldn't peel away the dream fogging her senses. Riley's touch lingered on her skin, the imaginary sensation of her lips on Ella's. Her tongue…and how good it felt sliding between her legs.

Ella's hand dipped into her pyjama shorts. Yep. She was incredibly wet.

With a sleepy sigh, she brushed over herself, the images fresh in her brain. Her dream might not have been real, but the way Riley had caressed her shoulders and chest earlier was. Her touch was somehow firm and soft at the same time. Meaningful.

Her clit ached thinking about Riley's strong hands.

Would she fuck me the same way?

God. Ella felt herself get wetter. She heard it as her own fingers quickened their movement, and she kicked the blanket off her legs.

Warmth rippled outwards, tension building in her muscles. Her libido had finally sprung from its hiding place and now demanded her full attention.

She'd been in a tangle over whether Riley was attracted to her or not, but the woman's flushed face and adorable awkwardness had confirmed it. If Ella hadn't been knocked off her game from the Maeve incident, she might've kissed her there and then.

Riley *was* attracted to her, and that gave Ella a boost she desperately needed. Self-care had multiple forms, after all.

The dream kisses filled her mind again, but it was like having an itch that she couldn't quite reach. Ella didn't want to indulge in the fantasy; she wanted the real deal.

But for now, this would have to do.

She closed her eyes, picturing Riley's face as she rubbed circles over herself. The backdrop of Riley's cabin fleshed out her imagination as dream Riley pushed her back on her bed. There was no need for longwinded undressing here. Ella wanted it hard and fast, so that's what dream Riley gave her. Her tall and muscular frame leaned over her, her fingers exactly where Ella craved them. It wasn't long before the fuzzy feeling tightened in her chest, and her orgasm mounted. Her breathing was laboured as she hovered above release.

The one thing she couldn't get right was the sound Riley made. Would she moan or whimper? Groan? Would she talk dirty? Tell Ella what she wanted? *Fuck.* She'd like that. The thought almost made her combust.

"Riley," Ella murmured, and the sound sent shockwaves through her body. Riley's face became focused, fresh in her mind. She could see the slight widening of her eyes. The dimples in her cheeks. She said her name again, louder, meaning it as she brought herself to climax, and she tipped over the edge. She came hard, abs contracting and forcing her upright as the feeling consumed her.

The climax faded quicker than she'd have liked, but it still hit a spot. It'd been some time. She let out a chuckle as the dreamy fog lingered in her brain. *Riley,* she echoed in her head.

Maybe Winnie was right. A good shag was just what she needed.

***

Admittedly, the island's uncertainties made Ella nervous. She couldn't speak the language and imagined her feeble attempts resulting in finger-pointing and the locals' uncontrollable laughter.

But Senhor Arenoso's words breezed through her mind. *"You hold the keys to your own life."*

So, with her phone smashed and the idea of hiding in her room alone more embarrassing than being an English stereotype, she decided to push herself. With a new pep in her step, she ventured down to the courtyard, freshly showered and wearing a yellow sundress that brushed against her calves. Her skin still felt tight from sunburn, but Riley's aloe vera had eased the pain a little.

She heard the market before she saw it. Voices and chatter carried up from the courtyard in lively Portuguese. Rows of wooden stalls covered the stone slabs, and what must've been the entire island's population was milling between them, browsing homemade crafts and textiles displayed underneath large beige parasols.

Food carts served fresh seafood rice, grilled *bacalhau* with garlic, crispy cod balls, and roasted octopus, all caught off the island. Senhor Arenoso had spoken about the ebbs and flows of the wildlife, and ensuring a healthy balance between conservation and human cuisine. Ella inhaled deeply, the mix of garlic and seafood making her stomach rumble.

The stalls overflowed with fruits and vegetables of all colours. Nuts, rice, olives, and more beans than Ella knew existed. A friendly man greeted her as she browsed the fruit, and she replied with a shy *"boa tarde"*, her gaze roaming over large oranges, melons, apples, and cherries.

She bought a bag of juicy plums to snack on in her room, then followed a sweet, sugary scent to the next stall. There were people gathered around it, calling out their orders in Portuguese. When she reached the front, Ella understood why it was so popular. Fresh bread, cakes, and traditional sweets filled the shelves, and she practically drooled at the sight of doughnuts, sweet lemon *farturas*, and creamy Portuguese tarts with flaky pastry and sugared tops. Ella bought two tarts, hoping to gift one to Riley after her surfing class.

She smiled to herself as she pocketed her change; she couldn't help it. Was it wrong to chase the good feeling? The combination of her best friend's support, an afternoon nap, and a decent orgasm pointed towards the no.

She and Riley were both just human… Why not have a little fun?

That had been the initial goal of this holiday, anyway.

After circling every stall, admiring a collection of beautiful ceramics, hand-painted homewares, and patterned tiles, Ella concluded there was definitely no alcohol on sale. *Shame. A nice glass of white would go down a treat right now.*

She picked up a cork "I heart Portugal" keyring for Winnie, considered buying a gorgeous purple-and-white handwoven rug but decided it wouldn't fit in her suitcase, then headed back along the path to her cabin.

The sun was hiding behind the clouds, giving her a welcome respite from the heat. She didn't want to jinx it…but things were looking up. She even dared to say she felt happy. Her work worries seemed far away as she took a bite from the plump plum in her hand, savouring the fresh juices.

She wondered when Riley finished work—or if Riley even thought of it as that. Knowing her, she probably had some hippie philosophy that categorised it under a different name.

Ella wanted to see her again, but would turning up at her cabin be weird? She'd been off the dating scene a while, but even she knew the idea came off a little creepy. She could always ask her after their yoga session in the morning. She wanted to stay clear of any game-playing. She only had limited time on the island, better not waste any more.

She dug into her bag for her key, but as she got to the top of the hill, she found her door already ajar and twitching in the breeze.

A chill ran down her spine. Had somebody broken in?

She edged the door open with her toe. Her suitcase was spread wide, her clothes scattered across the floor in a mess. She wanted to say she'd been ransacked, but actually, this was how she'd left her room.

A strange noise came from inside. *That sounded quite like—*

She rounded the corner and halted.

A…goat.

There was a goat in her bed. And worse, it had her

big, comfy underwear in its mouth. The ugly kind that wasn't supposed to be seen by anyone and was reserved for days with cramps or bloated bellies.

The brown goat barely looked up when Ella entered, and that offended her a little. "Uh. Excuse me. Those are mine." She edged forward, and the goat's yellow eyes snapped to her. *Oh god. Do these things charge?* She swallowed. "Look. Just give me my knickers back and there's no hard feelings, alright?"

She tiptoed closer, the pungent smell of urine and dirt hitting her senses. Had it relieved itself somewhere in here? She glanced around the room but couldn't see anything obvious. Unfortunately, the goat took the small distraction by the horns and leaped off the bed, skidding across the floor and out the door—with Ella's big knickers in its mouth.

"Hey!" She sprinted after it, catching sight of its brown rear end as it dipped over the hill and headed towards the courtyard.

No, no, no!

She ran in pursuit, her sandals kicking up a cloud of dust in her wake. As she descended the hill, she was met with a raucous sound. A mix of screams, shouts, and bleats. *What the hell is going on?*

What was once a peaceful market now resembled a manic petting zoo. Goats ransacked the fruit and veg stalls, running around with broccoli and potatoes in their mouths, being chased by angry people. The stall-holders' efforts were futile, as the goats jumped on top of the displays, crashing them to the ground.

Ella spotted her goat wielding her underwear like a flag and followed it further into the chaos. The stench of urine intensified, mixed with an assault of seafood, garlic, and a smell that could only be identified as goat. Someone screamed to her right, and Ella looked just in time to see a goat rip a pineapple from Pauline's hands and scamper off.

An elderly man cornered one of the animals, but it leaped on top of a table and pushed off a bag of flour, sending a cloud of white into the air. When the mist descended, Riley appeared at the top of the steps, her eyes wide as she took in the crazy scene. Her gaze met Ella's, and she ran over to her, her long hair wet and slicked back over her shoulders.

"What happened here?" she asked, shouting over the noise.

"I've no idea. I was just…" Ella spotted the goat trotting past, still chewing on her underwear. "Minding my own business."

Riley shook her head. "This has got Romeo's name written all over it."

"What do we do?"

"We need to herd them somehow, but everything is too manic. There are goats everywhere."

Ella combed the scene, thinking of something to use. "I've got an idea. You ring the yoga gong and get everyone to meet at the yoga cubbies."

"I don't think breathing exercises are going to calm

the goats."

Ella nudged her in the ribs. "Not for bloody breathing exercises. Just do it and meet me there."

Riley sounded the gong, gathered the locals' attention, and then instructed everybody over to Ella. The locals resisted, looking on at the destruction the goats had caused in horror. They muttered in Portuguese, giving Ella uncertain looks.

"You'll have to translate for me," Ella said to Riley, then cleared her throat. "Okay, everyone. Grab a yoga mat, and let's round these goats up. We've got to work together to form barriers, and then we can guide the goats back to their pen."

The people looked on while Riley translated, and understanding dawned on their faces. A few gave Ella nods of approval, but she was trying not to melt at Riley speaking in Portuguese. *Is there anything this woman can't do?*

Ella and Riley handed out yoga mats from the cubbies, and they started organising themselves into groups to pin the goats into one place. Thankfully, apart from one particularly naughty goat that could ascend the walls, the mats held strong. With a quiet focus descending on the group, and a dedicated team sent to rescue the escapee from the roof, the goats were rounded into submission and guided back up the path to their pen through the wide-open gate.

Once the last goat was inside, everyone cheered, offering Ella hugs and kisses on the cheek. Under usual circumstances, Ella would rather eat rusty nails than touch a stranger, but their genuine appreciation for her struck a chord, lighting a small flame in her chest.

They headed back to the courtyard to start the clean-up, but Riley lingered at the back, a huge grin on her face.

"Well done," she said, securing the lock on the gate and giving it a tug. "That was a clever idea."

"Thank you." The praise fanned the glow in Ella's centre, but she tried to brush it off. "The free-thinking voodoo of the course must be rubbing off on me."

Riley chuckled, glancing down at her feet. "Then Senhor Arenoso will be pleased."

"And you?"

"Me too."

Their eyes locked, and the air around them buzzed. Ella could almost sense Riley's hands on her back, feel the dusting of breath at her neck. She wanted more.

"I want to thank you again for yesterday. I really appreciated making a phone call." She swallowed. "And the aloe vera."

"You're welcome." A blush coated Riley's cheeks, but she wouldn't look at her. Instead, she cast her attention to the courtyard behind them. An unsettling feeling gripped Ella's insides. Being around Riley was like riding a loop-the-loop rollercoaster; she never knew which way was up.

"Shall we go help clean up?" Ella asked.

Riley looked over the fence at the goats grazing the pasture like they hadn't just wreaked havoc on Sandy

Springs. "Oh…uh, I think you've done your part. There's no need for that."

The comment stung, dropping Ella back to Earth abruptly. "Don't you want me there or something?"

"Ella…" Riley scratched at the back of her neck, and the sinking feeling enveloped Ella's whole body. "I just… You… There's no easy way to say this—"

"Here we go." Bile crept up her throat. This might be a new record for Ella rejection. What would the reason be this time? Too loud, too fat, too emotional, too much? How had she got this so wrong?

"It's not like that," Riley said, but she still wouldn't look at her, and that made anger twist in her gut.

"Riley, if you've got something to say, just say it. I'm a big girl. I can take it." Ella gritted her teeth. She didn't really want to have this conversation now, to shoot the possibility of exploring her relationship with Riley in the foot, but the feeling steered her, and the words tumbled out. "Why are you fighting this? I know you feel something here." She took a step towards her. "Tell me I'm wrong."

The goats bleated in the background. Riley shuffled her feet.

"Ella, I just…can't." Her gaze finally met Ella's, and the sadness there struck her. "I can't do this with you."

The rejection stung, slapping Ella across the face and pouring salt in old wounds. Tears threatened her eyes, and she suddenly felt very, *very* stupid. How many times was she going to put herself in this position? Just to get torn down by a beautiful woman?

"Tell me I'm wrong," she said again, a quiver in her voice. When she was met with silence, she scoffed, shaking her head. "You're a coward, Riley."

And she spun on her heels, putting as much distance between them as possible. Horrible, ugly sobs crept up her throat, but she held them in until she was out of sight.

No more women. Ella vowed never to let someone hurt her like this again. This was stupid, *so* stupid.

She cursed, realising that everything people said about her was right.

She was stuck. She had no purpose. She was looking for a quick fix. Something to make her feel better and to stick a plaster over the problems. But all that meant was the next time it was ripped off, it stung twice as badly, pulling off all the ugly scabs.

Her feet moved quicker, taking her further away from Sandy Springs and up the hillside. She didn't know where she was going, but she didn't care. Sweat beaded her forehead and ran down her neck, but she pushed on, until her feet ached and her lungs struggled to breathe.

Winnie had said a good shag might sort Ella out, but she realised she didn't want that. She didn't want a rebound. She wanted something that would last, like what Maeve and Annabelle had.

God. Now I'm jealous of them?

She admitted the truth. She longed to find someone who wanted her for who she was. Not a condensed version of herself—a quieter, thinner, smarter Ella 2.0—but an

Ella who was intrinsically Ella. With all her loudness and flaws and imperfections.

Ella didn't need to fly all the way to Portugal to be rejected again. She could've easily done that back home. She brushed the tears away with the back of her hand.

You need to break the cycle.

She heard Senhor Arenoso in her head and cursed, shouting to the wind. It frustrated her because he was right. If nothing changed, then this was going to be her life. Ella didn't want that.

She needed to focus on herself.

That hit her brain like a skimming stone, reverberating outwards.

I need to focus on myself.

This whole time, she'd been chasing something she thought would make her happy. Getting back with Maeve. Sleeping with Riley. The easy fix. A dopamine hit that would ultimately leave her feeling shitty. She couldn't do that anymore. She needed to put herself first.

A new sense of energy rushed through her. Her world of possibilities was blown wide open.

Ella could do anything she wanted to do, and she knew exactly where to start.

***

Pauline was right—the ruins were stunning. Ella ran her hands over the cool, crumbling stone and let out a sigh.

She didn't know how long it'd taken her to get here—she had no watch and no phone now that it'd been smashed to pieces—but judging by the sun's position in the sky, hours had passed.

Huge overgrown bushes sprouted colourful flowers around the ruins, nature finding its way back through the cracks in the masonry. She made a mental note to ask Pauline about the history here; she'd not been listening to her before and probably owed her an apology.

A profound sense of calm descended on her as she walked through the ankle-length grass and looked out over the cliff edge. Dark clouds gathered above, but that feeling of foreboding never came. It felt as though each wave lulling against the shore far below was reaching out to her, coating her in a calm she'd never felt before.

She hadn't meant to snap at Riley, or call her a coward, but she'd hated the feeling of her pulling away, and she hadn't been able to stop herself. Still, she shouldn't have done it. She knew better than anyone how mixing work and pleasure brought many complications, after all.

After a few more minutes of watching the waves, she started her journey home.

Luckily, the worn path had been easy to spot on the way up, and the castle's towers poking out from the trees had acted as a good guide. Ella could do the same with Sandy Springs on the way down and use the village as a guide. She followed the path as it wound down and around the hillside but stopped dead in her tracks when it disappeared into a body of water.

Weird. I'm sure it was this way.

She spun around, looking for another option, but the lone path that joined the two hills was now hidden by the tide.

Shit.

The water lapped at the earth around her. Was it still rising? She retreated up the path and concluded, after a few minutes of watching, that, yes, it was.

A prick of fear crept up her spine.

Not ideal. But she could make it work. Her tree-climbing skills were proving to be competitive—as long as she didn't drop anything—but having no water or food might be a bit worrisome.

Her belly rumbled on cue. With all the goat—and then Riley—palaver, she'd missed dinner.

Her hopes sank along with the light in the sky as the tiniest of raindrops landed on her skin. Were there wolves in Portugal? She couldn't remember. It would be quite the tragedy to finally rediscover her mojo and then be eaten alive by a rabid pack.

She supposed she'd find out; she was going to be stuck here all night.

CHAPTER TEN

Riley

Riley's hair whipped back across her face as she soared over the waves on a jet ski. She bobbed with the movement, spray spitting up and coating her clothes, but she could barely feel it. Her focus flicked between the dark clouds crackling in the sky above, and the place where the path to the ruins should be.

What was Ella thinking?

Riley couldn't believe she'd visit the ruins so late, especially at high tide. *Especially* when the weather was turning.

Actually, she could believe it. It was exactly the kind of stupid idea that had Ella written all over it.

Anger brewed in her belly. It was like the woman had a death wish. If Duarte hadn't spotted her on his way back from a supply drop, she'd have been stuck out there all night.

What if something has already happened? A chill spread down her spine, and she made the engine go faster, gaining height over the choppy waves. If their last conversation turned out to be the way they left things, Riley would never forgive herself.

Because Ella was right. Riley was a coward.

But we're focusing on Ella's stupidity here, not mine.

If she thought about confronting Ella about her feelings or admitting that, yes, she was attracted to her, she might just throw up.

Riley had cut off any matters of the heart years ago. Why was the fiery redhead interested in her? It didn't matter, anyway. She didn't want to be a holiday throwaway. She couldn't be. That wasn't the way she operated.

So why was she racing across the sea like a madwoman, trying to rescue her?

I should book another session with Marco Marcos.

The hillside came into view as a flash of lightning crossed the sky. *Shit.* She needed to be quick. She pulled the jet ski around the land, her eyes combing the path leading up to the ruins.

"Ella!" she called, losing her voice to the wind. Ugh. She'd have to get closer.

She drove the jet ski onto the grass, slipping and sliding and tumbling off onto the ground. She dragged it further inland and, after making sure it was secure, started jogging up the path to the ruins. She called her name again, her chest already heaving from the exertion and adrenaline pumping through her veins.

Her hair whipped around her face like a hurricane, and a clap of thunder rolled through the sky. If she didn't find Ella soon, they were going to get caught in a storm. The last place they wanted to be was on the water.

She pushed herself, feet slapping the ground underneath and carrying her closer to the ruins. The stone structure poked out above, guiding her. When she crested the top, moving aside the overgrown branches arching over the path, a purple fork cracked across the sky.

"Ella!" she shouted, her voice hoarse and breathy from the journey up. She ducked her head into the crumbled structure but came up short.

If she wasn't here, what was she going to do?

Dread smothered her stomach again, and she called louder, the wind thrashing in her ears. A small raindrop landed on her nose, and she lifted her head up just as the downpour began. The water quickly soaked through her T-shirt and shorts, but she continued shouting.

"Riley?"

The voice was so soft, Riley thought it was a figment of her own imagination at first. But then she turned, and

Ella stood under a fallen doorway, soaked to the bone in her yellow summer dress.

"Are you alright?" Riley closed the distance between them, relief coating her, followed by trepidation.

"What are you doing here?" Ella asked.

"More like what are *you* doin' here, Ella?" She waved her arms. "Are you trying to get yourself killed?"

The softness in Ella's voice vanished in an instant, replaced with a fiery rage. "Actually, Riley, I was trying to give myself to this stupid course, and it's just trying to kill me!"

Unbelievable. "You can't keep blaming the course for this. You should know you're not supposed to come here at this time. Did you even read the booklets we gave you?"

Ella's face said it all, but she continued to scowl.

"Do you have any idea how dangerous this is?" Riley huffed, the rain continuing to pound the ground around them. "I could shake you."

"Well, I could shake you too," Ella grumbled, folding her arms across her chest. "Do you have any idea how frustrating you are?"

"I can't be half as bad as you."

Their gazes locked, more electricity flowing between them than was racing across the night sky. The wet, earthy smell filled Riley's nostrils, as another booming thunderclap surrounded them.

Riley broke contact first, walking past Ella and into the stone structure. Most of the roof had fallen away, but branches of a nearby tree hovered over the top, providing a little bit of shelter. She stood under it and sighed, feeling a brief respite from the pelting raindrops.

Ella followed her in and rested her hands on her hips. "What are you doing?"

"Waiting." This woman's naivety started to grate on Riley's nerves.

"I agree this place has its quirks, but I don't fancy staying here all night."

"Ella." Riley ground her teeth. "If you haven't noticed, there's a storm going on above our heads right now. We have to wait it out."

"Can we make a fire?"

"Everything is wet."

"So what are we supposed to do?"

"Wait," Riley snapped.

Rain pattered on the leaves above them, branches twisting and wailing in the wind. They didn't speak for a few minutes. Riley's body started to ache, the cold seeping into her bones. Ella wandered around the space, peering at the crumbling walls. In the streaks of moonlight dappling through the cracks, there wasn't much to see.

"Well, I'm so thrilled you came to rescue me. The conversational wizard herself." She stopped walking and turned to face Riley.

"You could be more grateful." Riley pushed off from the wall where she'd been leaning. "Do you have any idea what I'm risking for you? If Senhor Arenoso knew we were here?"

To her surprise—and absolute outrage—Ella scoffed.

"This isn't a joke to me, Ella."

"This isn't a joke to me either, Riley." Ella's voice quietened, and she stepped towards her. The moonlight glinted on the hair plastered to her face, but the look in her brown eyes made Riley pause. "This is not what I thought I'd be doing with my life at thirty-three. I lost my job, my ex-girlfriend/ex-boss got engaged to the woman she cheated on me with, and then, to top it off, a goat ransacked my cabin, stealing my knickers."

A goat stole her underwear?

The detail seemed less important when Ella took another step towards her, close enough now that they could reach out and touch. Her gaze held Riley's, and it was impossible to look away.

"It's hard to believe in myself," she continued, "when my mum and best friend both think my life is in such a state that I need this…intervention. It's even harder to realise everything they were saying is absolutely true. And then there's you."

Riley swallowed, suddenly aware of her breathing. She was hanging on Ella's every word.

"My heart has been stabbed, stomped on, squished and sawn into teeny tiny pathetic pieces more times than I can remember. All my life, I've been too stubborn, too loud, too little, too much, and this time I wonder if they're right. If everything they say is true and needs fixing. Why else would I be here, stuck in the middle of this storm, cold and pissed off at the world, with yet another person who thinks I'm all of those things?" Her eyes became glassy, teeth snagging on her wobbly bottom lip as she looked away. "But when I see you…it's like all that bad stuff is forgotten for a second. When I see you, my heart still reacts. I can't help it. Maybe that's stupid, or naïve—or both—whatever. But it reminds me that maybe I'm not so broken after all." She flicked her attention back to Riley, pinning her in place. "Maybe I am some of those things, and that's okay. I'm not afraid to admit I'm not perfect. I'm just me."

Riley's cheeks burned as Ella moved closer, the air fizzing with energy.

"So I'll ask you the same question, Riley. Do you have any idea what I'm risking for you?"

Riley couldn't speak. Or find any cohesive thoughts other than taking Ella in her arms and kissing her. She hated that anyone had made Ella feel small. She hated even more that she'd added to that. Or that she could ever think she was too much. Ella was an all-powerful lifeforce of energy, so strong and so bright that most people probably didn't know how to compete with it. She wore her heart on her sleeve, her struggles, her desires. She was human. Real. Beautiful and flawed in the ways humans should be.

But Ella mistook her silence for something else, and she shook her head. "That's what I thought." She turned away, her footsteps soft on the mulch underfoot as she put distance between them.

Distance that Riley didn't want.

"Ella, wait."

"You know what?" Ella spun to face her, taking quick steps to get back in her face. "This whole course is about finding yourself and getting out of your comfort zone. But why don't you practise what you preach?" Her voice stung, cutting straight through Riley's heart. "When was the last time you ever got out of your comfort zone?"

Ella's chest heaved, those wild eyes flicking between Riley's.

She was right. Riley always bit her tongue, always tried to keep control. She couldn't say anything in reply. Words wouldn't cut it. Pushing all her doubts and reservations off the nearby cliff, she reached out, placing a hand on Ella's waist.

The gasp was soft in the pattering of the rain around them, but Riley still heard it. She pulled Ella closer to her. Delicate hands landed on Riley's chest. Riley's breathing malfunctioned, alarms blaring in her head, heart racing like Ella was petrol and Riley's body a waiting match.

Before she could change her mind, she leaned in, pressing her lips to Ella's and lighting the flame.

Ella's soft mouth kissed her back, and Riley's stomach plummeted. Time slowed. Freefalling in the best way possible. The chatter in her head fell away, leaving the feeling lighting her up head to toe, fire engulfing all of her senses.

Ella's grip tightened on Riley's T-shirt as she kissed her deeper, her nails grazing through the fabric of her soaked shirt. She opened her mouth to her, and heat filled Riley's belly, curling the tips of her toes. She welcomed it, delving deeper, feeding the kiss with everything she wanted to tell her but couldn't. She loved her sweet taste. Her plump, pillowy lips. How she wore her heart on her sleeve and kissed just the same. She wished she were as brave.

Her hands drifted from Ella's waist to the curve of her bum. Every touch elicited a new, breathless sigh, and Riley wanted it all. She cupped Ella's jaw, pushing the slick strands back from her face, her kisses becoming desperate. She couldn't get enough, and dragged her lips along her soft neck, inhaling her scent and placing a firm kiss to her pressure point.

Ella's gentle moan woke Riley's clit with a throbbing ache, and she pulled back to look her in the eye, noting the moon reflected in her dark irises. Something knotted deep within her loosened, and she leaned in to kiss her again and again.

The wind swirled around them, but Riley hardly noticed it. Every sense pointed to Ella, singing a song that was uniquely hers. Her body hummed, pleasure and arousal searing every nerve ending. Why had she been fighting her instincts so hard?

They finally parted for breath, hearts beating wildly. Riley missed her touch immediately.

"That's better," Ella commented, her breath tickling Riley's mouth.

Riley smiled, pressing her lips to hers and pulling her closer, two wild flames burning bright in the pouring rain.

CHAPTER ELEVEN

Riley

Riley closed her cabin door behind them and flicked on the light. The rain continued to hammer against the roof, but the worst of the storm had passed. Ziggy meowed from his spot on the bed, squinting against the brightness, and Ella scampered over to him, leaving drip marks across the floorboards.

"Hello there, handsome," she murmured, scratching behind his white ears.

Riley stood still on the welcome mat, raindrops

rolling down her forehead and arms. The whole ride home, she'd soared higher than the birds in the sky as they'd skipped over the waves, Ella's arms tight around her waist.

Their kiss had electrified her, filling her veins with a shot of something she hadn't even known she needed. Hand in hand, they'd sprinted through the rain as it bounced around their ankles, and Riley had brought them both here on autopilot.

But back inside the familiar space of her cabin, reality descended on her, swirling her mind like the storm's black clouds.

What am I doing?

Ella glanced her way, probably wondering why she hadn't moved or said anything since they stepped inside.

Riley slipped her sodden shoes off and cleared her throat. "I'll just get us some towels."

She pulled two fresh, fluffy ones from the bathroom and handed one to Ella. Now the adrenaline had started to wear off, she could feel the cold seeping through her soaking T-shirt and shorts. She rubbed the towel over her hair as Ella fussed Ziggy. His loud purrs could be heard even over the pouring rain.

Riley's eyes wandered over Ella's body. Her yellow dress clung to her curves like a second skin and was incredibly distracting. Especially when she noticed her firm nipples pressing through the material. *God.*

"Would you like a change of clothes?" she asked.

"That would be great, thanks."

She pulled out two clean T-shirts and two pairs of pyjama bottoms and left Ella's on the bed. "I'll just get changed in the bathroom. Give you some privacy."

She left and closed the door before she could cringe over herself. Why was she suddenly being so formal and…strange?

Or was the more apt question, why had she invited a dripping, see-through, incredibly attractive Ella into her cabin after midnight?

Her heart stuttered in her chest, and she leaned forward, grasping the porcelain sink to stare herself in the mirror. Her breathing fogged the glass, terrified blue eyes staring back at her.

What's the big plan now, Riley?

She should tell Ella to leave. It'd already gone too far.

The memory of her lips made her stomach somersault, and she tightened her grip on the sink.

Being around Ella had a unique effect on her. As though all the chaos in her mind quietened when they touched. It was dizzying but not unclear. Quite the opposite—it was as if she'd put on a pair of Ella-glasses, and everything had come into focus for the first time in years.

But the reality of that was immobilising.

Senhor Arenoso's furrowed brows and deep-set frown popped into her head. She had to tell him…but he'd be so disappointed. She couldn't afford to lose the only person she thought of as family. Or her job. She couldn't be like António.

Her mind was running away with itself. But what could she do? The thought of sending Ella away after what she'd said at the ruins made her want to vomit. And more importantly, she didn't want Ella to leave. She didn't want her own fear to be the reason this feeling ended.

She sucked in a few deep breaths, letting the sensation wash away the negative energy clogging up her veins. Then she slipped off her wet clothes and got changed, hanging the sodden ones on the radiator.

Sensing she'd been a while, she opened the bathroom door, stopping herself halfway through. "Er—you all good in there?"

Ella laughed. "Sure. You can come back into your own apartment."

Ella was sitting on the bed, dressed in Riley's oversized navy T-shirt, one of her old surfing ones from back home. She'd pushed her red hair back off her face, which was flushed and still a little pink from sunburn.

Seeing Ella in her clothes made Riley swallow. She was perfect.

Not helping, brain.

Ella's dark eyes were focused on her. Even now, in the comfort of unflattering oversized clothing, electricity sizzled between them. She wondered what thoughts were occupying her mind. Was she overthinking this as much as Riley was? Or was this something that happened to her often?

Since she and Elodie broke up, Riley couldn't even think about putting her heart in the firing line again. How could she do that when Ella was going to leave in a couple of weeks?

Ziggy hopped onto Ella's lap, and she giggled, delighted. The sound shot endorphins straight into Riley's heart as she scratched at his chin, his purrs loud enough to send tremors through the cabin. Riley tucked her hands into her pockets, not knowing what to do with them. Why did it feel like she'd never done this before?

"Would you like a drink?" she asked.

"What do you have?"

"Teas, coffee, water…whisky."

"What?" Ella's sudden jump in volume startled Ziggy, and he ran under the bed. She stood, closing the distance between them.

Riley feared for her life.

"This whole time, you've had whisky in here?" She shook her head, her eyes wide, but Riley caught the quirk of her mouth. "How many more secrets are you keeping?"

Riley chuckled nervously, retrieving the bottle from the cupboard and pouring two small glasses. She didn't like to talk about herself. It opened too many trapdoors.

But what did you expect would happen, inviting her back here? Eejit.

Ella checked out the label, letting out a low whistle. "Sixteen years? Nice. You know your whisky."

"Not really. My dad." She handed Ella her glass.

"Are you two close?"

She shook her head. "No. Not really."

Perhaps sensing she'd stepped into a sensitive topic, Ella didn't pry, much to Riley's relief. She swirled the amber liquid with a smirk. "I can't believe you've had this here the whole time. What about Senhor Arenoso's rules?"

"Let's just say I know a guy." She forced a smile she wasn't really feeling. The implications of all the rules she was breaking piled on top of one another, pushing her further into sinking quicksand.

Did Ella expect them to have sex? What if Riley disappointed her? What happened when Ella left? Should she tell her about the anniversary? About Elodie? How the biggest secret was that she didn't really have anything together at all?

What was she supposed to do?

Nausea rose in her throat, and her breaths came quick and fast, the glass shaking in her grasp.

What if someone found out and she lost everything again?

"Riley." Ella's voice was soft. "Do you want me to leave?"

Riley opened her eyes. Ella's gaze studied her, the frown line etched deep into her forehead.

"It's just…a lot."

Ella pressed her lips together, her eyes darting over Riley's features. "I'm not expecting…anything, you know. This is all far more than I deserve."

"Please don't say things like that." The sharp edge in

Riley's voice surprised them both.

"I'm just saying. You've already saved me twice." She stepped forward and caressed Riley's cheek. "As long as we're on the same page, we're fine. Talk to me. What do you want?"

Talking was so simple, yet so foreign. But as Ella stroked her cheek with her thumb, the stress and sickness in Riley's stomach slowly ebbed away. She leaned into the warmth with a sigh, the soft touch grounding her. The intimate gesture soaked into every fibre of her being, with Ella's big, emotion-filled eyes looking back at her, searching, yearning to go deeper. Their connection seemed to surge between them, radiating from the point of contact on her skin, speaking of something that stretched for several lifetimes, a feeling that scientists could never quite explain.

Her energy. Just…everything that was Ella. Riley couldn't fight it.

She met Ella's gaze and uttered softly, "I want you to stay."

They sank down into Riley's sofa, and she pulled the orange blanket over them. Ella tucked her legs underneath her, her knees resting against Riley's. Even that was enough to send flutters to her chest, even through two layers of pyjama bottoms.

Riley sipped at the whisky, hoping it would ease her nerves. With the blinds drawn, the only light came from the lamp she'd acquired from the market, casting a soft, warm glow over the room. The rain continued to thud on the roof, and Riley realised she'd completely lost track of time.

Luckily, tomorrow was Sunday, her one day off in the week, so she didn't need to worry about that. Or the implications of any of this. The fact that a client was sitting on her sofa, in her cabin, wearing her clothes.

Or the fact that she'd kissed her, and now she was tracing Riley's forearm with her fingertips.

She tuned back into the feeling, chastising herself for worrying about work. She needed to be present. Who knew how much time she and Ella had? How fast things would change?

Time is a storm in which we are all lost.

She met Ella's gaze, feeling her heart speed up at the soft swirl in her irises. "I'm sorry. I don't do this…like, never do this."

"That's okay. I don't either."

"Really?" She found that hard to believe. Ella laughed, and she straightened her face out, feeling it pinched. "But you're gorgeous."

The corners of Ella's mouth curled. She brushed her fingers down to Riley's wrist, leaving tingles in their wake. "I could say the same thing about you. Have you looked in a mirror recently? You're like an Irish beach babe Thor but like…hotter."

"I don't think so." She chuckled and shook her head, wet strands tickling her back.

"I do."

Their gazes locked. Ella's hand stilled on Riley's.

Her focus fell to her lips, and all she wanted to do was kiss her again. To feel her body light up the way it had at the ruins. To explore this with her without any fear.

But fear had her in a chokehold.

"Did you mean what you said at the ruins?" she asked instead, her voice barely audible over her thundering heart.

"Which part?"

"All of it."

Ella looked down at her lap. "I mean, yeah, it's true my life fell to shit, and that's why I'm here. But I think I'd been living like that for a long while before."

Riley recalled what she'd said about her ex-girlfriend/ex-boss. Was that who she'd wanted to phone the other day?

"I guess I never realised how much I was doing just to please other people," Ella continued. "What I thought I should do. Taking a step back, I can see that a lot of those things weren't making me happy. Not really."

Riley knew the feeling.

After what happened with Elodie, she'd chase anything to take her mind off the pain. But running only takes you so far; she had to stop and walk through it to finally see she was just feeding and extending the process.

Some habits she still fell into from time to time.

Her gut soured at the sight of the glass of whisky in her hand. She didn't want to be like her dad. She downed the liquid so she didn't have to look at it anymore, then set her glass on the table.

Ella followed suit, spluttering a little as it slid down her throat—an action Riley found far too endearing—and they fell back onto the sofa together, limbs entwined. Ella's hair had curled from the rain and fallen over her face. Riley's hands itched to reach out and move it, to trace her jaw with her fingertips, but she wasn't brave enough.

"Did you mean what you did at the ruins?" Ella asked, and Riley realised she'd been staring at the woman's mouth again.

Heat flushed her cheeks, nerves multiplying in her belly. Though she was fairly certain of where Ella stood on the kiss, she could never be one hundred percent sure. This was not exactly an everyday situation they found themselves in.

"The kiss, I mean," Ella confirmed, then adding in a whisper, "Do you regret it?"

Riley's hand folded over Ella's instinctively. "I don't regret it. I kissed you because I wanted to."

"Okay. Good. Because I don't want to be something you regret, Riley."

Riley's heart fluttered. Ella's vulnerability called to her in a way that made her want to be brave as well. She looked down at their entwined hands, Ella's small and warm underneath hers. "I won't lie to you and say this doesn't scare me—because it does. I feel completely and utterly out of my depth and…" She chuckled, remembering Ella's words at the ruins. "Out of my comfort zone."

The curl of Ella's lips told her it was the right answer. Her brown eyes flickered to Riley's. "What about now?"

There were many things Riley could say to that, complicated and tangled in a mess of other things, so she answered simply. By capturing Ella's lips with hers.

When she switched off her mind and followed her body's instincts, it was a no-brainer.

Ella sighed into the kiss, her fingers threading into Riley's hair and pulling her closer. Her soft lips explored Riley's, parting her mouth to brush their hot tongues together.

Oh my god.

Everything inside Riley turned to jelly. Soft, pliable putty that Ella could shape in her hands. She played her like her favourite instrument, lighting up music all over her skin, with a loud thumping drum pounding between her legs.

The kiss started softly, quickly intensifying, lighting a fuse that burned all the way up Riley's spine. Her pulse quickened, the heat blooming outwards, leaving them breathless when they parted.

Those deep brown eyes, flecked with caramel under the warm light, stared back into Riley's. Her body hummed with Ella's energy, craving more, needing more.

Those kisses were dangerous. Riley would sign over her soul to Ella as long as she kept kissing her like that.

She hadn't felt this way in a long time. Not since—

Her brain jolted awake, feeding her with warnings and flashing lights, and she looked away. The boy's screaming. The headlines. Picking a bloody and drunken Elodie up from the pavement. How a split-second accident upturned their whole lives.

Ella cupped her cheek gently, and the touch grounded Riley, quietening the voices.

"So, how are we going to do this?" Ella asked. "I know we're not in normal dating circumstances, but…" Riley's eyes flickered to hers, and a warm, gooey honey spread around her heart. "I don't want this connection to go to waste."

"I don't either." She sighed, feeling shaky from the adrenaline and endorphins pounding through her system. "And I don't want to distract from your experience here. The course and everything."

"Me neither." That surprised Riley, and Ella laughed at her expression. "Shocking, I know. But I actually want to—god, I can't believe I'm saying this—but…I want to *surrender* myself to the course. Like Senhor Arenoso said. I really do want to work on what makes me happy."

Something like pride washed over Riley, and she smiled. "I'm glad to hear that."

Ella brushed a hand through Riley's hair, and she shivered at the touch. "And I obviously don't want to do anything that would jeopardise your job and life here."

Riley nodded. No one could know if they explored this further. As the thought passed through her mind, the urge flared to run and hide herself away. There was so much at stake, and she couldn't end up back where she was four years ago. But she didn't want to get caught up in the details of the future and the dos and don'ts.

She wanted to be present.

She wanted to be brave.

If she let Ella slip through her fingers without even exploring what their connection could be, it would go against everything she believed in. Not only would she be a hypocrite, she'd also be the world's biggest eejit.

"I don't do any of this lightly, Ella," she said, the fuzz of the alcohol descending on her. "I could lose my job." Her eyes passed over Ella's face, studying her expression. Her emotive eyes, full cheeks, soft lips. *Those lips.*

Ella took her bottom lip into her mouth and bit down on it.

Lord, Jesus.

"That sounds like a lot to risk." Her hand brushed up Riley's arm, and the hairs stood to attention, sending a shiver up her spine.

"It is." Riley tried to focus on the physical sensation instead of her mind threatening to unravel. "But I don't think I could live with the regret, knowing we both felt like this and did nothing about it. I don't meet people like you."

Ella's alluring eyes flicked to hers, and liquid heat slipped and curled inside Riley's belly. "Me either."

But she couldn't get too attached; Ella was going to leave in a few weeks.

Shut up, brain.

She cleared her throat. "Okay. So how about we keep

the days for the course, and we can see each other in the evening? Keep it separate?"

"That works. I don't do anything in the evening anyway, apart from listen to Pauline's gossip." Ella gave a soft smile, tracing gentle circles over Riley's skin. "And I won't tell anyone about us. Well, apart from maybe my best friend Winnie. Or my mother if she asks. But actually maybe n—"

Riley raised her eyebrows. "You're gonna tell your mum about me? That seems pretty fast," she teased.

Ella laughed. "Fine. No mothers. No days. And no telling people."

The confirmation made Riley shake her head. *What am I doing?* She exhaled, letting the voice fade into the background and focusing on Ella. A grin crept onto her face. "Well, maybe not *all* days. I think it's only fair you have to step out of your comfort zone, too."

"Oh, no. Why do I not like the look of that smile?"

Riley chuckled. "I think you should come to one of my surfing classes."

Ella groaned. "Riley, have you not witnessed this island trying to kill me—on more than one occasion?"

"And I've saved you—on more than one occasion."

Their gazes locked, and the charged current sizzled between them, fanning the flame already burning in her chest.

"I suppose that's true."

"So, is that a yes?"

The corner of Ella's mouth lifted, and Riley leaned forward to kiss her.

She could get used to that.

CHAPTER TWELVE

Ella

Ella woke to something swatting her face. She squirmed, blinking away dreams of giant goats chasing her through Manchester Airport to see a fluffy paw hit her square between the eyes. Ziggy's chest rumbled as he brushed himself under her neck, suffocating her. She chuckled, manoeuvring his body away from her airways and waking up Riley in the process.

Though they hadn't had sex last night, they'd slept in the same bed together, and in a way, that felt just as intimate. She got the sense that Riley never shared her spaces, and yet here Ella was, lying between the soft sheets of her bed, basking in the warmth of her body.

Ella was wound up tight—who could blame her after all of those toe-curling kisses?—but she couldn't rush anything. The last thing she wanted was to scare Riley away.

Small slivers of light peeked out from under the blinds. The rest of the cabin was still cloaked in darkness.

Ella fought off a yawn with the back of her hand while the other tickled behind Ziggy's ears. "What time is it?" she mumbled.

Riley brushed her hands over her face. "Quarter past six."

Ella groaned. "Doesn't your cat understand the weekend?"

"My personal alarm clock doesn't take days off, I'm afraid." Riley laughed low in her throat and stretched, flexing her arm muscles. Ella's mouth went dry.

It's far too early to be getting caught in those thoughts, Ella.

"How'd you sleep?" Riley asked, and to Ella's horror, she flung back the sheets and jumped out of bed. Ella missed her warmth immediately. "Can I get you a drink of something?"

Ella's temple throbbed. As much as she'd thought she'd missed drinking, she did not miss the consequences plaguing her the next day. Combined with their lack of sleep—they'd stayed up until the early hours talking—her mind was running on a small delay.

Ziggy jumped after Riley, rubbing himself against her legs as she chopped oranges into halves. She popped a slice into the juicer and, without missing a beat, poured some food into Ziggy's metal bowl, moving on autopilot with a bounce to her step.

Cute.

Normally, Ella would kill for a coffee, but the idea of fresh juice sounded better, even if the whirring noise made her want to hold a pillow over her head. She sat up and observed Riley cooing over Ziggy, making plaid pyjama bottoms and an oversized black T-shirt look remarkably attractive. But she had the kind of body that would be flawless wearing a Tesco carrier bag.

Seeing her so at ease, especially after their conversation last night, warmed something in Ella's belly. *Is she always so carefree in the morning?*

There'd been a shift in the air between them, and finally, they were on the same page. That thought sent excited sparks all over Ella's skin.

When the machine stopped whirring, Riley made her way back to the bed, carrying two glasses of freshly squeezed juice, and hopped in next to Ella.

Ella let out a small moan as the cool liquid slid down her throat. "Wow. That's delicious."

"No better way to start the day."

Ella could think of several. Starting with curling up back under the sheets with Riley and exploring every inch of her sculpted body with her mouth. Heat crept between her thighs at the thought. Maybe she needed a cool shower.

She finished her juice and cleared her throat, angling herself towards Riley. "So today's your day off. What are you going to do?"

Riley placed her glass on the bedside table. "Actually, I was hoping to spend some more time with you." She smiled sheepishly. "So, what do you want to do?"

Ella pushed away the dirty thoughts infiltrating her mind. She glanced around Riley's cabin, at all the bits and pieces that made her Riley. She wanted more of that.

"Why don't you show me what you usually do on your days off?"

"Really? It's not that exciting."

"I think so."

She locked eyes with Riley's blues. When she grinned, it touched someplace deep in her centre.

"Alright," she agreed. "But I warn you now, there are no refunds for the tour."

They had a quick breakfast of eggs and toast, Riley packed a bag, and they headed out into the sunshine. Ella borrowed some of Riley's cargo shorts and a vest. Not her usual choice of attire, but her sundress was still soaked from last night.

Clouds rolled over the sky, chasing the last of the storm away, but the humidity hung thick in the air.

Riley led them up the side of the cabin to join another gravel track leading through the trees and dipping back down into the valley on the other side. The grass grew long in places, overgrown trees hiding the mountains from view.

Ella smelled the grove first. The sweet, citrus scent swirled around her, and then the path opened up into an orange grove with dozens of trees bearing fruit.

She spun to face Riley. "You really come here on your days off?"

"If I've run out of oranges. And we finished my last few today." She reached up to pluck one from the tree and threw it towards Ella.

It slipped from her fingers and rolled across the ground. She picked it back up, laughing, and squeezed it.

"Smell it."

"What?"

Riley grinned. "Just do it."

Ella brought the fruit to her nose and breathed in the sweet, aromatic fragrance. "That's the most...*orange*-smelling orange ever."

"They're the best-tasting ones too. Try it."

Ella peeled the skin, then hesitated before taking a bite. "Isn't this stealing?"

Riley brushed her hands through the leaves, giving each fruit a squeeze before tugging another from the stem. "They belong to the island. There are actually afternoon orange-picking classes in the activities...which you'd know about if you read the damn booklets we gave you."

Before Ella could comment, Riley cast a cheeky smile in her direction and joined her side. She peeled her orange, cheersed them together, and they leaned in to take a bite.

Ella's teeth sunk into the juicy flesh, sweetness lighting up her tastebuds and running down her chin. She wiped at it with her fingers, nodding. "God, that's good."

Riley chuckled, her blue eyes flitting over Ella's face. Then she pulled her deeper into the confinement of the trees, gripped her waist and planted a citrus kiss on her lips.

Oranges might just be Ella's new favourite fruit.

They collected more produce from the trees, stored them in Riley's rucksack and then sat back on the grass overlooking the grove.

Puffy white clouds drifted overhead, stretching across the sky. Ella extended her toes, letting the grass tickle her feet.

Riley dug out two small square canvases from her bag, quickly followed by a portable paint tray, and a packet of brushes.

"You paint here?" Ella asked.

"There are so many beautiful places to paint on the island. Here seems as good a spot as any."

Ella had to agree. Surrounded by trees, the warm sun overhead, and the heavenly scent of oranges, it made for a pretty perfect setting.

Especially when paired with the gorgeous blonde sitting beside her.

Riley handed her a canvas.

Ella frowned, poking it away with her finger. Devin

had always been the creative sibling. "Can't I just watch you paint? I'm kinda awful at this stuff."

She shook her head. "You wanted a day in the life. No backsies. Besides, I could never concentrate with you ogling me."

Ella snorted. Who knew it would take just three little near-death experiences to bring Riley out of her shell—and yes, Ella was counting the tumble down the cliff on her first day. It had hurt. But she could totally get on board with this confident, cheeky Riley, even if she was the butt of the joke.

"Fine," she said. "But you're going to have to teach me."

Riley tucked one leg under the other. "First. Get comfy."

Ella scoffed. "There's no way I can sit like that. I'll break my back."

"You don't have to sit like me. Just find what works."

Ella laid on her stomach, moving the canvas in front of her. She could at least work on her tan if nothing else. "Alright. Let's do it."

Riley chuckled. "I usually sketch the scene first. Just a quick outline for positioning." Her hand moved across the canvas, black pencil lines marking the white. "Don't try to paint everything, but pick a focal point and think about what it is you're trying to capture."

Ella wished she had the capacity to capture the details in Riley's expression. The way the tips of her eyebrows raised in concentration. Her lips, and how they puckered as her sharp blue eyes flicked across the landscape and back to the canvas. The flex of her long fingers as she worked, the twitch in her strong forearms, the way her vest clung to her body like it was sculpted to her. Watching her at work drummed something fierce in Ella's heart, and she found it hard to look away.

Riley looked at her, her eyes sparkling in the sunlight. "What?"

Oh god. I am ogling her. "Nothing."

Feeling flushed, she picked the spot in the orange grove where Riley kissed her and worked outwards, drawing the two trees and their outstretching branches. The lines came out messy and wobbly, unlike Riley's precise, effortless ones.

They moved to painting, starting with the shadows in the scene, like Riley suggested. Ella was a little heavy-handed with her colours, and her attempts to even them out only ended with paint licking up her forearms, much to Riley's amusement.

In between stealing glances, an ease fell over the two of them as they chatted beneath the afternoon sun, shadows stretching across the grass. Admittedly, Ella's painting wouldn't be winning any awards, but time passed quickly, and spending time doing something Riley loved warmed a little space in her chest.

"Are these your favourite clouds?" she asked, dabbing her brush in the white and trying to recreate the soft texture in front of her. "Crickets or something?"

Riley offered a playful smirk. "Cirrus. And no, these look more like cumulus clouds. They've got those lovely puffy heads, see?"

"I just see Simon Cowell on a skateboard. Looks like something's chasing him."

She cocked her head, squinting up at the sky and biting her lip. "A dog, maybe? Or an angry contestant."

Their eyes met, and everything around them faded away. Riley's brush stilled in her hand, and Ella set hers down. She wet her lips, feeling suddenly dry. "Well…I think I've finished."

Riley snapped out of her trance and turned her attention to Ella's painting. She beamed, her dimples popping. "Hey, it's good."

The paint had glooped in parts, and the trees resembled angry monkeys more than the peaceful pull of the orange grove, but Ella appreciated her enthusiasm, nonetheless. She'd actually really enjoyed creating something. She snuck a glance at Riley's canvas, and her eyes bulged.

"Oh my god, Riley."

The mix of greens, oranges, peaches, and blues brought the grove to life. Riley had managed to capture the location with realism while giving it a dreamy quality. The hues of the mountains merged into a half-finished blue sky, swirls and dabs giving the canvas texture. How on Earth had she painted that in the same time as Ella?

"Hey, it's not finished yet." Riley moved it out of her view, but it was no use, she'd already seen it.

"You're so talented." She angled her head to peek back at the canvas. "You could sell that."

"No one would want to buy this."

"Yeah, they would."

Riley's brush stilled in the paint, and she shook her head, letting her chin drop. Ella moved to catch her face and stroked her thumb over her cheek. A new habit she couldn't seem to shake. "I'm not joking," she continued. "You're really good."

"I don't think so." She peered at her through thick lashes. "It's just a hobby."

"It could be more than that if you wanted it to be. If I could paint as well as you do, I'd be living in a millionaire's mansion right now with fifteen flamingos."

"Fifteen?" Riley blew out a small breath of laughter, and Ella dropped her hand. "That's a lot of names to remember."

"I love how that's your response and not 'why do we need fifteen flamingos?'"

Ella hadn't realised what she'd said until Riley's gaze warmed her face. "I'm there too in this wee mansion of yours?"

Her heart thundered against her ribcage, and she attempted a playful shrug. "Yeah. Who else is going to massage my feet and pick up all the flamingo poop?"

Riley chuckled, tucking her hair over her shoulder. "You know, I could think of worse ways to earn a living."

"Deal." Their eyes locked, and Ella arched an eyebrow. "You'd also have to worship me three times a day."

"I don't see that being a problem, either." Riley's gaze swept over Ella's features, fanning heat inside her navel. Her mouth parted, pink tongue darting out to wet her lips, and a strong tug behind Ella's sternum almost took her breath away. It seemed as though Riley was going to say something more, but then her mouth curved, and her hand jumped back to life, swiping blue across the canvas.

Ella watched her work for a little while, soaking up the feelings swirling around her like watercolour paint. Every second they spent together was multi-layered; she loved that. But she couldn't understand why Riley, with all her positivity about life and her encouragement of others, couldn't see her own talent.

"So you've seen my day," Riley started, lifting her eyes above the canvas to find Ella's. "What about you? What does a day off in Ella's world look like?"

Caught off-guard, Ella went blank. She pulled a bottle of water out of Riley's bag and had a sip. Her old life felt like a disjointed memory. She couldn't even remember the last time she really had fun. She and Winnie always had a good time, but truthfully, Ella always had work or Maeve or her parents to complain about.

What did she actually do for fun?

There must be something.

She felt Riley's gaze land on her when she didn't say anything.

"I hang out with my best friend Winnie a lot, and…"

She didn't want to talk about their nights spent getting wasted, or the time she'd spent stalking Maeve and Annabelle on social media. Other than that, all she could think of was late nights at the office, followed by watching Netflix in bed. She used to play netball at school, but she always preferred watching it to playing. Ella and her mum still liked to watch the Netball Super League together, but she'd cancelled a lot in the last few months. Work had sucked up so much of her time, like a boring old vacuum cleaner.

"And…erm." Ella sighed, chewing at her lip. "I don't know. My family are always doing something. Mum loves to cook for us."

Compared to Riley's daily life, hers had all the excitement of a rusty fax machine. That left a sour taste in her mouth.

"That's sweet, actually," Riley said. "Are you close with your family?"

"Yeah," she started. But then her mind wandered. When was the last time she didn't cancel plans on her mum or make excuses not to see her brother? There were only so many times she could fend off unwanted questions about herself.

They were always pressuring her. *Weren't they?* She sat up a little straighter, trying to recall her mother's words. *I just want the best for you.* Ella had assumed she was being patronised, implying "the best" was "to be like Devin". But the more she thought about it, the more she wasn't sure. Her mum had never pushed her to change careers or relationships. She just asked a *lot* of questions. A lot of questions Ella didn't have the answers to.

Huh.

"What is it?" Riley asked, looking up from her painting.

Ella swallowed, then had another swig from the water bottle. "I…just realised I need to put in some more effort with them."

Riley nodded. "This place has a way of doing that to you."

Didn't she know it. Ella was one more epiphany away from a brain haemorrhage. "Are you close with your family?" she asked tentatively, remembering their conversation about Ireland.

Riley hesitated before saying, "No."

"What happened?"

She continued to paint, her eyes focused on the canvas. "My mum left when I was young, and my dad…he's a drunk."

That surprised her. She reached for Riley's thigh and gave it a squeeze, the urge to comfort her overpowering any overthinking about first-date etiquette. "Riley, I'm sorry… Do you wanna talk about it?"

"He's always been the same. For as long as I can remember." The birds singing in the trees around them filled the silence while Riley chewed at her lip. "The house was a mess. His friends were constantly around. We didn't speak for a long time, and then…" She furrowed her brows. "Well, I thought he might change. But he never will. Leavin' was the best thing I did."

Ella's heart pulled, imagining a young Riley having to deal with that on her own. "You deserved much better than that."

"Thank you." Their eyes met, tingles running along Ella's skin. She realised her hand was still on Riley's thigh, burning heat through the touch. "Senhor Arenoso gave me an alternative," Riley went on. "He showed me that there's more to life. That's why my family here are so important." She offered Ella a small smile and gave her canvas one more look over before announcing, "It's done."

Ella wanted to ask more, but she turned her attention to Riley's canvas. "Can I see?"

After a little more encouragement and some batting of eyelashes from Ella, Riley spun the painting to face her.

"Riley…it's breathtaking."

The finishing touches and white highlights on the leaves and sky elevated it to a whole other level—one that Ella couldn't even put into sensical words.

The two of them packed away their things and headed back up the path towards Riley's cabin. The sun warmed her neck as it dipped in the sky, the soft pad of their footsteps blending with the chatter of the birds in the treetops.

Riley was a little quiet once they started walking, pushing Ella's mind into overdrive. Had she said something to upset her? Or was she itching to get back and get this date over with? Maeve sometimes ended their time prematurely, claiming an early start, only for Ella to see she'd been active on Facebook hours later.

She brushed her hand against Riley's, making her turn around. "Everything alright?"

"Yeah, sorry." Riley observed the view over Ella's shoulder before giving her a small smile that didn't touch her eyes.

"You sure? You sound like you just dropped your ice-cream cone on the floor."

Riley sighed and glanced behind them before hooking her hand behind Ella's neck, beckoning her closer. The corner of her mouth ticked upwards. "You're not the only one this island makes reconsider their life choices."

In Riley's strong hold, Ella's body was no longer her own. She felt herself leaning closer, losing herself in the woman's orbit. She couldn't look anywhere else apart from those blue eyes, their flecks of green and brown visible in the sunshine. "How so?" she said in a breathless whisper.

Riley shook her head, dimples forming in her cheeks that made Ella want to kiss her all over. "You're very direct, do you know that?"

"Sorry."

Riley's other hand cupped her chin when Ella's head dipped. "No. It's a good thing. You're making me realise how much I've been hiding away. Sharing this with you…has been the best day I've had in ages." She grinned, the dimples sinking deeper. "Which is not something I would usually admit on a first date."

Ella's belly flip-flopped. "Nothing about us is usual, anyway."

"That's true—"

Ella leaned in, melting against her soft lips. Her whole body hummed at the sensation when Riley kissed her back, warmth radiating over her skin. Riley's fingers threaded into her hair, kissing her deeper, and when they parted for air, Ella's lungs emptied completely.

Those kisses should carry warning labels.

"*Atenção!*" a voice shouted from the path above them. Screeching brakes kicked up dust into spirals in the blue sky. "Watch out!"

A bike hauling a wooden cart was speeding down the hill, heading straight towards them. Riley pulled Ella out of the way, tripping over a boulder and landing in a bush. Ella collapsed on top of her with a grunt.

A loud crash cut through the air, followed by groans and the whir of spinning tyres. A murky cloud bloomed into the sky where the cart had tipped over, narrowly avoiding a tree.

Riley opened her eyes, grimacing. "Are you okay?" she asked Ella.

"I'm fine. Are you?" Ella stood up, offering her a hand and tugging her to her feet.

"Oh, no. No, no. *Merda.*" A tall boy was sprawled across the path, his long dark hair flopping across his face. He scrambled up, dirt covering his legs and shorts, and put his head in his hands. Remembering the two of them, he spun round and ran over, slipping over the gravel in his clunky sandals.

"Sorry. *Peço imensas desculpas.* So sorry." His face fell in relief when he spotted Riley. "Ah, Riley. *Graças a Deus.*"

Riley dropped Ella's hand like a hot potato. "Romeo! What are you doing coming down the path like that? You could've killed someone."

This *is the famous Romeo?*

Ella's eyes narrowed, softening when she took in the boy's round, chubby cheeks and fluffy facial hair. He couldn't have been more than a teenager.

"I'm sorry. Sorry. The brakes are a little stiff, and I was late collecting the oranges." His chocolate-brown eyes flicked to Ella. "Miss. I'm so sorry. Are you good?"

Good wouldn't necessarily be Ella's choice of word, but she nodded anyway, and the boy bowed his head in apology.

He turned his attention back to his dusty bike and wooden cart and let out a groan. "My bike. What am I going to do?"

Riley inspected the damage, eyebrows pinching. "It's just the tyre, Romeo. You've bust it."

"Oh, no. Senhor Arenoso is going to kill me. *Estou feito.*"

"I can fix it. I have some tools at my cabin."

His face lit up, and he crushed Riley in a hug. "Yes! *Obrigado.* Thank you. So lucky it was you." His gaze moved between the two of them, lingering on Ella.

"What—"

"We were orange picking," Riley blurted out before he could say anything further.

"Ah." He brushed a hand over his sad moustache. "Okay."

"Come on, before anyone sees what you did to the bike. Push it up here." Riley cast a glance towards Ella, but it was distant. Empty. Making the fuzzy feeling in her chest sink like stones into the soles of her feet.

They made their way back up the path. Romeo pushed his squeaking bike and cart, with Riley leading at the front and Ella trailing at the back, like a scolded child. When they reached Riley's cabin, Romeo wheeled the bike into the garden, leaving the two of them alone on the path.

"I'm sorry to cut this short," Riley said, her voice low.

"Me too."

"But I had a great time."

"Me too."

They lingered for a moment, their gazes moving over one another.

"I'll see you tomorrow," Riley said.

"Yep. See you." Ella gave her the best smile she could muster, then headed down the trail.

She should be walking among the clouds right now. Riley was into her. They'd slept in the same bed, had the best first date—if they could call it that—she'd ever had, and shared kisses that lit her whole body on fire, and yet…her heart quivered like a deflating balloon.

The crashing cart had knocked the wind out of her sails. The fear and panic in Riley's voice rang clear in her ears, and Ella didn't like the way she'd snapped back from her like an elastic band.

This was going to be harder than she'd originally thought. She kept her eyes down on the path, moving towards her own cabin at a glacial pace. Her head and heart were arguing with one another. So much so, she didn't notice Pauline until she let out a curdling coo in her direction.

"Ella! Where've you been?" Her attention fell on Ella's outfit, her eyes widening. "And what the dickens are you wearing?"

CHAPTER THIRTEEN

Ella

To Ella's surprise, the morning's yoga class helped clear her brain fog. Doubts about whatever was going on with her and Riley fell to the back of her mind, despite the gorgeous woman's voice calling out breathing timings for the group. Maybe whatever was developing between them had come at the wrong time. Ella needed to want change for herself, not for Riley, and she needed to focus on that.

Maybe it's perfect timing, her heart called back at her. Maybe they were meant to meet here. Even now, sparks crackled in the air between them, dancing, waiting for that moment for their eyes to connect and the feeling to swarm around her like butterflies.

Regardless, Ella needed to focus on herself first. Beautiful blondes after. That was the deal.

And for god's sake, she had to enjoy her time here. A week had already passed, and before she knew it, she'd be back traipsing the rainy English streets with only memories of the sunshine to keep her warm.

That was why she'd agreed to attend Riley's surfing class this afternoon, even though the thought terrified her. Her body wasn't made for exercise, especially not "trying to stay balanced on a moving board hurtling over the waves" type of exercise.

Riley called the class to a close, and Ella opened her eyes, catching her watching from the front of the courtyard. Riley grinned, and the electric sizzles spread through Ella's veins, giving her wings. Really, she couldn't believe her luck that Riley was into her at all. She needed to remember that.

She rolled up her mat and stored it in the cubby, Pauline following close behind her and breathing down her neck like a wildebeest.

"That was a great class. Don't you think?" She wedged her purple mat next to Ella's. "I can feel my mind settling more and more with every session." She brought her hands together in front of her face. "*Namaste.*"

"That's great, Pauline."

She puffed out her bosom. "And I only had twenty-six thoughts about Albert."

"Nice. That's fifty better than last time."

They made their way to the front of the class, and Riley looked up as they approached. Nervous jitters surged in Ella's gut, making her skin tingle. It was impossible to switch off, despite her brain urging her body to behave.

"Good session, ladies." Ella caught the quirk of Riley's mouth before she addressed Pauline. "You're making great progress with the lion's breath."

"Thank you," Pauline gushed, letting out a shrill schoolgirl giggle that pierced Ella's eardrums.

Riley's gaze flicked to Ella. "I'll see you at the surf class later."

Ella nodded, trying to ignore the butterflies. "Yep. See you then."

They bowed and then headed their separate ways. Pauline chittered in Ella's ear as they headed to breakfast.

"My eyes aren't as sharp as they used to be." She linked her arm through Ella's, and her flowery perfume invaded her nostrils. "But I'm sure Riley was wearing the same shorts you were yesterday."

Ella tensed. *Oh fuck.* Pauline had given her the third degree when she got home—until she'd managed to distract her with the cakes she'd bought from the market.

"Not this again," Ella grumbled.

"I'm just saying, hun. Quite the coincidence is all." Her sandals clunked against the stone underfoot. She nudged Ella in the ribs. "I think she likes you."

Ella sighed. The woman rivalled Miss Marple

lately—if Miss Marple smelt like talc and loved to wear mismatching prints. "I don't think so."

"I saw the way she smiled just then. The smile of young love."

"Pauline." Ella rolled her eyes and let out another huff. "You don't know what you're talking about. Maybe she's smiling at you. Checking out that neon tennis skirt."

"Hmm. Perhaps it's possible she does like an older woman. I read that's popular among the LBQGT+."

Ella laughed. "LGBTQ+. And yeah…she's not wrong. Maybe Riley likes that too."

Pauline giggled, something resembling a horse's whinny. "You really think so?"

Shit. Ella didn't mean to take the heat off her by throwing Riley under the lovin'-older-ladies express, but something about the idea had tickled her. And it worked—Pauline spent the majority of breakfast discussing the many ways to let Riley down gently.

Afterwards, Ella met Senhor Arenoso at his hut on the cliffs. As before, he was sitting cross-legged in the centre of the room, a soft breeze through the open doors swirling his burgundy kaftan. But instead of his dark hair brushing past his shoulders, today, it hung in a thick braid down his back.

Ella waited outside the door, looking out over the waves as they crashed against the rocks. *Hopefully that won't be me later.*

"Ella." His deep voice beckoned, and she turned her head. "Welcome back."

"*Bom dia*, Senhor."

His eyes combed her face, and the tips of his moustache twitched as he smiled. "Good morning, indeed. It seems the island is serving you well."

When he didn't expand, Ella swallowed. Did he mean Riley? Did Romeo say something?

"What do you mean?" she asked, her voice small as she took a seat on the same chair she'd sat before. A mix of sandalwood and cinnamon was burning away on the shelf, pillowing small plumes of smoke into the air.

Senhor Arenoso rose to boil the kettle before turning back to her. He interlaced his fingers, and she briefly admired his selection of gold rings. "I sense your chakras unblocking. You've taken a step onto your path. How does it feel?"

She let out a breath, relieved she didn't have to spin a Pauline-Riley distraction story here, too. "Good."

He nodded, his impassive face not giving anything away. "So, Ella, tell me. What is it that you want?"

Her horny brain projected Riley's strong legs wrapped around her head, but she looked past it, ignoring the pulse awakening between her thighs.

She needed to focus on herself. God dammit.

Her mind argued that Riley making her come *was* focusing on herself.

It was going to be one of those days.

She scrambled, trying to find something intelligent to say and ignore the throbbing in her underwear. Her eyes locked on the owl totem hanging around his neck.

"Is that your familiar?" she asked.

"Yes." He stroked the metal, his curious eyes studying Ella's face. "Is that something that you want to get in touch with?"

Ella nodded, and Senhor Arenoso turned to make the tea. Admittedly, she was curious. If Riley was a dolphin, what would she be? A tiger? A shark? A wolf? She'd been told on more than one occasion that she had a sharp tongue.

"That's good," he murmured, before asking over his shoulder, "would you like the same as last time?"

"No, thank you. I'd like Yorkshire Tea, if you have it."

He chuckled, a warm, throaty sound that seemed to echo in the small space. "As luck would have it, I do."

All she needed now were some Jaffa Cakes, and it'd be just like home.

Once he'd made the drinks, Senhor Arenoso handed Ella a mug and leaned back against the table.

"The owl is a powerful familiar," he started. "It has a deep connection to wisdom and the ability to see things most cannot. However, that doesn't mean it isn't without its darkness. Everyone is a balance between light and dark, no matter who they are.

"Guides come to us in many forms, but their common focus is to help us back into alignment with the universe. To do that, you have to listen. The guide is part of your inner self, Ella. If you shut that out, then alignment is impossible." He tilted his head. "Even in one week, I can feel you starting to listen to the world around you again. Would you agree?"

The island had pushed Ella to her limits, turned her inside out, and frustrated her, but yes, being in nature and away from her phone had eventually made her feel more like herself again. Whoever that person was.

When she didn't elaborate, he sipped from his tea. "I understand you still have resistance. Resistance to happiness. Resistance to freedom. Resistance to love."

Her eyebrows furrowed, and her mouth opened before she could stop it. "I don't resist love. Love is all I've ever wanted." Heat spread up her neck at the admission.

She hated the idea of wanting to be loved. It felt weak and pathetic, like admitting she wasn't worthy enough for it just to be a given. Winnie seemed to find love wherever she went, sticking to her like Velcro.

But Ella had to fight to keep Maeve's attention, twisting herself into someone she thought she wanted her to be, trying to latch onto things that ultimately just weighed her down.

It wasn't just Maeve, either. Ella had to work twice as hard at everything to even hope to come close to Devin's achievements. Without anything to show, she feared her parents might retreat, turning their love into a supermarket checkout transaction. One promotion equals one belly rub and a pat on the back.

It was exhausting trying to be what she thought she needed to be all the time.

Senhor Arenoso was watching her closely, as though he followed her every thought. "Humans rely on fear as a way of protecting themselves from disappointment, hurt, and heartbreak. You probably don't realise it half of the time, but when we function from places of fear, our thoughts and actions pollute the energy around us, and that's what we attract back. Shedding those fears and resistance is where the real Ella, the Ella hidden deep beneath all those layers, can heal and love freely."

Ella wanted to tell him he was wrong, but the words wouldn't form in her mouth. She knew she needed to change. The island had alluded to that many times. But more than that, she felt it herself. It was time for Ella 2.0.

"I suppose you're right," she admitted, tracing her finger over the mug and feeling the heat beneath the ceramic. "What do I have to do?"

"Unpicking and unlearning habits take time. There's no easy route. But opening up to the world and recognising your own limitations is a great place to start."

"I don't want the easy route. I want to do this properly."

"*Excelente.*" He grinned, revealing a small gap in his teeth, before adopting a more serious tone. "The difficult part will be remembering all this after you return to the busy modern world. When you receive your totem and learn of your guide at the fire ceremony, this is how you will keep the peace within you. They're already there, Ella. Here with you in this moment. You just have to listen."

Ella squeezed the mug tighter. She didn't want to be disrespectful, but she wondered why her guide was so keen on playing hide-and-seek. And why they were so incredibly horny. "Okay. I'm ready. Let's do this."

Senhor Arenoso sipped from his mug with a nod. "We are making excellent progress. Let's continue."

***

Ella's mind had taken a beating at Senhor Arenoso's class. Now, it was time for her body.

The gentle waves helped ease her fears of being swept away in the ocean current again, but lying on the sand pretending to surf did little to ease her fear of looking stupid. Luckily, there were three others doing the same, so she went for it. Unluckily, she was lying next to Pauline, whose joints popped and clicked with every movement, like a one-woman percussion band.

Ella wondered if the older woman's sudden interest in the sport had anything to do with Riley.

After practising positioning on the sand like marooned whales, they took the boards into the shallow water, getting a feel of the waves. Lying-down surfing seemed the way to go. The rush of the waves cresting around her as they pushed her body along were much more appealing than the thought of falling and ending up with body parts in different places.

Riley waded through the water to her, dimples deep

in her cheeks. "You're looking good out there."

"Don't sound too surprised."

Riley grinned, sweeping a hand through her long hair so it fell down her back. Ella's eyes were drawn to the toned muscles in her arms, then the tight swimsuit caressing the rest of her tanned body, until Pauline's excited screams made them turn their heads. Her limbs were spread like a starfish as her board crept onto the sand in slow motion. She lay there for a few seconds before struggling to her feet.

"Did you see that, Riley?" she called.

"Great work, Pauline. Keep it up." Riley turned back to Ella, an inquisitive look in her eyes. "I have to admit I was surprised to see her sign up for this. Has she said anything to you?"

So much for "letting Riley down gently". Ella bit her lip to stop the chuckle forming in her throat. "Maybe her guide is a dolphin, like you."

"Or a starfish, perhaps."

Their eyes locked, and a slow smile spread across Riley's face. One that made all of the world shrink around them and Ella's insides turn to jelly.

As though she suddenly remembered they weren't alone, Riley broke contact, swishing her hands through the water before returning Ella's gaze, but this time her expression was much softer. "You ready to give standing a go?"

"Really? Already?"

"I think you can handle it."

Ella felt the fear creeping up her spine but exhaled, embracing it. If it all went tits up, at least it was an excuse for Riley to manhandle her again.

They paddled further out into the ocean so they were waist-deep. Ella clung to her board as Riley recapped the instructions. She needed to lift her chest, keep her balance and focus her eyes where she wanted to go.

Riley squeezed her arm. "You've got this, Ells."

Ella's head swivelled at the nickname, and her heart swelled. *Ells.* There was something about the personal touch that gave her wings. She flashed Riley a wink, then started paddling forward, cutting her arms through the water. The wave lifted the board, and she hesitated, fear immobilising her muscles.

"Pop up!" Riley encouraged.

She forced her legs to move, straddling the line in the middle of the board. She wobbled, legs shaking as she stepped into a crouch. She leaned left, almost stumbled, but managed to right herself. Spray coated her, some saltwater going in her mouth. She glided forward, trying to spit, the board wriggling with a life of its own underneath her. She hit a bump and almost tumbled headfirst into the sea.

"Ahh!" she shouted, tearing her eyes from the board to look at the shore.

But she was already there. She'd made it.

The group applauded and whistled, Pauline's voice carrying above the others. Not sure how to dismount, Ella flopped off, landing in the shallows on her arse and splashing everyone nearby. But she didn't care. Nothing could wipe the smile off her face. She'd never thought of herself as athletic. Now, she could add it to her résumé.

Riley ran towards her, the gay equivalent of a *Baywatch* babe, kicking spray in every direction. "That was amazing!"

Ella laughed, throwing her head back and taking in the blue sky above them. It fucking felt amazing too.

They stood, chests heaving, taking in each other's smiling faces. Flooded with the urge to kiss Riley's gorgeous mouth, Ella's body hummed. Did she have to look so utterly kissable? She wanted to taste every inch of her perfect freckled skin, trace the lines of her muscles with her tongue. She dug her nails into her palm to focus on something else.

From the way Riley's gaze continued to focus on her lips, Ella wondered if she was in the same predicament. She hoped so.

"You coming in for another?" Riley asked.

Ella shook her head, feeling the ache in her muscles. "I'll think I'll end on a high today." She lowered her voice, even though the others were far enough away in the sea. "But why don't you go show me how it's done?"

Riley's mouth quirked. "Would you like that?"

"Definitely. Any excuse to ogle you."

Riley laughed, threw Ella a wink that made her insides clench, then grabbed her board and paddled out into the sea. The waves were only small in this area of the beach, supposedly easier for learners to grasp, but within seconds, Riley caught one, popping up onto her feet.

She weaved effortlessly over the wave, turning left and right, her hair flowing out behind her. The cocky bastard even threw a smirk in Ella's direction, and she loved it. The woman was sexy as hell.

"Riley, look at me!" Pauline shouted, sliding onto the shore with the elegance of a sea slug. "Ahh!"

Riley glanced behind her, and her board slipped from under her feet, catapulting into the air. It spun and twisted before landing on top of her with a splash.

Shit.

Ella scrambled towards her in the water, breathing out a sigh of relief when her head popped up through the waves. The relief was short-lived when a groan left Riley's mouth, and her hands flew up to cup her nose. Blood seeped through her fingers, trickling down her neck and into the water below.

CHAPTER FOURTEEN

Riley

"That wasn't exactly what I had in mind." Riley propped up the pillows in her bed and laid against them. Her blonde hair was still a little damp from the water and cascaded down her front, tickling her chest.

"Me neither." Ella laughed, rolling onto her front and jiggling the mattress. "You just showed me how *not* to surf."

"We skipped ahead a little. How to hit yourself in the nose with the board is supposed to be lesson three."

Ella laughed harder, giving a snort, and the sound made Riley grin. She loved it when she did that. Ella covered her mouth with her hand and groaned. "Sorry, I'm snorting again."

Riley grabbed her wrist and pulled it away, revealing Ella's pursed lips. "I think it's cute."

Ella's gaze combed Riley's face. Then the corner of her mouth twitched. "Well, I think it's cute that you tried to show off and failed miserably."

"I must be spending too much time with you."

Her eyebrows arched, her voice squeaking. "What does that mean?"

Riley struggled to bite back her amusement. "That your clumsiness is rubbing off on me."

Ella dug her fingers into her ribs, scowling when she didn't react. "Don't tell me you're not ticklish."

"Nope."

Ella's hands pressed harder, searching up and down her torso for a reaction. When Riley continued to watch her with amusement, she grumbled, resting her hands on her stomach. Her pouting face was pretty adorable. Her deep brown eyes flicked to hers. "How are you feeling?"

Riley felt the bridge of her nose. "It doesn't even hurt anymore. Just a little nosebleed."

"It was quite a lot of blood."

"I've had worse." Memories of the accident tried to prise their way into her mind, but she pushed them away. *Not now.*

Ella brushed her hands over Riley's abdomen,

grounding her. "Have you ever broken a bone?"

She swallowed. "Just once. Here." She pivoted her wrist to show her the scar running down her skin.

"God." She grasped it, tracing the white line softly with her fingertips.

Riley shivered at the touch. Screeches ripped through her eardrums. Glass smashing. Elodie's scream. The wailing sirens. Heat spread up her neck. Her lips felt suddenly dry. She moved to sit up, but Ella stopped her.

"What do you need? I'll get it for you."

The kindness in Ella's eyes pinned her for a moment, and she let out a breath. "I'm okay. I don't want to be a nuisance."

"You're not. The medic said you shouldn't do anything strenuous."

"But—"

"Just…let me take care of you. What do you need?"

She acquiesced, softening under Ella's gaze. "Just some water, please. Thank you."

Ella filled a glass with water in the kitchen and returned to her, waiting until she took a few gulps before placing it on the wooden bedside table. She rejoined her on the bed, leaning on one elbow, the other hand draped over Riley's torso.

The cool liquid soothed Riley's throat. "Thank you."

"You don't have to keep thanking me." Ella traced the geometric pattern on Riley's T-shirt, moving dangerously close to her hip bone. "I…like taking care of you."

Jesus. Ella's fingertips running over her made her swallow. How could such an innocent movement send shivers down Riley's spine? Her breathing quickened, but Ella continued, unaware. Gentle. Soft. Teasing.

Riley's breathing hitched when she grazed the bare skin where the cotton had ridden up.

Ella glanced up at her. "Are you okay?"

Dammit. Her mouth was dry again. Her focus dropped to Ella's fingers, now still on her skin.

Ella suddenly burst into a grin. "Wait. Is this tickling you? I knew it!"

Riley chewed at her lip. "Sorry to disappoint. It's quite the opposite." Her heart thumped loudly against her ribcage, making her unsure how to articulate the feeling curling in her belly. "It's...nice."

Ella raised an eyebrow. "Nice? Oh..." A mischievous look sparkled in her eyes, and her fingers started tracing over her abdomen again. "*Nice,* huh?"

Tingles spread over Riley's arms, and when Ella eyed her, searching for permission to continue higher, she nodded, her chest pulling tight.

"You know..." Ella began, lifting Riley's T-shirt to expose her belly button. Her warm fingers grazed just above the top of her boxer briefs, and Riley sucked in a breath. "I'd like to take care of you in other ways too."

A deep ache rolled through Riley's stomach, heat slipping between her thighs.

Ella's eyes held hers. "And you can just...lie right there."

"Mmm." The idea of Ella touching her made all the blood rush to her clit, and she couldn't form anything cohesive.

Ella hooked her finger underneath the waistband of her boxer briefs, her eyes glancing back at hers. "Keep talking to me. Tell me anything you're not comfortable with."

"I trust you." The words rushed from Riley's lips. But before she had time to overthink their meaning, something flickered across Ella's features, locking them both in a swirl of energy, and any anxiety melted away.

Keeping eye contact, Ella moved her hands along Riley's navel, drawing goosebumps over her arms. She smiled, confidence sparkling, and craned her head to kiss Riley's stomach. The soft press of her mouth seared her, the heat leaving her skin tingling. Then she lifted Riley's leg and adjusted herself so that her pretty face nestled between her thighs. Riley couldn't tear her eyes away.

Ella caressed her thighs before squeezing. Riley let out a small groan, and a wave of arousal rolled through her, pulling her into deeper depths.

"I love how strong your legs are," Ella said. Her fingers dipped under Riley's T-shirt, lifting it higher and exposing her abs. "And your stomach." She traced over the muscles, her tongue flicking out, wetting her lips.

Then she pressed a kiss to Riley's belly. And another. And another.

God. Riley tensed underneath her touch, her chest tightening. It'd been so long, she was hypersensitive.

Or maybe it was because it was Ella touching her.

Ella pulled a hairband from her wrist and scooped her red hair into a bun. Their eyes connected, and the corners of her mouth curved into a seductive smile, sending a jolt straight into Riley's clit.

Is this really happening?

The shot of panic wasn't enough to overpower the throbbing between her legs. Sure, Riley wasn't the type to just "fool around", but if she admitted it to herself, she did miss romantic connection. It was a side of herself that had lain dormant for so long now, she wasn't sure it was still there. But she used to love the push and pull of control, the way two bodies connected and spoke to one another through touch. The possessiveness.

Ella slid her hands up her top, letting her nails drag over her abs. She was watching her carefully, testing the waters before doing it again, a little harder, making Riley hiss and squirm.

Jesus. Yes, she wanted this.

Ella's fingers gripped the waistband of her shorts, and after a nod of confirmation, she shuffled them down Riley's legs, leaving her in her black briefs.

When Riley had pictured this before, lying in this bed or daydreaming out on the island, her mind had hijacked the fantasy. Her thoughts had always found their way into the spaces, taking any Ella fantasies and drowning them deep in the depths of the sea. At this moment, Ella held all of her concentration. Every touch. Every lingering look was making the feeling swell deep in her centre, begging for attention.

Ella dipped her head, just a breath away from touching her, and Riley gasped. Anticipating the feel of her mouth, she fidgeted, feeling more wetness pool in her underwear. She didn't just want this; she *needed* it. She needed Ella. Desperately.

A loose strand of hair fell from Ella's bun, and she tucked it behind her ear. "I want to taste you," she murmured, low in her throat. Those big eyes commanded hers, pupils blown wide. "Can I?"

Riley's cheeks warmed, words impossible to form. She swallowed and nodded, and Ella wasted no time in closing her mouth around her clit. Riley moaned at the contact. Even through the soft cotton of her boxer briefs, her whole body reacted. Her hands gripped the covers, and Ella kissed her harder, letting her tongue swipe over her.

Arousal peaked in her centre, making her ache everywhere. *Fuck.* She might combust at this rate.

"Please," she begged, unable to stand the pressure building in her clit.

Ella slipped off her underwear, the cool air hitting her as her hungry eyes raked over her exposed skin. Time seemed to slow before she buried herself back between Riley's thighs, and the relief from her hot tongue was immediate. She couldn't contain it.

She whimpered, tightening her grasp as Ella took turns to kiss, lick, and suck at her. Her fingers spread Riley's legs wider, and she angled her head so she could meet her gaze.

Their eyes locked, and a tremor of pleasure swelled below Riley's navel.

"Do you want it soft?" Ella asked. Her tongue snaked out to brush delicately over her, and Riley cursed. "Or hard?" She sunk her tongue into Riley, then swiped harder against her clit.

Riley pulled back. "S–soft. Ish," she managed.

Ella's lips quirked, and the sight of her there between Riley's thighs sent another surge between her legs. Her tongue flicked back and forth over her clit, a teasing pressure that hit her just where she wanted it.

"Like this?" Ella asked.

"Mmm." Words failed her, but her hands gripped the back of Ella's neck. Ella hummed at the contact, and the vibrations pinged pleasure along Riley's skin.

Ella's tongue slicked and lapped at her, and more wetness flooded her thighs.

"God. You're soaked." Ella drew a lazy swipe up her folds, her eyes flicking to hers. Before Riley could feel embarrassed, she added, "I fucking love it."

Ella's lips and tongue worked to draw whimpers from her, Riley's chest coiling tighter as she got closer and closer to climax. Her hips bucked, her muscles clenching. Ella's hands brushed her abs, hips, and squeezed at the tops of her thighs, as she pulled herself closer. Deeper.

"Mmm." Riley closed her eyes, moans catching in her throat as she hovered above release. Her thighs trembled.

So close.

Her heart beat furiously against her ribcage, breaths coming hard and fast.

Come on.

She was drenched, evidence of that slicked up her thighs and Ella's face—and it felt so good—so why couldn't she finish?

You feel too guilty.

Oh, no. The slip opened up the pathway for Riley's mind to intercept her thoughts, and now the flow barraged her with them. One after the other.

You shouldn't be doing this.

It's all going to end badly.

She opened her eyes and focused on Ella. Her gorgeous mouth brought another hit of pleasure, which almost pushed her over the edge. Her lungs burned.

Ella's going to leave you.

Her arousal plummeted off a cliff, and she let out a deep sigh, relaxing her legs as they started to cramp. Sensing a change, Ella switched her focus to her face, and she slowed.

Riley bit her lip. "Sorry… I, uh. I'm not sure I can…finish."

"That's okay. There's no pressure to come." Ella pressed her lips to her thigh, her mouth glistening with Riley's wetness. "I just wanna make you feel good."

"You do. You did." Riley felt herself scowl. "I was so close as well, but…"

"Hey." Ella brushed her fingers over her abdomen. "It's okay."

"Sorry. It's just frustrating."

"You really don't need to apologise."

"It's just been…a while." Tears pricked behind her eyelids, and she wished them away.

Ella propped herself up on her elbow again. "It has for me too."

Probably not three years, though.

Embarrassment crept up Riley's spine, flushing her neck. *Jesus.* Suddenly, she felt very vulnerable, and she covered her face.

Ella climbed up her body to pull Riley's hands from her eyes. She planted a kiss on her palm. "Getting to touch you in any sort of way is rewarding for me. Just being around you is. With or without clothes on." She offered a soft smile. "We can do anything you want. At whatever pace. There's no pressure."

Her fingers cupped Riley's face, her thumb stroking her cheek.

Riley inhaled and exhaled, letting her breathing return to normal. She leaned into Ella's touch. "I do want this." She blew out a big breath, trying to push her negative thoughts away. "It's just…dusting off the cobwebs, I suppose."

"Cobwebs." Ella raised a teasing eyebrow. "That's some sexy talk."

Riley chuckled, feeling more at ease. Ella had a way of doing that. "I know. You're very lucky."

"I am." Her fingertips traced along Riley's jaw before settling back on her chest. "And I don't expect anything from you, either. Like you don't have to touch me if you don't want to."

"But I do." The words tumbled out before she could help it. But sometimes, she didn't want to think, she just wanted to do. To follow the signals firing through her body. And everything inside her pulsed with the energy of Ella.

Their eyes connected, and the air in the room shifted.

Riley suddenly remembered Ella's body, pressed on top of hers, and she started throbbing again. Taking it slow, she let her hands drift lower, over Ella's curves, and cupped her round bum, giving it a small squeeze.

Ella didn't need much more encouragement. She adjusted herself so that she pressed against Riley's clit and rocked her hips. *God.* Riley tightened the grip on her arse, her eyelids dipping.

"You like this too?" Ella asked, her voice a breathless whisper. Her eyes studied Riley's face, her lips pursing. "You can ride me. Use me to make you feel good. Whatever way you see fit."

Riley's stomach rolled. Any other thoughts melted away.

"Within reason, anyway." Ella's mouth quirked, her gaze fixed on Riley's face. "But I like that," she whispered, shooting shivers up Riley's neck. "Whatever makes you feel good makes me feel good."

Words stuck in Riley's throat as Ella continued to

grind their hips together. She needed to get her out of those shorts.

Now.

Ella gave out a little shriek as Riley flipped her onto her back. Looking up at her with wide eyes, she gasped, before Riley captured her lips in a kiss. She moaned into her mouth, her hands reaching for Riley and pushing their centres back together.

Riley broke the kiss to tug Ella's shorts off, lingering at the sight of her hot pink underwear. Riley could never, but they suited Ella to a tee.

She rolled them down her legs, sucking in a breath at how wet Ella was.

Riley was the lucky one.

The thought struck her, knocking her from her rhythm. She used to be confident in this area of her life, but in the last few years, it'd become less of a priority. The idea of ever being close to someone again made her want to run for the hills. But Ella's dark eyes looked back at her, her face tanned from the sun, her plump lips parted.

She was so beautiful.

Perhaps noticing her hesitation, Ella grazed her bicep, giving her a small pull to join them back together. Riley propped herself up on her hands, their faces so close, Ella's breath tickled her nose.

She kissed her, and Ella wound her hands in her hair. Riley lowered herself as she took Ella's lip into her mouth, biting when their hot, naked centres finally brushed together.

She almost collapsed at the sensation. The sound. The *feel* of Ella's wet pussy sliding against her clit had her already quickening the pace of her thrusts.

"Oh my god." Fingers tightened in her hair, teasing at her scalp. "That feels so fucking good."

Riley pulled back to look at her. Ella's eyelids fluttered, combing over Riley's form as she rocked her hips, combining her wetness with her own. Pleasure rolled through Riley's abdomen, and she felt an orgasm building again.

"I love feeling how wet you are."

"I do, too." Hearing Ella voice it out loud made it all the more obvious. She gave in to the craving completely, sliding over her and letting the feeling drive her.

Ella let out a moan as Riley ground harder, nails raking across her skin. "Just like that." Her hands moved to Riley's waist, brushing her muscles as they contracted. "Mm, Riley."

Riley locked eyes with her, feeling a strong tug behind her sternum. A mix between a whimper and a grunt came from her throat as they came together. All of her senses blazed, feeling nothing but Ella.

She moaned, circling over her. The slippery friction built in her core, threatening to spill everywhere. "*Fuck*...Ella."

Ella cursed, too, legs quivering underneath her.

Riley's clit ached, begging for release. She gripped the headboard, unable to support her shaking limbs, and pushed harder against Ella. Everything pulled taut, threatening to unravel.

"Oh, shit, Riley. Like that," Ella moaned, her nails digging into her back. "Ah, shit. I'm coming—"

The sound of her orgasm pushed Riley over the edge, too, and with a long, drawn-out moan, hot, blinding heat pulsed through her. She tightened her grip on the headboard, her body trembling. Pleasure exploded in waves, rippling through her muscles and squeezing the air from her lungs. She couldn't stay quiet if she tried. Ella's orgasm melted into hers, and they rode it out, gasping and struggling for breath until Riley collapsed on top of her.

A dizzying wave fell over her, coating her in a feeling that buoyed her high up in the ceiling. She didn't ever want to come down.

"Oh my god." Ella sighed, stretching her body out like a cat. "That was so fucking hot."

Sweat beaded over Riley's forehead, and she pulled back to take her T-shirt off with a chuckle. "We didn't even get fully undressed."

Ella laughed, the sound light and airy, and Riley's heart squeezed. "That's proof of it being some time." She wrapped her leg over Riley, and they snuggled closer together, despite the heat in the room.

"True." A weight vanished from Riley's body, making her light-headed. Her orgasm lingered, and she couldn't stop a grin from stretching across her face.

"Though I'm not sure that's what the medic had in mind when he said no strenuous exercise." Ella planted a kiss on her shoulder, and she pulled her closer.

She turned her head to take Ella in. Cheeks rosy, eyes glistening, mouth pink and perfect. "Nothing wrong with breaking the rules from time to time."

Ella mock gasped, laying a hand across Riley's chest. "Who are you, and what have you done with Riley...?" She pinched her eyebrows together. "I don't even know your last name."

"Murphy."

"That suits you."

"So does yours, Miss Cargill."

She shook her head. "Wait. How do you know that?"

Riley shrugged, feeling heat warm her neck. "I saw it on your suitcase."

"Oh, yeah." Ella poked her playfully. "I knew you liked me."

She raised an eyebrow. "Who says I do?"

Ella dug her fingers into her ribs before remembering she wasn't ticklish. "Dammit." Her eyes brightened. "I know a different way of tickling you now, though." She traced her fingertips down Riley's sternum, stomach, and hips, rippling goosebumps everywhere.

Riley let out a small groan and caught the way Ella's mouth parted.

"You're right, though," Riley said, mouth curling. "That was really hot."

Ella hummed, wrapping an arm around Riley's waist. "You like it when you hear me come?"

Riley's clit twinged, sending a jolt through her body. "I do."

"Maybe you can do it again sometime. If you're lucky."

Riley grinned, leaning forward to kiss her. "Maybe right now."

Ella squealed as Riley rolled her onto her back. She kissed her again, savouring the taste, bathing in the happy feeling swelling in her chest. She didn't want to lose this moment—or the new confidence firing through her system.

So she followed the tug of her heart, worshipping the woman in front of her, hoping that luck was on her side for once. Praying that the noises in her head wouldn't come back and chase it away.

CHAPTER FIFTEEN

Life on the island fell into a beautiful rhythm. Ella woke with Bernardo's crowing, stepped out into the sunshine, and breathed in the fresh air. Morning yoga settled her mind and body—and the eye-candy instructor was an extra bonus. Senhor Arenoso commented on her energy shift, Marco Marcos actually started making sense, and she still hadn't hit herself in the nose with the surfboard.

Opening up to the island meant the island was opening up to her.

Evenings were her favourite, though. Spending one-on-one time with Riley in her cabin felt like being on another planet, an alternate universe where good things happened to her. She worried that one day she'd wake up in her own bed back home, and this would all have been a dream.

She found herself walking lighter, smiling more, carrying a happiness inside her that she hadn't felt in a long time. Winnie would blame it on all the amazing sex she was having—which definitely helped—but it was more than that. It was the way Riley made her feel.

The only trouble? Ella's time on the island was passing far too quickly.

And she didn't want to think about what would happen when it ended.

"Come on, slowpoke," Riley called, striding ahead and throwing a grin over her shoulder.

"How much further?"

Riley waited underneath the bow of a tree, its leaves shading her from the afternoon sun. She handed Ella a bottle of water, which she gulped hastily.

Though the sun wasn't at its hottest today, and a cloud of mist hung over the valley, heat flushed Ella's neck from the hike. Riley had insisted on showing her the neighbouring village, but so far, all they'd seen were endless trees and red and yellow wildflowers as the path cut through the mountains.

She handed Riley the bottle back, and she slotted it into her backpack. Ella adjusted her bikini strap as it was digging into her shoulder, then leaned into Riley. The scent of sea salt and lemongrass made her swoon as she wrapped her arm around her.

How did she always smell so good?

Riley kissed her forehead, then angled Ella's body to face down the mountain. Her gaze combed the canopy of trees, the fog in the valley obstructing the view.

Unsure what she was supposed to be seeing, Ella asked, "What is it?"

Riley brushed her arms with her fingers, and she squeezed her. "Just wait."

Frankly, Ella could use the rest. So she leaned into Riley's shoulder, admiring how the woman always smelt like the fresh sea breeze, and waited. The fog slunk over the mountains, revealing what looked like steam rising into the sky at different points from down below. Ella peered closer, spotting slanted orange and brown roofs spaced among the trees.

"Is that the village?" she asked.

"Yep. You made it."

They descended into the houses. Below the clouds, patterned cobblestones led them between the buildings. Women busied themselves in the gardens, tending to the flowers and bushes and offering greetings as they passed. Farmers tipped their hats as they pulled along carts of vegetables and fruits, young children waving from the seats.

Fresh pastries caught Ella's attention through a window, and Riley steered her towards a bakery with two huge baskets full of pink and purple flowers hanging outside the doorway.

"*Boa tarde*, ladies," a young woman called from behind the wooden counter, working at pace but keeping her attention on the two of them, her hands moving in a blur. A cute yellow butterfly clip held her dark hair from her face.

Riley nudged Ella as she took in the range of cakes and pastries. "What would you like?"

How could she possibly choose? "You pick."

Riley engaged with the woman in Portuguese, and Ella's libido flared. She loved hearing her speak the language and contemplated tearing her clothes off right there and then, knocking over the bread rolls, and taking her on the counter. Riley caught her eye with a grin, reading her mind, and brushed her fingers against hers when the baker's back was turned. Heat shot through with the touch, and Ella flushed like a schoolgirl. Riley bought two Madeira cakes, and they headed back out onto the cobbles.

Music drifted through an open window as they tucked into the spicy honey and cinnamon cakes. They were a little dry, but Ella finished hers with pleasure as they took in the view of the sea beyond the buildings. Riley had mentioned the possibility of going for a swim, and she wondered if the sea was any different on this side of the island.

They explored the rest of the shops—Ella noticed three rainbow stickers in the windows, which pleased her—and shared a laugh at the "No Goats" sign hanging outside the pottery studio. Riley conversed with the locals while Ella managed "*boa tarde*" and "*obrigada*", and Riley promised to teach her some more Portuguese.

They browsed art in one of the shops, and Riley pointed out some of her favourite paintings, telling Ella about the different locations on the island.

"Which painting do you like?" she asked.

Ella studied the collection—mountain and sea views, hydrangeas, lakes and beaches—before turning back to Riley. "I prefer yours," she answered honestly. "You could easily sell paintings in here, too."

Riley smiled but shook her head before continuing to wander around the shop.

Ella caught herself watching her in this environment, a strong sense of longing overcoming her. Like the day they'd spent together on Sunday, getting to experience time with Riley in this way made it seem like this was *their* life. Like there wasn't an expiration date or a timer ticking away in the back of her head.

Riley's blue eyes flicked to hers, and Ella's heart fluttered. Even in a casual T-shirt and the cargo shorts she favoured so much, there was something about Riley that drew her in. A warmth and an electricity from deep within her that she wanted to chase.

Riley's mouth curved, showing her dimples, and then she made her way towards her, something hidden behind her back. As she drew closer, her grin only got wider, and then she dropped something onto Ella's head.

The floppy material fell over her eyes, and she laughed as Riley adjusted it.

"What is this?" Ella pulled at the edges of the hat, and Riley guided her towards a mirror.

"It's like the one you lost, isn't it? On the boat ride over with Duarte?"

Ella stood, taking in her reflection. The oversized straw hat did bear a likeness to the one she'd lost overboard. But this one had a thin strip of ribbon trim— the same blue as Riley's eyes.

She swivelled, catching Riley's gaze in the mirror. "I love it."

Riley paid for the hat, waving away Ella's protests.

"Thank you." Ella brushed her hand against hers, but she moved it away.

"Sorry. We need to be careful in the village. Sometimes Jane and Kristoph eat out here."

The words kicked out the air from under her, and the happy feeling shrivelled in her chest. "Ah, right."

Riley grimaced at her change of tone before masking it with a smile. "But don't worry. I have a surprise for you." She thanked the shopkeeper, checked her watch, and then started walking.

But Ella didn't follow. The reminder crushed her, squeezing and squishing her into something small. She didn't want to have to hide any part of her away. Ever since coming out at sixteen, Ella had vowed to never shield those sides of her. The reminder made her feel like a tiny bug that'd been stepped on. Small. Insignificant.

Emotions she'd felt when she'd dated Maeve. Maeve's hard gaze cut through her thoughts, mouth downturned in a frown as her firm hand squeezed her thigh. *"What did I say about keeping quiet?"*

Ella hadn't meant to bring up politics at dinner, but she couldn't help but step in when Maeve's uncle suggested putting metal spikes outside the office to deter the homeless. Her suggestion of rehabilitation internships had been met with sneers and laughter.

So Maeve had kept Ella away from her family gatherings. She was too loud, too much, too Ella. Good enough for private but not for public. She didn't want to do that again.

Don't think about that lanky grasshopper.

Deep down, she knew Riley's intention wasn't to hide her away. Riley wasn't like that. This was her job…her whole life. Ella could understand why she was being careful. She'd already risked a lot for her. Ella shouldn't ask for more.

Riley turned to call her on, and Ella awkwardly jogged to close the distance. Riley checked her watch again.

Somewhere to be?

"Where are we going?" Ella asked.

Riley tapped her nose. "You'll see."

She led them out of the village and up a small incline through the trees. Under the shade of the canopy, goosebumps prickled across Ella's arms. She breathed in the earthy scent and caught something else, reminding her of her favourite pub from back home.

They trekked a little further until Ella spotted a wooden cabin. Humidity licked her skin, and as they took a few more steps, big clouds of steam slunk between the trunks. *Is it…on fire?* Riley didn't seem concerned and linked her fingers through hers. This time, Ella flinched at the contact but tried to hide it.

Now they were in private, it was fine to touch her again?

Unaware, Riley tugged her closer to the cabin, eager for her to see around the corner.

Steam floated up from a small pool in the ground, the heat warming Ella's skin. Patterned tiles ran around the perimeter, the same workmanship she'd spotted around the village. Tall conifers and ferns spread their leaves, giving them a little privacy from the building.

"Welcome to one of the island's best-kept secrets," Riley said, turning towards her. "Pires' hot springs. Or *termas*."

"It's beautiful." Ella's gaze wandered over the rocks and the lush greenery, following the steam as it poured up into the skies.

"And it's all ours."

Ella glanced at her. "What do you mean?"

"I made a deal with the owner, Senhor Pires." She gave a light shrug and tugged Ella closer to the pool. The steam swirled around them. "For another…forty-six minutes."

"Riley…you shouldn't have." She watched the

turquoise water, unsure how to feel. She wished she could let this uneasy feeling float away with the steam too. She swallowed the lump that rose in her throat. So, was this about hiding her? Making sure no one could see them together?

Or a nice romantic gesture?

"I want you all to myself. Can you blame me?" Riley pulled her T-shirt over her head and placed it on one of the rocks. "And this way, we can properly relax."

Ella's eyes were drawn to her blue bikini top, then down her defined abs. Riley took a step towards her, and Ella marvelled at the way her body moved.

Riley is not Maeve, she reminded herself. *This is a good thing.*

She raised an eyebrow as Riley's hand found her waist. "So this is why you wanted me to wear my bikini."

Riley's mouth curved in that Riley way that made Ella want to kiss her. "Yes," she said. "Can I?" She gripped Ella's T-shirt between her fingers and, after she'd nodded, lifted it over her shoulders, placing it on a rock with her own. With a grin, she set Ella's new hat back on her head and ran her hands over her stomach and thighs. Ella sucked in a breath as she dipped to kiss her neck.

"You sure this is okay?" she asked breathlessly. Riley's lips brushed down her skin, and she sucked at her pulse point. Ella's knees wobbled, and she let out a groan.

"We're all alone," Riley whispered against her neck.

Vibrations spread down Ella's spine, fluttering between her legs. "What about the building?"

"Don't worry. Senhor Pires takes privacy very seriously." Her tongue brushed Ella's neck, and she sucked at her sensitive skin again.

Ella's belly rolled. All her previous trepidation evaporated into the air. She gripped the waistband of Riley's shorts, pulling their bodies closer together as an idea formed. "Then how about we make this more interesting?"

Riley straightened up, hitting her head on the rim of Ella's hat. They burst out laughing, and Ella threw the hat like a frisbee to land on their other clothes. She held Riley's gaze as she reached behind her own back to tug at her bikini strings. They loosened, and the material slipped from her breasts, exposing her. Her nipples hardened in the air.

Riley's voice stuck in her throat. "You want to skinny-dip?"

Ella popped open the button of her own shorts, tucking her hand inside. "You don't?" She grinned as she slid the material over her legs, catching Riley's eye before doing the same with her bikini bottoms.

"God. Ella." Riley's attention fell to her nipples, her waist, her bare legs, then landed on her mouth. "You're so unbelievably sexy."

Ella flushed at the compliment. Suddenly, Riley's mouth was on hers, silky and soft and drawing another moan from her throat. A low pulse throbbed between Ella's thighs, encouraged by Riley's wet tongue. Her fingers searched for Riley's bikini string and she pulled it, letting it drop to the floor.

She kissed her slowly, purposefully, controlling the pace as her hands worked to undress her until they were both naked on the edge of the hot springs. She let her fingers trace across Riley's skin, gentle and soft enough to raise goosebumps, remembering the effect it had on her the first time.

Riley inhaled, her irises soft and swirling. "I've never done this before," she admitted.

Ella leaned back, taking in her small breasts and perky nipples. She let her gaze dip lower, past the amethyst necklace lying against her sternum, over her firm stomach and sharp hipbones, the adorable little freckles decorating her tanned skin. She was truly a goddess. "You live in paradise, and you've never skinny-dipped?"

"Nope."

"Well, I'm more than happy to be here for your first."

Riley nodded. "After you."

Ella dipped her toe into the water and let out a heavenly sigh. She sunk lower, the water coating her like hot silk. *Oh my god.* All her muscles relaxed as she delved deeper.

Riley joined her, taking a seat beside her in the springs. She chuckled, floating her arms through the water. "It feels so different naked."

Ella tilted her head up to peer at the sky through the leaves. Overhead, the trees shaded them, but streaks of sunlight filtered through, casting patterns across the water. She let out a deep breath. "Freeing?"

"Yeah."

"This is amazing." She turned to find Riley already watching her. She brushed a strand of wet hair off her forehead. "It looks different from the brochures."

"So you *did* read the brochures?"

Ella shrugged. "I skimmed."

"Those are the tourist springs. This is for the locals."

"Ooh. The VIP experience. I like it."

Riley's hand found Ella's thigh under the water and gave it a squeeze.

The heat from the spring wasn't the only thing warming Ella's centre. She swivelled her body so she could climb onto Riley's lap, catching the way her eyes widened.

"Definitely the VIP experience," she teased.

Riley kissed her, and she wrapped her arms around her neck, deepening it. When she slipped their tongues together, Riley clawed at her back.

"Ells," she breathed against her mouth, making her tingly everywhere. The steam floated around them, making it even harder to breathe.

Ella ground against her, their bodies slipping together under the water. She took Riley's soft lips in hers, before moving across her jaw and neck, kissing away the water droplets, enjoying the mix of sweat and perfume on her skin before sucking at the same spot Riley had earlier.

Riley pulled back, looking into Ella's eyes with a

wild ferocity that electrified her. Her hands held her back with a strong grip, her chest heaving as her focus darted between Ella's mouth and eyes. "We…we can't."

Ella's body hummed. Making out with Riley, feeling her strong touch, her body underneath her, was more than enough to set her off. If there was nobody here then…"Why not?"

Riley nodded, and Ella turned to read the sign sticking out of the ground. In big red letters, it read:

No sex

No pastries

No goats

Ella cracked out laughing. "What is it with the goats on this island?"

Once they couldn't stand the heat anymore, they climbed out, using the towels from Riley's rucksack to dry and redress. Riley disappeared into the building, returning a few minutes later with a small man wearing a dark orange polo shirt and too-long khaki trousers that bunched at his heels.

"Ella, this is Senhor Pires."

"*Boa tarde*, Senhor," Ella greeted him.

"Call me Henrique, please." He extended his hand, shooting Riley a look with his eyebrows raised. "She's a pretty one. Now I understand why you want private." He winked, shaking Ella's hand a little too vigorously. "Come. Come. Food is ready."

Food? Ella cast a glance at Riley, but she just raised her eyebrows as they followed Henrique behind the building, where more purple and blue flowers filled baskets hanging beside the windows. A dozen tables and chairs were set out on a decking overlooking the forest, where several holes had been dug into the ground. Mounds of dirt were piled high like giant anthills. Ella hoped that whatever created them wouldn't be on the menu.

Henrique showed them to their seats, although the rest of them were empty, and pulled out Ella's chair for her.

"*Obrigada.*" She sat awkwardly, shuffling her bum along the wicker, her hat flopping with each movement.

He clicked his tongue. "Ah, polite, too." He flashed them a toothy beam and clapped his hands. "So, who is hungry?"

Riley leaned across the table. "Henrique makes the best *cozido* on the island."

"Psh." He waved his hand. "Best in the *world.*"

"And he makes a vegetarian version, too."

"*Cozido*?" Ella asked, as Henrique approached one of the holes and started shovelling the dirt from the top.

"Mariana!" he shouted, seemingly to the sky.

Riley chuckled. "It's a type of stew. It's buried underground and then cooked by the heat of the volcano."

"What? That's amazing!"

Riley's eyes sparkled. "I thought you might like it."

A bang and a clatter from the door behind them turned their heads, and a tall woman appeared carrying two metal poles. She exchanged some fast words with

Henrique in Portuguese, and then, with a grunt, they used the long poles to lift the pot out from the hole.

More chattering voices sounded, and Ella swivelled to see a handful of people walk into the restaurant, greeting them before taking their seats. While Henrique and Mariana prepared the dishes, the seats filled up. Ella recognised some of them from the village, including the baker with the yellow butterfly clip.

It really did seem to be the place the locals frequented.

"How…" Ella looked around, struck by how quickly the place had filled up.

"Everyone knows it's *cozido* time. It takes hours to cook underground."

Ella's belly growled at the hearty scent of stew, and Henrique brought two enormous portions over to them. Steam poured out of the bowl, and she peered in, spotting cabbage leaves.

"*Bom apetite.*" He shot them a wink and joined Mariana in dishing out the other bowls.

Ella dug in, tearing apart the cabbage leaves to find a selection of other vegetables inside, soft and perfectly cooked. She spooned the stew into her mouth and let out a groan at the juicy, flavoursome broth.

Stew wasn't what she'd imagined she'd be eating when she daydreamed about Portugal on the plane. More like endless pizza slices, chips, and margaritas while lying horizontal on a beach somewhere, as the sun washed away all her problems. But that sounded boring in comparison.

She didn't want that anymore. From pushing her comfort zone, she'd discovered more qualities about herself that surprised her.

She caught Riley's eye across the table, and she grinned. Stew had been the least of her surprises on this trip. She smiled back at her, trying to be thankful for this moment, with the delicious food and even more delicious company, as the crackle of conversation buzzed around them.

By the time they got back to Riley's, Ella's feet ached all over. She collapsed on Riley's bed, disappointed not to see Ziggy bound towards her. A kitty cuddle would have been perfect right now. He must be out exploring.

She let out a heavy sigh. "I'm fucking knackered."

Riley chuckled, packing away the contents of her rucksack. She hung the towels in the bathroom to dry and then sat on the bed by Ella's feet.

Ella pulled her gaze from the ceiling to look at her. "Thank you for today. I had the best time."

"Even though, and I quote, your feet 'feel like slabs of concrete'?"

"Yep. Totally worth it." She moaned as Riley massaged the sole of her foot. "Oh my god." She closed her eyes, unable to stop the noises leaving her mouth.

"You know…" Riley began. Ella peeked and caught a cheeky grin spread over her face. "You took care of me. How about now, you let me take care of you?"

Ella's heart stuttered. Riley continued to rub circles over her feet, making it hard to concentrate. "What…what do you have in mind?"

Riley hummed, her eyes drifting over Ella's body in a way that made all the air in the room thicken. "I think we'll start by removing some clothes." Her hands caressed Ella's calves and then up her thick thighs. The breath caught in her throat. "And then you can just…lie there." Riley's eyebrow quirked, and her hands drifted between Ella's legs, parting them. She rubbed soft circles, barely touching her clit, and Ella bit her lip.

Fuck.

She swallowed, remembering the cool touch of Riley's fingers on her chest when she had sunburn. Imagining them caressing other parts of her body sent a strong flutter between her thighs. "Anything else?"

"Actually, yes." Riley's eyes lit up. "I've got an idea to make this…interesting."

CHAPTER SIXTEEN

Ella

Ella lay on her front, wearing only her underwear, with her face down in the pillow.

"No peeking," Riley insisted as she rattled something under the bed. "I want you to relax."

Ella lifted her arms above her head and let out a breath. She sank a little further into Riley's mattress, but her ears pricked at every sound, wondering what the woman was up to.

There was a rustle and a click and then Riley's voice.

"This might be a little cold."

Smooth, cold hands ran up Ella's legs, and she flinched at the contact as they glided up over her thighs, fingers teasing under the material of her underwear and the curve of her arse, before dropping back down to her calves. Riley squirted more oil on Ella's back, then rubbed either side of her spine and across her shoulder blades, dipping down her arms to the tips of her fingers.

"Oh my god," Ella groaned, her muscles crying out with relief. "That feels incredible."

"Good." Riley caressed her thighs in circular motions and leaned close to Ella's ear, her breath tickling her neck. "Your body is unreal."

She was glad her face was squashed into a pillow so Riley couldn't see her reaction. She was still learning to love her body for the way it was. Riley's enthusiasm for her curves and wobbly bits made it easier for her to relax, knowing she wasn't judging her—but actually enjoying it too.

Riley pressed harder, slipping her hands over her oily skin. "How's the pressure?"

"G–good." Ella could barely string a sentence together. Her body was levitating somewhere above her.

"Let me know if anything is too much."

"I will."

Riley worked magic over Ella's muscles, her strong hands rubbing out knots in her back and taking her to a higher plane as weightlessness spread through her limbs. Every touch brought pleasure along her nerve endings, and she couldn't hold in how good it made her feel.

Riley paused for a moment, the mattress jiggled, and then she mounted her, a leg on either side as she continued to massage. The extra pressure was welcome. She glided her thumbs up her spine, leaning forward to rub over the dip of her neck, and Ella let out another moan.

Riley's breath ghosted over her skin. "I love hearing you," she whispered. "It really turns me on." She nibbled on Ella's earlobe, and Ella grasped the pillow. Then she kissed her neck, erupting tingles everywhere, but pulled away too soon. Before Ella could complain, she resumed her pressured movement over her back, and Ella let out another involuntary whimper.

Riley had her in the palm of her hand. Literally.

Riley adjusted herself, spreading Ella's legs so she could kneel between them. A deep ache twinged through her clit, and she fidgeted under her touch. Fingers worked at the heel of her foot, sliding over her calves, thighs, and then rested at Ella's underwear. Riley slid her fingers underneath, inching closer to her pussy.

Ella bit her lip as she traced the outside with her thumbs, delicately, then let out a gasp. *More.* Heat rushed between her thighs, and her clit started to throb. Riley inched closer, teasing at the sensitive skin before grabbing her arse with force.

"Fuck," Ella cried, her voice muffled in the pillow.

Riley's firm hands squeezed before dipping down to brush at her entrance through the crotch of her underwear. Ella inhaled, turning her head to look at her.

Riley's long blonde hair was tied up, her eyebrows furrowed in concentration. Her jaw was held tight, and when her eyes flicked to Ella's, she felt herself clench.

"Is this okay?" she asked, her voice a low hum.

"Yes." Ella squirmed underneath her, wanting more.

The corners of her lips ticked upwards, then she pressed a little harder, and Ella fell further into the mattress. She was so wet already and felt it soaking through. "God."

Riley hissed, rubbing her through the material, and Ella squeezed her eyes shut, biting at the pillow. But then Riley stopped.

There was another rattle, and then a humming vibration filled the room.

Ella had her fair share of practice to recognise that sound.

Her pulse quickened, anticipating the touch. But Riley made her wait. She cursed, her core pounding. Just when she was about to beg for something—anything—the vibrator brushed against her crotch. The lightest touch. And it sent Ella feral.

She pushed herself onto her knees and backed into Riley, needing more contact. The vibrations sent tremors of pleasure through her, but Riley pushed her back onto the bed.

"Please," Ella whined.

"Lift your hips."

Ella obeyed, Riley's commanding tone only arousing her further. Her clit throbbed with a deep, consuming ache, slick gathering in her underwear. "Please—"

No sooner had the words left her mouth than the smooth length of the vibrator teased at her, and she gripped the sheets with a groan.

"So greedy," Riley commented. She pressed the toy harder, the pleasure intensifying in Ella's centre. "Do you trust me?"

"Fuck." Ella couldn't concentrate on anything other than the electricity pulsing through her. "Y–yes."

"Then let me take care of you."

She slid the length of the toy along her, and Ella was surprised at its size. She bit back a whimper, the cloth barrier providing excellent friction around her clit. But she needed more. She didn't have the patience for much more teasing.

Riley's fingers inched her underwear to the side, slowly, torturously slowly, and Ella nipped at her lip, tightening her hold on the sheets.

Then the toy eased inside, filling her. Ella moaned, a guttural sound clawing out of her throat.

Riley fucked her with the dildo, sliding it in and out at a steady pace. Ella's obvious arousal echoed through the room, but she didn't care. All she cared about was the way Riley touched her, making her pant into the bedsheets.

Pleasure coated her head to toe as the vibrations pushed her to the edge, threatening to spill everywhere already. "Ah, fuck." Her lungs strained, her breath catching in her throat as she hovered.

Then Riley pulled out, and Ella gasped, her body a quivering mess. She tugged Ella's soaked underwear down her legs, pushed her up, and slipped the shaft back inside. When Ella cried out, Riley fucked her harder, and she gave into it completely, clinging to the sheets and letting her pound her into the mattress. Riley's hand gripped her hip, fingers curling around her soft flesh as her other hand sunk the toy deeper. Soft, breathless groans slipped from Riley's mouth, and Ella's core tightened. The hard, deep thrusts, combined with the sound of Riley's exertion, tipped her over the edge with a cry. She came hard, tightening around the length as Riley continued her pace.

"Fuck…fuck…fuck…" She rested on her elbows, blinking away the spots in her vision as her legs trembled. Without Riley's hands on her, she'd completely collapse.

Riley slowed, before pulling out completely, and kissed Ella's back. A shiver shot up her spine, her body somewhere in another dimension. Heat and pleasure leaked everywhere, and she bathed in it.

There was another rustle, and the vibrations started again. Riley kissed her shoulder, then her neck. Her voice sounded low in Ella's ear. "Because you're so greedy, do you think you have another for me?" She brushed Ella's hair away so she could get better access to her neck, and Ella's toes curled as she grazed her teeth over the sensitive skin.

Riley pressed a small silver bullet into Ella's hand, and she thumbed over the smooth surface. "I want to feel you come this time."

God. Ella nearly choked. Exhaustion robbed her of her voice, but somehow, her pussy still tingled.

"You start yourself off." Riley's lips dragged across her neck, making her shiver. "Tell me when you want my fingers."

She could hardly say no to that. So she shifted the vibrator in her hand, angling it to brush over her clit.

"F–fuck." She flinched from the sensitivity but pushed through, letting the vibrations work their magic. Riley continued to plant kisses across her shoulders, sucking hard in places, making Ella gasp and clutch the sheets. Her strong hands caressed her, her nails dragging across her quivering skin. Heat peaked between Ella's legs, and she could already feel another orgasm starting to build. "Now," Ella breathed.

Riley moved behind her, then slicked her fingers in Ella's wetness before sinking into her. Slow and steady. Ella quivered, and Riley groaned at the sensation.

"Jesus. You're wet."

She pumped her fingers, and Ella circled the vibrator around her clit. God. She loved how Riley's fingers felt inside her. She pushed into her, revelling in the feeling as it grew. Her heart beat wildly in her chest, her breathing ragged. She could hardly keep grip on the bullet as it slipped around her. The muscles in her legs and arms burned as she edged closer. She was going to need another massage after this.

Riley quickened the pace, hitting her deeper, and Ella

let out a moan.

"I can feel you," Riley murmured, her free hand resting on Ella's neck. "Tightening around my fingers."

Ella could too. She gasped as another jolt of pleasure cracked between her legs, and she bucked, almost collapsing as her orgasm claimed her. The vibrations started from the inside, rippling out in beautifully violent tremors, wracking her whole body into a shuddering mess.

She wound the sheets tighter in her grip as the waves washed over her, finally lowering herself down onto the bed, with a spent sigh. "Oh…my…god."

"My thoughts exactly," Riley murmured. Her hands grasped Ella's hips, forcing her up again.

"Riley." Ella laughed. "My legs…"

"I promise you can rest in a minute."

What? Surely the woman was satiated. Ella wasn't sure she could handle much more.

Riley lifted her back to her knees, her legs shaking and barely supporting her weight. She loved Riley's strength. How easily she could move her around. She laughed at her trembling body, but the sound melted away when Riley lay down on her back, sliding to position herself underneath her, those strong hands cradling her thighs.

"What're you…"

Riley smirked, and Ella's focus was drawn to her dimples. Their eyes locked, and the possessive darkening of Riley's irises almost made Ella come again. That, and the fact that her gorgeous face rested between her legs.

Riley's gaze commanded her. "Sit."

Ella did as she was asked and allowed gravity to take the reins. Riley guided her, gripping her hips and sliding Ella over her face. Her hot tongue sunk into her, slow and controlled, her soft lips kissing and lapping at the mess between her thighs.

"Oh, god, Riley…"

She plunged her tongue deeper, taking her time as her hands roamed up Ella's waist, cupping her breasts. She hummed against her, the vibrations teasing, and Ella's eyes nearly fell out of her head.

After a few torturesome moments, satisfied, Riley lifted Ella off her, rolling her onto her back. She had no say in the matter, her shaky body a slave to Riley's strength. Everything ached in the best way possible, a warm fuzz coating her skin all over.

Her soul slowly seeped back into her body, and she turned to Riley, those blue eyes sparkling. "What?" she asked breathlessly.

Riley leaned closer, capturing her mouth in a tender kiss. The gentle gesture floored her almost as much as the second orgasm. Something about the intensity of it made her stomach completely bottom out.

Riley's breath tickled her face. "Making you come is quickly becoming my new favourite thing."

That'd do it, too.

Riley's mouth curved into a smile, and Ella traced the grooves of her dimples with her fingertips. She turned to kiss them, making Ella chuckle.

"Or making you laugh," Riley said. "A close call. I love that, too."

Ella's gaze flicked over Riley's freckled face, her cheekbones, those lips. For once, she didn't have anything to say. Words didn't seem enough for all the emotions surging through her system. She could only look. She could only feel it.

She'd give anything to keep floating high in this bubble they'd created in Riley's cabin. The outside world was overrun with piercing edges, sharp stingers, and nosy beaks, threatening to burst it. Ella's luck was bound to run out sometime.

But as she admired the woman next to her, heart swelling in her chest, she hoped the weightless feeling was enough to keep them both flying high for a while longer.

Ella knew it'd be a long way to fall.

CHAPTER SEVENTEEN

Ella

"So, Ella." Marco Marcos clasped his hands together, and Ella's attention was drawn to his hairy knuckles. The man could make a family set of jumpers out of all that hair. "You're halfway through your time here at Sandy Springs. How's things?"

She leaned back in the squeaky chair, mulling her words before answering. "Better. It just feels like time is going too fast."

He scratched at his beard, regarding her over his

square glasses. "If you *could* slow down time…what would you like to do with those extra hours here?"

Her mind jumped to Riley. Every moment they'd spent together, even the bad days, Ella wished she could do them all over again. Every touch, every smile, every time those kind blue eyes flicked to hers. The first time she'd made Riley laugh. The first time they'd had sex. Ella wanted it all back. She didn't want to think about the lasts that were edging over the horizon.

She sighed, chewing at her bottom lip. Despite her best intentions to focus on herself and avoid a holiday romance, she couldn't help falling for the tall Irish yoga instructor.

But she was also falling for the island too.

The wild sea and sandy shores, the calls of the birds dipping over the sculpted cliffs, the friendly locals, and the smell of the orange groves. Bernardo the cockerel, the mischievous goats, all the beauty hiding in plain sight. How she spent more time looking up at the sky instead of at her phone. How being here, feeling the wind in her hair and the sun on her skin, made her believe in herself again.

Her gaze refocused, pulling her back to the room. "I would just…be."

He twirled the pen between his fingers. "Can you expand on that?"

"I'm really enjoying my time here. I would just keep doing what I'm doing."

Marco scribbled in his pad, eyebrows pulling together in concentration. He tapped his pen on the paper and clicked his tongue. "When you first arrived, Ella, you said you needed a break. Do you feel you've been successful with that?"

She nodded. Her days of pencil skirts and expensive coffee seemed like another lifetime. All those nights spent staying late with the computer screen, making herself miserable as Maeve pranced Annabelle in front of her face. The last thing she'd want would be to go back to that. Not that she could, anyway. She was very much unemployed. "Definitely," she said. "I feel distanced from my old life, but in a good way. Like my perspective has shifted. I feel…lighter."

He hummed. Scribbled some more. Then he looked up. "You mentioned your perspective has changed. What things have you viewed differently since being here?"

"Most things." He waited for her to continue, studying her face with intensity. Ella let out a humourless laugh. "I think I'd been putting my energy into the wrong places." Maeve sprang into her mind, all taunting long legs and sharp features. The thought of her passed without leaving an acid trail in its wake. "I let those places drain me, and then didn't fill the space up with anything that actually made me happy. I can see why my mum and best friend thought I should come here. I'm…grateful for that."

"Good. Sometimes the only thing we have control over is perspective. How we utilise that can be powerful." He flicked his pen as if to emphasise his point. Then his gaze softened. "Would you like to expand on that?"

Ella sighed. Since her conversation with Riley in the orange grove, the relationship with her mum had been playing on her mind. "I always thought my mum was pressuring me to be like my brother. Rubbing his achievements in my face. Wishing I could be more like him, but…I think that was how I chose to see it. I put that pressure on myself. I wasn't happy with my life, so I pushed my family away. I hated how that made me feel." Emotion swelled in her chest, and she paused, taking a moment to feel it. "Being here…I don't blame Mum. I'm trying not to blame myself, but…there's still a lot of hurt there."

"That's understandable. It takes time to let that go. Don't rush yourself. Everyone heals at different paces." He observed her carefully. "It's also important not to overlook how your mother's behaviour shaped this feeling. Your feelings are valid, and it's important to express them to build healthier relationships."

Ella nodded, picking at the pocket of her shorts. "I'm going to have a real talk with her when I'm back and get everything out on the table. I want to be closer with her again." She could use Riley's landline phone to call her mum, but some things were better saved for in person.

"I'm happy to see you making progress." The smallest of smiles inched onto his face as he made notes. Then he glanced back up, pinning her with his steady gaze. "We can practise some run-through scenarios if you'd like. That might build your confidence to fully address the conversation once you're home."

Home. The word punched straight into Ella's ribs, leaving her breathless.

As much as she wanted to see Winnie and her family, the thought of going home made everything inside her shrivel like a prune. She couldn't stay here forever. The course was three weeks, and she'd known that from the start—but what she hadn't known was how much she'd love it here. How much she'd love the version of Ella that had bloomed on the island.

Going back to her apartment, jobless, with no real purpose, made her chest tighten. Would she lose all her progress? The very idea wound its way into her lungs, sucking out all the air, suffocating her. Throwing saying goodbye to Riley into the mix—possibly forever—pricked the back of her eyelids.

How could I ever say goodbye to her?

She swallowed the lump that'd wedged in her throat but couldn't find anything to say. The scraping of Marco's pen intensified in her ears. Scratch. Scribble. Scratch. What could he be writing about this? Did he know? Could he see the fear in her face? The clock ticked loudly from the wall opposite, reminding her of every second slipping through her fingers.

"You look like there's something you want to say." Marco's gravelly voice cut through the mania swirling in Ella's brain.

Her gaze flicked from the wall to his piercing stare, and she opened her mouth to speak, to scream, to let everything out that was building and building—because she couldn't understand how a feeling that was so amazing could also feel so incredibly terrible.

She forced a small smile. "I'm fine."

***

Ella's sandals slapped against the path as she put as much distance between Marco Marcos's office and herself as possible. Conflicting emotions surged through her. On the one hand, she was mad that she'd predictably fallen for someone who, while wonderful, couldn't give her what she needed. Riley would never leave the island. She'd said multiple times how much Senhor Arenoso was like a father to her, and thinking of the island without Riley there would be like stripping away the sun from it.

Ella didn't want to impose on Riley's life, either. If she did stay—assuming Riley would even want that—what would she do? Sure, she could lounge about all day and roam the island, but it would become tiresome eventually. She was a worker at heart. She needed purpose. A challenge. She could hardly teach yoga.

Ella had taken the path up to Riley's cabin without thinking about it. She wouldn't be in; she was having some sort of meeting with Senhor Arenoso and had seemed pretty nervous about it. But that meant Ella had time to recuperate, away from the afternoon people traffic, and hopefully get some Ziggy cuddles too.

She hopped up the steps, breathed in the sweet floral

scent of the bushes, and sat cross-legged overlooking the sea. The trees swayed their branches in the breeze, creaking and blending with the cry of the birds diving over the waves.

Marco Marcos's session had sent her mind into a tangle, but Ella had new techniques for sorting it out. Closing her eyes, she focused on her breathing. The air filled her lungs, stretching out and touching every section of her skin before she released it, imagining the particles floating up into the blue sky.

It's a shame that this technique will always make me think of her.

She'll forget me.

But I won't forget her.

The lines between Ella's eyes deepened as she squeezed them tighter. Her heart quickened in her chest as she caught on a thought.

Is she going to forget me?

She wanted to trust her gut instinct and believe that Riley felt the same as she did. But her instinct had led her down the wrong path before. Look at her and Maeve.

What if this was part of Riley's work cycle? Picking up a woman down on her luck and waving goodbye before the next plane landed?

Riley isn't like that.

Are you sure?

Images of Riley flashed behind her eyelids. Taking other faceless women with beautiful bodies to the hot springs, laughing and flirting and touching skin. Would she teach them how to surf? How to paint? Skinny-dip together? Share Madeira cakes and massages and let them share her bed?

No. Even the thought was too much. Ella let out a sob, feeling a tug from deep in her chest. She opened her eyes and looked out at the sea, letting the tears slip silently down her cheeks. She followed a dozen waves as they rolled, frothed, and collapsed on the shore, then closed her eyes again, letting her breathing take centre stage.

A while passed before her mind emptied, each thought tugging Ella in another direction before she let it pass by on the breeze.

"Ella." Riley's voice jolted her, and she spun to see her standing in the doorway, surfboard under her arm. Her damp hair hung loose over one shoulder of her swimsuit, her cargo shorts spotted with drips.

Ella's heart skipped until she caught the frown lines either side of Riley's mouth. "Is everything okay?" she asked, pushing herself to her feet. She groaned as fire spread through her limbs. She'd been sitting on the stone too long.

"You tell me." Riley put her surfboard down, leaning it against the window. "Why have I just had Pauline bring me flowers?"

She grimaced. "Is that what your meeting with Senhor Arenoso was about?"

"What?" Riley's eyebrows drew together. "No. No... She brought them to me as I left the beach. Luckily."

Ella imagined Pauline serenading with a bouquet of roses and let out a laugh.

"This isn't funny."

"I know. Sorry." Ella squashed her mouth into a line but could still feel laughter tickling the edges.

"Would you know anything about it? Why Pauline felt she had to 'let me down gently'?" She used air quotes to puncture her words.

Ella blew out a breath. Riley's seriousness sobered her. "She may have mentioned something about it—"

"Ella. Why didn't you say anything?" She threw her hands up. "Do you have any idea how bad this could look for me if Senhor Arenoso finds out?"

This again. Yes, she knew all too well. She was sick of having to hide all the time. It drained her, and even though she knew Riley wasn't like Maeve, it still caused an ache from somewhere within her heart. But she gritted her teeth; she didn't want to say anything she'd regret. Their time was already dwindling. "It was just a bit of fun. She was saying stuff about me and you, so I just steered her off the scent."

"Wait. Is that why she came surfing?"

"I think so."

Riley shook her head, chewing at her lip. Ella didn't miss the lines etching deeper into her forehead. "You can't mess with people's feelings like that. I just had to explain the rules between staff and clients to her and give the flowers back. It's embarrassing and awkward, and I just feel like..." She let out a heavy sigh. "Such a hypocrite."

Ella reached out an arm to comfort her, but she took a step towards the door.

"I think you should go." Riley's gaze was cast to the floor. She wouldn't even look at her now?

"I'm sorry. I wasn't thinking."

Riley lingered in the doorway but didn't react. "I've had a long day. I just need some space."

Ella swallowed the lump in her throat. "Okay." *It's already happening.* "Sure." *You're too much, Ella.* She took a step back, and Riley went inside, leaving Ella standing awkwardly on the stone. She spun and descended the steps two at a time, her heartrate climbing. Her mind bombarded her with thoughts again, but this time, she couldn't stop them piling and piling and making it harder to breathe.

The end was coming, and all she wanted to do was run. Why delay the inevitable?

CHAPTER EIGHTEEN

Riley

Without Ella in her bed, the nightmares were back with a vengeance. Riley woke covered in sweat, her sheets wrapped around her limbs like they were trying to suffocate her. Jane had offered to be with her today to take her mind off it, but Riley hated needing a babysitter. She should be better by now. She groaned, pushing herself into a sitting position and brushing her hands over her wet eyes.

It didn't erase the images. Or the feeling that came

with the smashing together of two vehicles. The piercing screech and the screams. The before and after.

It was always going to be at its worst today. Memories of her dad even joined in the nightmare, his taunting sneer as he peered over the wreckage with a bottle in his hand. *'Look at what you've done. And ye say I'm the monster?'*

Ziggy chirped at Riley's movement, hurrying over to rub himself against her face, and she tickled his chin. She could make out enough of his features from the morning sun streaming through the blinds to see his green eyes rolling back in his head. He loved nothing more than a chin tickle.

She scooped him into her arms, trying to hold him like a baby, but he pawed her and scampered under the bed. He used to let her carry him when he was a kitten, but less and less now.

She sighed, then completed a round of breathing exercises to try to clear her brain fog. The memories of the accident were replaced with those of Ella. She didn't know when this had all become so complicated.

What did you expect?

She was irked that Ella had said those things to Pauline, but deep down, she knew she didn't have bad intentions. Riley had pushed her away on impulse. The combination of the anniversary of the accident and the realisation of her feelings was a recipe for disaster.

Riley liked Ella. She *really* liked her. But in a week, she'd be leaving the island for good. Back to her normal life. Her life without Riley.

She hadn't even told Ella about the anniversary. Was there any point? If she was just going to leave, should she even bother?

Her gut twisted, tightening into knots that built on top of one another to form a big, ugly tangle of dread. She had known this was going to happen, that Ella would leave, but she hadn't realised it would impact her on such a level. She'd been far too naïve.

Ella wasn't hers. Never was.

So what actually was the point? She was following in António's footsteps and risking losing her job for nothing but a good old-fashioned stab in the heart.

She groaned again, louder, and rolled over in a big huff, inhaling a hint of Ella's scent, which lingered on the pillow next to her. Without her realising, it was happening again. The ache of loss. A before and an after.

Before Ella. After Ella.

Riley didn't want to think about the after.

She didn't want to think at all—or feel—or do, well, anything. But she couldn't do that, she wouldn't be like Elodie, so she forced herself out of her bed and dragged her heavy feet to the shower.

Inside, the hot water coated her skin, and she imagined it washing all the bad dreams away. She wished it were that simple—that the water could cleanse her, soothe her, create a barrier that would make all the bad just slip and slide away. But the bad always found a way in. It would pool in the anniversary cracks, forcing them open until the feelings spilled inside her, drowning her in their weight.

She couldn't be happy-go-lucky Riley today.

No longer feeling the benefits of the water, she turned up the heat, letting out a hiss when the droplets landed on her skin like needles. Steam filled the bathroom, and her mind jumped to Ella. Her gorgeous naked form standing on the edge of the hot springs.

Her stomach coiled again, the knots squeezing. Was everything going to remind her of Ella when she left? When she used the blender in the morning, would she see the scowl on Ella's face, then her smile when she had her first sip of juice? Would the citrus scent of the orange groves always bring back memories of kissing her, the ocean always replay Ella's delighted laugh when she first caught a wave? Would her bed always plague her with the sound of Ella coming undone?

She felt another crack form in her chest. Perhaps the anniversary of Ella's goodbye would have the same effect as Elodie's, too, and she was destined to be haunted by the memories of people she loved who'd left.

She tilted her head to the shower stream, letting the hot water scorch her face. She wasn't sure what she could do. Ever since the António triplet scandal, Senhor Arenoso had made the rules on client/staff relationships very clear. If she told him the truth, she'd lose her job, her home, her close bond with the man who'd helped her in her time of need.

But hadn't she already jeopardised all that by

pursuing Ella?

Fuck. She was torn. Her head and heart were tugging her in two opposite directions. *What a mess.*

She switched off the shower and stepped out, drying herself with one of the fluffy towels hanging on the back of the door. She wasn't thinking about how she and Ella had dried themselves off after being caught in the storm. Or their first kiss at the ruins. And how all the world's energies seemed to pull them together.

She wiped a hand over the fogged glass and looked at herself in the mirror. Her cheeks were red from the heat of the shower, but her stare reflected sadness. She took in the circles under her eyes, her puffy eyelids, her blonde hair slicked down over her back. She sighed, fogging the glass again. She needed to get out of here.

She threw on some joggers and an oversized T-shirt and took the back paths down to the cliffs to avoid seeing anyone. Inside one of the crumbling and unused huts, she let out a happy sigh, hearing nothing but the waves crashing beneath her. She eyed the stack of surfboards piled in a corner. The storage space didn't hold much apart from a workbench and the box of wax. Luckily, that was all she needed.

With painting out of the question—even that reminded her of Ella—she just needed something to occupy her mind. Rewaxing these old boards should do the trick.

She lifted the first onto the bench and dusted it off with an old towel before running her hand along the clean surface.

"A good wax is a surfer's best secret," her dad's gravelly voice reminded her.

Riley's only happy memories of her dad were when he'd taught her to surf. The rugged Irish coastline and the cold, fierce waves biting at her skin. When she was nine, they'd taken a road trip to the southwest coast with one of her dad's poker buddies and his son, Kenan. Her days were spent dipping in and out of the sea, racing Kenan along the sand and building sandcastles. But the nights were long. She and Kenan huddled together, making earplugs out of pillows to try block out their dads' vicious laughter as the bottles emptied and glasses smashed.

Riley blew out a breath, letting the memory leave with it. She picked up the wax and started drawing horizontal lines, cross-hatching close together up to the stringer in the middle of the board. She used to dream about her mum coming home and storming through the door, wrapping her up in the big purple coat she'd only seen her wear in photos, declaring they were running away together in dad's camper.

But she never came. And her dad pawned the camper to pay off gambling debts.

Riley picked up the pace with her movements, feeling herself frown as she concentrated on the circular top coat. Before she knew it, she'd already finished two boards.

"I thought it was supposed to be your day off today?"

Riley jumped at the voice. She spun, almost

propelling the surf wax at the man in the doorway. But it wasn't the wide, barrel-chest image of her father. Senhor Arenoso lifted a hand in greeting, his deep green kaftan swaying around his ankles.

She plastered a smile on her face, thrown off by the interruption. "*Bom dia*, Senhor," she greeted, brushing her hands on her trousers.

"Good morning, Riley." He combed her with his eyes before landing on the stack of boards behind her. He gave a gentle nod. "But you know you don't have to call me that in private."

"Right, sorry, Danilo." Riley was so used to calling him by his work name that his first name still felt terribly informal.

He's checking up on me. She swallowed, feeling nervous.

Since they'd had their meeting yesterday, agreeing to Riley's day off for the anniversary, she hadn't expected to see him, never mind him turning up here. *How did he know where I was?*

His surprise visit had her wondering if he suspected something was out of the ordinary. Had Romeo told him about seeing Ella at the groves? Or Pauline about the flowers? Had someone been following her? *Oh, Jesus.*

"I'm sorry to intrude on your day, but I thought I might find you here when your cabin was empty. I know you prefer the quieter places on days like these."

"It's alright." Riley's chest tightened. His other-worldly senses always caught her off guard. It made her all the more nervous he might know something else was amiss.

He regarded Riley with careful eyes. "How did you sleep?"

"Not great," she admitted, unable to hold the man's dark gaze.

He ducked his head. "I'm sorry to hear that. I know how hard today is for you. I wish there were more I could do to help." He reached out and squeezed her hand, and tears immediately pricked Riley's eyes.

The small act of comfort meant the world to her. She felt most people couldn't understand the way the anniversary haunted her, but Danilo always made her feel seen. He was the complete opposite of her own father.

"I feel I've failed you in a way, Riley."

"What?" She shook her head. "That's not true."

He seemed to study her, looking deeper beneath the layers. "With all your time here, I thought we could break the cycle. To help you move on from your fears. It hurts to still see you suffer."

"I'm a lot better." Which wasn't a lie. She knew she still had a way to go, but compared to a few years ago, it was light and dark. She wondered if Ella had anything to do with it.

"You know the course is my soul child, but I care about you. All I want for you is happiness. I sense a change on your horizon." His dark eyes found hers again, and he waited, as though he was going to say more. He frowned, tapping her hand twice before moving it away.

Then he let out a sigh. "What I am saying is, I would understand if you decided that your happiness is no longer at Sandy Springs."

Fear shot up Riley's spine. "Danilo, that's the last thing I'd want. This is my home, please, I—" A sob escaped her throat, and she put her hands to her eyes.

She couldn't lose her home, her job, her life here. It was the only thing keeping her sane. Had he finally realised she was an imposter? A fake? Incapable of teaching the course because her own life was a mess?

"I'll do better," she said. "Please…don't fire me."

"Fire you? Riley, why would you think such things?" She slowly lowered her hands and found his eyebrows pulled together. "I'm just saying I would understand if you decide that Sandy Springs is no longer for you. I just want you to make the right choices. To be happy."

Happy. Riley wanted to be happy, too.

Despite all the baggage and negativity that the anniversary brought to her every year, this time had been different. Ella's face popped into her head, that slow half-smile spreading across her lips, and for a second, all the darkness shifted. Hope flickered.

But just as quick as it shifted, it reverted back. Ella was just a temporary fix. Ella leaving meant the new happiness would leave too. What was Danilo trying to tell her? Did he know? Was he trying to tell her to go?

The man had a heart of gold, but he was a stickler for the rules. He even said it himself, the course was like a child to him. He'd do anything to protect it, even if it meant letting Riley go. But she wasn't ready for that. How could she be?

She sniffed, trying to find some composure. With a sigh, she began, "Sandy Springs is my home. I appreciate everything you're saying, but I'm not going anywhere."

He smiled, his moustache curling with the movement. "That's nice to hear." He tapped her hand again, then turned to look out at the ocean. "I hope you know how much I value you. Not just as an employee, but as a friend." He reached into his pocket and pulled out a necklace with a black crystal. "Obsidian is believed to be a protective stone. Its energies can help get rid of emotional blockages and digest bad experiences, providing clarity. I hope it helps."

He held the necklace out for Riley to take, and she felt herself getting choked up again. Her own dad didn't even remember her birthday, but Danilo was such a sweetheart. How could she ever let him down?

"Please," he said, giving the necklace a little shake. "It's the least I can do."

"Thank you." She accepted it, rubbing her thumb over the cool stone.

"I won't tell you what to do, but I hear Marco Marcos has some spare slots tomorrow if you're interested. Maybe it would help to talk about it again."

"I'll consider it, thanks."

He touched the owl pendant hanging around his neck thoughtfully. "I know you don't always agree with your familiar. But the dolphin, like you, find ways to ride the waves of life. They might swim along unnoticed for a while, but they always rise above, bringing joy and strength to those who witness it. You bring great harmony to those around you, Riley. My hope for you is that you remember to save some for yourself." He nodded, gave her a smile, then made his way to the open door. He spun before he reached the threshold. "Be kind to yourself today. What happened wasn't your fault." And then he left, leaving a swirl of energy thickening in the hut.

Riley exhaled, rubbing her hands over her face. There was so much to unpack in that conversation, she didn't know where to start. She sighed, sucking in several deep breaths. Then, a new lick of life straightened her spine. Inspiration had struck her like a lightning bolt.

A short while later, she was standing at the top of the cliffs overlooking the beach. The sea breeze caressed her, twitching her hair about her face. Her hand moved with a mind of its own as it danced away, bringing the image to life.

The blues, purples, and whites created zigzag waves. Chaotic swirls and edges rose as the brush worked in fierce, precise movements. At the bottom of the canvas, the sea was as dark as charcoal, lightening in colour towards the surface. A lone form leaped out of the water, the golden sun casting long streams of light across its body.

A dolphin.

Everything swirled around Riley's brain. In the tangle, a few thoughts separated themselves.

Is Senhor Arenoso trying to tell me something? To leave? To stay?

The man liked to be cryptic at the best of times, but their conversation earlier had left her uncertain. What she did know was that he wanted her to figure it out.

Is my guide struggling to lead me? She knew that in order to receive guidance, she needed to be open. The truth was she'd struggled to see what harmony and strength Danilo saw in her for some time.

Her hand blurred as she swiped more white across the chaotic roll of the waves, and she smiled, letting out a shaky breath. She felt like she was starting to understand. Just like everything else in the universe, all these things were connected.

When Riley first met Ella—the shrieking woman who had just tumbled down a hill with a suitcase on top of her, sticks and twigs caught in her wild hair—she knew she would invite chaos into her life.

And that was exactly what happened.

But Riley was realising something—sometimes, a bit of chaos can be a good thing. It's said that the flap of a butterfly's wings could be capable of starting a hurricane on the other side of the planet. One small, seemingly insignificant action can make a big change over time. Meeting Ella and inviting that chaos in had already started to change her.

With Ella's fire and direct nature, how she wore her heart on her sleeve, Riley couldn't help but be drawn to her. In her own process of healing, Riley had hidden parts of herself away. Being around Ella brought colour back to those spaces. She made her feel more confident, more playful, like she could express her sexuality again and give in to the desire. Ella's heart, her beautiful and enormous heart, could hold so much love, Riley was afraid of it.

Because her past had taught her that in the blink of an eye—of a flutter of a butterfly's wings—those things can disappear.

But they can also ignite.

In order to find the balance she was searching for, Riley needed a little chaos.

After another swipe of paint, dabbing the bristles side to side to add more texture, she let out another breath.

She knew what she had to do.

CHAPTER NINETEEN

Ella

Ella wasn't surprised when Riley didn't show for yoga class, but it still hurt. Had what she'd said to Pauline affected her that badly? Or was something else going on? Ella had only meant for it to be a joke, not taken to heart, but watching the replacement instructor in Riley's space at the front made dread sink deeper into her stomach.

The woman, Jane, was nice enough, but she wasn't Riley.

Sleeping in her own bed had felt strange, too, without

Riley's long, warm body to snuggle into.

Better get used to it, she supposed. Her king-sized bed was waiting for her back in England, but she'd give the world's comfiest mattress a miss to be able to keep sharing Riley's.

She tried to focus on holding her balance, but her shaky breathing threw her off, and she nearly toppled over. Jane's attention landed on her, but she forced a smile, hoping she wouldn't come over and give her any advice. She didn't want to speak to anyone.

She couldn't spend what was left of her time on the island like this.

Jane closed the session, making a joke that made everyone laugh but made Ella even sadder, and people started packing away their mats. Ella lingered at the back, dragging her feet, when a familiar oversweet perfume bombarded her senses. She looked up to find Pauline, wearing fluorescent green-and-yellow spandex with a black kimono. It was giving funeral and eighties disco all in one. But the woman's face was the most surprising. Her dark eyebrows were drawn together worriedly, the frown lines etched deep beside her mouth. After a quick glance over her shoulder proved that no one else was around, she leaned in to whisper, "Ella, I think I might have done something to upset Riley."

Her mouth wobbled. Her pleading eyes full of concern. *Dammit.* The fact that Pauline was blaming herself for this just made Ella feel even more terrible. She fought the pricking sensation forming behind her own eyes, but it was no use, and a lone tear slipped down her cheek before she could brush it away. She pulled her oversized hat down over her face. She'd worn it in an attempt to make Riley smile, but now it doubled as a shield from prying eyes.

But Pauline jumped into action, her own sadness vanishing as she wrapped her arms around her, suffocating her in her bosom.

"Oh, sweetie. What's wrong?" She gave Ella another squeeze, making her grunt, then tugged her away from the courtyard.

With their roles now reversed—Ella being the sniffling snot monster while Pauline encouraged her on— Ella hardly registered where they were going until they stepped inside. Pauline's cabin was immaculately clean, with not a sock out of place or a single crease in the bedding. But the collection of flowers and home-crafted items dotted about the space made it feel very homely. Ella recognised some of the designs from the local markets, the colourful patterns and detailed craftsmanship. Had she bought all of these?

"Take a seat, bestie."

Ella sniffed, catching a strong whiff of Pauline's perfume, which seemed to pillow out from every direction. She didn't want to sit on the bed and ruin it, so she perched awkwardly on the end of the wooden frame.

"What are you doing?" Pauline asked, peering at Ella hovering over the bed like she was about to squat and cough. "Sit your bottom down."

Ella did as she was asked, and another tear slipped down her cheek.

Pauline collapsed on the mattress, legs kicking in the air. She righted herself, blew out a breath, then commanded Ella with her eyes. "Tell Pauline everything."

Ella didn't have it in her to comment on Pauline speaking about herself in the third person or tell her how much she shared her mother's inherent love for gossip. It was hard to find any words in the depth of all the sadness swallowing her.

"I'm sorry, Pauline," she started, unable to look the woman in the eyes.

"What are you sorry for?"

"I owe you an apology. I've not been fair to you." A swell of emotion rose in her chest, and she bit her lip. "I shouldn't have made those comments about Riley to you. They were untrue, but I didn't mean to hurt anyone's feelings. I was just deflecting and making a joke." She forced her eyes to meet Pauline's. "And I'm sorry if that hurt you. You've been a good friend to me since being here. And I've just been a cow."

"You haven't."

"I have, and I've been selfish—"

"Listen." Pauline pressed her lips together, then breathed a long, heavy sigh, taking Ella's hand in hers. Ella tried not to mind that it was clammy. "Thank you for your apology. I appreciate that." She paused, selecting her next words. "But I won't have you talking negatively about yourself. I know I'm not the easiest person to be around, but you've been kind and listened to me talk about Albert. You carried my suitcase and gave me a shoulder to cry on, and I won't let you think you're not a good friend to me, because you are. You've a good energy around you."

Ella laughed, sniffing loudly. "You've been spending too much time with Senhor Arenoso."

"Maybe a kitten's whisker. Anyhoo, do you want a tissue? I have plenty."

Ella accepted and dried her eyes, allowing her body to relax. Relief swept over her. She didn't want to be the reason that anyone else was upset; Riley was bad enough. Her face drooped, and Pauline poked at her mouth with a plump finger.

"What happened there?"

"Sorry." Ella rubbed the spot she'd touched and sighed.

"Is this about Riley?"

Ella hesitated. As much as she'd grown to like Pauline, Riley didn't want anyone to know about them. If she wanted to leave the island on good terms and protect Riley's job, she needed to keep it a secret. "No," she said, wiping at her eyes with her sleeve and hoping Pauline hadn't noticed the long pause.

"Probably for the best. I am a nosy Noreen, but I'm not the best at keeping secrets. Albert would attest to that. I told everyone we knew about his affair in our family Christmas card."

Ella glanced at the woman, seeing her in a different light. She might have her flaws—the wailing, snotty crying, and gassy tendencies—but she had a kind heart. "Sounds like Albert deserved worse."

Pauline's mouth erupted into a toothy grin, and she pulled Ella in for a hug. "There she is. My bestie's back."

Ella chuckled into her shoulder and then hugged her, wondering how Winnie was going to take the news.

After chatting for a while longer and after Pauline had tried on different outfits for the fire ceremony at the end of the week, Ella left her cabin feeling reenergised. Patching things with Pauline had been the hors d'oeuvre; now it was time for the main. She just needed to find Riley.

A funny feeling lingered in her belly. One she couldn't quite place. But if she'd learnt anything on this island, it was to listen to herself and follow her heart. Senhor Arenoso had been right. Ella had many reservations and had put walls up, trying to protect herself, but they'd just stopped her from getting what she desired. She didn't want a quick fix anymore. She wanted something that would last.

She wanted Riley.

She let out a laugh, a mixture of relief and amusement, because the very idea that Ella had fallen for her was both ridiculous and oh-so-predictable. But she didn't care what her mother or even what Winnie would think. Yes, admittedly, she still had plenty to work on, but this time, she wasn't shying away from it. And a connection like theirs came once in a lifetime.

Ella knew what she wanted; she just hoped Riley knew too.

She pressed her nose up against the cool window of Riley's cabin, knocking her hat to the floor. The lights were dark, but she just wanted to be sure, in case—heaven forbid—anything had happened to her. Her heart sank a little. The fact that Riley had had a day off today without saying anything felt…strange. Was she reading too much into this? Being too forward? She didn't want to be too much and scare Riley away.

Her heart skipped in her chest as her mind tried to pull its old tricks on her.

But she took in a breath, refocused, and remembered what Senhor Arenoso had said to her. *Surrender to the process.* If she followed her heart, she could leave the island with no regrets. No matter what the outcome was, she would survive. She always did.

She wouldn't let her brain get in the way of her trying.

With newfound focus, she looked out over the sea, breathing in the fresh air. *Where would Riley be?* She picked up her hat and started walking, hoping her intuition was right.

A short while later, feet in the sand and the sea breeze in her hair, she tilted her head up to the cliffs, catching a head of familiar blonde hair. *Riley.* Her heart skipped a beat, insides squeezing. All the confidence she'd felt on her walk over drained out the soles of her feet.

You can do this, Ella.

She walked towards the rocks, nerves building with every step. Memories of stumbling up these boulders after Riley had rescued her played in her mind. The electricity that'd warmed through her veins just from being around her—maybe from the near-death adrenaline, too.

Her fingers gripped the rough grooves, and she pulled herself up, the sun warm on her back. She remembered it being trickier than this, but maybe that was because she'd been terrified of falling and crushing the handsome yoga instructor. But no, she felt stronger. She *was* stronger. Both mind and body.

She could do anything. Even super scary things like telling Riley how she felt about her.

With a heave, she approached the top and found a hand waiting. She looked up and met cool, blue eyes, almost stilling her heart.

"Need a hand?" Riley asked.

She pulled her up and set her on her feet. Ella smiled when she didn't move her hands away. The time apart must have done them some good.

"I'm sorry about what happened with Pauline." The words burst from her throat like gunfire. "I had a really nice talk with her, and we're all good, and I just don't want anything to come between me and you, ever. Which I know is a bold statement considering I'm leaving in less than a week. But it's true. I really like you, Riley."

Riley gave her a dimpled grin, her hands tight on her waist. Paint licked up her arms with a small spatter on her jaw. "I really like you too, Ella."

Looking into Riley's eyes, Ella felt buoyed by the gentle waves, swallowed in the blue depths. Caught in the swirl of blue, brown, and green, she could quite happily drown.

But the next words left Riley's mouth, and a cold wave crashed over her.

"But there's something I need to tell you."

Riley's mouth had lost its smile, her eyes abandoned their sparkle. All the lead weight in Ella's chest returned, almost buckling her knees.

She hated those words. Those words never bore good news, especially not when they began with "but", the worst conjunction in the English language.

It was lovely to meet you, but *unfortunately, you're not a match for our company.*

I love spending time with you, but *I think we should just be friends.*

I love you, Ella, but *sometimes things happen. You know Annabelle, the receptionist…*

She steeled herself, stiffening in Riley's grip. Her defensive walls twitched, ready to spring into action, pack the cannons and get ready to fire. But she steadied her breath and waited for Riley to continue.

"I should've told you earlier, but it's really difficult for me to say."

Ella's stomach dropped. *Please don't be married.* But when Riley's eyes filled with tears, she softened, caressing her cheek.

Riley leaned into the touch, breathing deeply, and then her eyelids fluttered open.

Ella thought she was going to be sick.

"Four years ago, a car accident changed my life." Riley blew out a sharp breath, her voice wobbling. "Me and my ex were leaving her parents' house. The country roads were challenging at the best of times, never mind in the dark, but Elodie knew them like the back of her hand.

"Then someone tried to overtake us, but the cars came together, flying through a wall and crashing in a farmer's field." Tears fell down Riley's cheeks. Ella brushed them away with her fingertips, her chest tightening at the pain in her voice.

"The crash…was horrific. Luckily, all we came away with were a broken bone, scrapes, and bruises. But the other car…they weren't so lucky."

"Oh god." Ella held Riley tighter while she collected herself.

"The driver was fine, but the passenger… The kid was only ten. The way the car folded trapped him in his seat, and he had to have his leg amputated. I can still hear the screams, the sounds, every year."

"Riley, I'm so sorry." With the slightest tug, Riley collapsed into Ella, knocking her hat onto the ground. She wound her arms around her.

"That one moment changed everything." She sniffed. "My whole life. Everything. I lost everything."

She buried herself into Ella and let the tears fall. Ella held her tight as a soft sea breeze fluttered around them.

She didn't know how much time passed until Riley pulled back.

"Do you want me to take you home?" Ella asked.

Riley rubbed her red nose, her skin blotchy from crying. She pressed her knuckles to her eyes. "God. I don't want anybody to see me like this."

"Here." Ella plucked her hat up off the ground and placed it on Riley's head. She let out a soft laugh; it didn't suit her, but it'd do the job. Then she covered Riley's painting with the sheet, careful not to look at it, and packed her paints into her bag for her.

They walked back to the cabin mostly in silence, other than Riley's directions to avoid the busier path. Riley's quiet sobs filled the air occasionally, and Ella gave her hand a quick squeeze.

Once back inside the walls of her cabin, Ella caught sight of the two canvases Riley had propped up on the bookcase. The day in the groves came swirling around her. It had felt like a milestone in their relationship: opening up, spending time together, feeling somewhat normal. The fact Riley had displayed the two paintings side-by-side, one a masterpiece and one a blotchy mess, squeezed something deep inside her. That day must've meant something to her too. It gave her hope.

But then Riley let out another heartfelt sob, and Ella brought her into her arms, rocking her as she nestled into the crook of her neck. This wasn't how she'd expected their encounter to go. Her heart hurt for the woman weeping in her arms, but she had more questions.

"I'm sorry you have to see me like this," Riley mumbled. "The anniversary, it just brings everything back."

"You don't have to apologise," Ella said, pulling back and brushing the tear-soaked hair from Riley's face. "I'm glad you're telling me."

She nodded, eyes red and puffy.

"You can tell me anything, Riley. I care about you." Their eyes met, and Ella saw an emotion she hadn't seen there before. Something darker. She remembered to breathe, then reached for Riley's hand and gave it a squeeze. "If you're ready to talk, I'm ready to listen."

CHAPTER TWENTY

They curled up in Riley's bed, the same way they had many times before, but now with an air of vulnerability surrounding them. Whatever shields and barriers they'd constructed, out of habit or necessity, lay at dust by their feet. There was nowhere else to hide, but Ella didn't want to. She had a feeling their next conversation would have an irreversible ripple effect.

For better or worse.

Her breathing came quick and loud in her own ears. She didn't know what to expect. Riley's revelation had come as a surprise to her, but it also made a lot of sense. They'd not spoken much about how Riley came to work at Sandy Springs. Riley had said she needed a lifestyle change, not dissimilar to the majority of people who found themselves here. She'd befriended the staff, and they were impressed with her yoga knowledge. The next thing she knew, years had passed, and she was still here.

Ella had never seen someone fall apart so easily in front of her, but then she imagined it hadn't been easy at all; it was more of an accumulation of everything Riley had been hiding. She tightened her arm around the woman's shoulders, combing her fingers through her hair. Her heart ached to think she'd kept all of this inside all the time. If nothing else, she hoped to make the burden lighter for her. Riley had done that for Ella when she'd found her at the bottom of the creepy fingers tree after finding out about Maeve's engagement.

So she waited, held her tighter, and continued to brush her nails against her scalp in soft circles.

Riley's arm draped over Ella's stomach, and her eye was drawn to the white scar tracing her wrist. She drew her fingertip over it and felt Riley exhale.

"Did this happen in the crash?" she asked.

"Yeah. But it was a clean break."

A moment passed between them. Ella continued to caress the line, evidence of the moment causing Riley so much distress. But she sensed there was more.

"What happened after the accident?"

"It was a mess." Riley exhaled again, and Ella heard the quiver in her voice. "The boy's mum, the driver, she sued Elodie. Claimed dangerous driving… Drummed up this whole media campaign spreading lies and hate about us for injuring a child." Her voice turned steely. "But it was an accident. It all happened so quickly. No one meant for anyone to get hurt."

"That's awful. I'm sorry you had to go through all that." Ella's mind stumbled on a question she was almost too afraid to ask. But she took a deep breath and asked it anyway. "What happened with you and Elodie?"

"I guess…sometimes traumatic events bring you closer together. Sometimes they break you." She was quiet for a moment. "She changed. Became a shell of herself. She started to believe everything the media were saying. That she was a reckless monster who deserved to rot behind bars." She shook her head, her words quickening. "I tried to help her. I tried so hard to help her, but she wouldn't listen. Started drinking heavily, acting reckless. I didn't recognise her anymore. I tried so hard, Ella, but it wasn't enough. I—"

"Hey, hey, it's okay." Ella pulled her into her chest, even though she was much smaller than Riley, and rocked her.

"I couldn't stop it all falling apart," she said in a quiet voice.

Ella's eyes watered, and she squeezed her tighter. She knew that feeling well. When you felt something slipping through your fingers, and you tried to claw it back, only to worsen the distance.

Maybe that was why she'd stayed at her job, close to Maeve, so she could still touch on that happy feeling when she needed to. But the feeling wasn't real. It was just an illusion.

Riley rested her chin on Ella's chest, and she kissed her temple, breathing in the smell she'd become so familiar with. She didn't want their relationship to slip through her fingers either, but that same fear gripped her own insides. Maybe Riley's aversion to having a relationship with a client was just an aversion to relationships in general. After having her heart broken, Ella could understand that. But it still scared her. Was she going to put her heart on the line just for it to be stamped on once more?

She wanted to tell Riley how she felt about everything, but today wasn't about Ella. It was about Riley.

"Thank you for being so open with me," she murmured against her hair, planting another kiss.

"I'm sorry. I didn't want you to see me like this."

"It's okay. Nobody's perfect all the time. In fact, I remember you saying that to me. Remember?"

"I guess I can't argue with that." Riley gave a sad chuckle, then sniffed. "I just don't do well on the anniversary. It reminds me of everything I lost."

Ella's heart flinched. It hurt to hear Riley speak about someone else in that way, but she understood. "It's alright. Let it out. I've got you."

They stayed like that for a long time. Riley curled up on Ella's chest, their limbs intertwined. When Riley broke their cocoon and reached over to the bedside table for a tissue, Ella met her gaze.

"Do you want to have some space?" she asked.

Riley dabbed at her swollen eyes and red nose, then her sad blues glanced back at her. "Would you stay? I understand if—"

"Of course I'll stay."

Her mouth curved, and Ella pulled her back into her arms again, arranging herself behind her.

"I've never been the little spoon before," Riley said, backing herself into Ella.

Heat flared between Ella's legs, but she ignored it, kissing Riley's shoulder. "I've never been the big spoon either. But I wanna hold you."

A beat passed, then Riley let out a big sigh. "That sounds nice."

It wasn't long until Ella felt Riley relax into the curve of her body, her breathing falling into a shallow rhythm. She must've been exhausted. Ella nuzzled closer, soaking in the heat, wishing she could zap all of Riley's sadness away.

As with several other moments in their time together, Ella sensed this openness didn't come easily to Riley, despite the things she taught on the course. Something about that made Ella like her even more. Riley wasn't perfect. She had her flaws and weaknesses, like everyone else. Getting to see those sharper, vulnerable parts cast her in a new light. One that spread into Ella's heart and firmly planted itself in its centre.

She held her a little tighter, careful not to wake her, and rested her eyes for just a moment. At one point, she felt Ziggy join the bundle on the bed, his soft fur tickling her nose before he curled up in between their legs.

Ella woke sometime later, the room darkened by the descending sun. Riley and she were still cuddled together, and as she blinked, their conversation slowly seeped back into her memory.

It was a lot of information to process—even after one of the best naps of Ella's life.

Her bladder demanded her attention, so she carefully shuffled away from Riley and peeled herself from the bed. She padded across the wooden floor to the bathroom and hissed as she sat on the freezing toilet seat.

Their situation had already been complicated, with Riley's work and Ella due to leave at the end of the week. Throwing in a haunting anniversary, with some unresolved trauma, just added more pieces to the puzzle.

Ella didn't want to be selfish, but she also needed to think of herself. She didn't want to be a replacement or a consolation prize. She wanted to be someone's number one; she wouldn't settle for second best again. Ever. She needed to think about her own happiness.

But didn't Riley make her happy?

Ugh. My head's a mess.

The creaking of floorboards jarred her from staring

at the white tiles. Riley must be up.

She forced herself to stand with a groan, flushed, then washed her hands. Her stomach bubbled. Why was she suddenly so nervous?

She found Riley at the kitchen sink, filling a glass of water. She gulped hastily, then ran a hand through her hair, pushing it back from her face. She turned when she heard the door, and the smile blooming across her face made Ella smile too.

"Hey, everything okay?" she asked, offering Ella the glass.

Ella took a swig. "I think so. Just processing."

"It's a lot. I get that." She observed her, as though she were trying to uncover anything hiding beneath the surface. Her eyes were less red, but the puffiness lingered.

"How are you feeling?" Ella asked.

"My mind feels lighter, but my body feels heavy. Like I could sleep for a thousand years."

Ella traced her jaw with her fingertips. "How about I run you a bath?"

Surprise flickered across her features. "Really?"

"Maybe we can channel the healing powers of the hot springs into your tub."

The corners of her mouth lifted. "Does that mean you'll be joining me, then?"

Ella smiled. "Sure. If that's what you want?"

She planted a soft kiss on Ella's lips. "It is."

Ella started to run the bath while Riley searched her cupboards for candles. She returned with a bag full of tealights varying from Christmas gingerbread to cherry blossom.

"They're old presents," she explained with a shrug. "I'm not really a candle gal."

Once the water was steaming and the flames were lit, covering the bathroom in a golden glow, they started to undress. Riley pulled her T-shirt over her head and hung it on the radiator. She slipped her shorts and underwear off too, and Ella couldn't help but stare at her glorious form. She wanted to commit it to memory. Every freckle, every hard line and sculptured muscle. The way her blonde hair fell over her strong shoulders. Her perfectly toned back. Those cheekbones and dimples, the blue eyes so full of emotion.

A surge of feeling rose in Ella's chest, and she turned away, focusing on undressing herself to distract her thoughts from derailing. She didn't want to forget a thing, but would these moments come back to haunt her?

Calm down, Ella. It's just a fucking bath.

"After you," she said, turning to find Riley had now pulled her hair into a bun. Ella always loved how it changed the shape of her face. It made her more vulnerable somehow when she didn't have all those waves to hide behind.

Riley climbed into the tub, steam pillowing around her, and let out a heavenly sigh.

Ella took in the curve of her biceps as the water coated them. How her hair glowed in the candlelight. Savoured the hums of pleasure as she sunk into the water.

Stop it.

Tears pricked her eyelids, but she wished them away. Letting go of someone who was arguably not right for her had been so difficult. How could she possibly let go of someone like Riley?

She swallowed the lump in her throat. "Where do you want me?"

"Here." Riley offered her hand, and Ella stepped into the bath, lowering herself into the hot water so she laid back against Riley's chest. Riley wound her arms around her, the water sloshing over the two of them, and they each let out another sigh. Warmth spread through Ella's body like balm to her soul. Lying here with Riley was everything. She'd never felt closer to her, but her mind kept prodding at the places that hurt.

"This is amazing," Riley whispered.

"It is," she managed, watching the shadows dance across the tiles. Her lip wobbled. She was relieved Riley couldn't see her face. *Don't ruin the moment, Ella.*

They didn't speak for a few minutes, just let their bodies relax.

Riley broke the silence first. "I already feel better. Thank you." Her hands glided over Ella's waist, and she gave her a squeeze.

"You're welcome." Ella wished she could say the same, but her mind wouldn't settle.

"Thank you for being so understanding and patient." She kissed Ella's cheek, nuzzling into her neck. "That means the world to me."

Ella bit her lip, tracing over Riley's fingers where they lay across her stomach. "Does this happen every year?" she asked.

"Yes. But it's been easier this time."

A spark of hope flickered in Ella's heart, and she cursed it. "How so?"

"Meeting you has opened my eyes to a lot of things." She caressed Ella's arms, moving her hands up and down, the water rippling around them. "I was doing fine here. In my eyes, fine is good. Fine is functioning. Surviving. But it's not really living."

Ella's pulse quickened. Riley scooped up water and washed it over the two of them.

"I've been scared to want more," she admitted. "Wanting something sets you up for disappointment. Not wanting anything is safe. It's…"

"Lonely?" Ella offered.

She felt Riley nod behind her, and how her hands stilled. "Yeah. It's pretty lonely."

"Being with the wrong people feels pretty lonely too, though."

"That's true. Has that happened to you?"

"With my ex, yeah. I wanted it to work with us so badly, but thinking about it now, I was just scared of being alone. I tried to force it, even though it wasn't working. But now…" She swallowed, her pulse quickening. "I know what I want."

The flames danced along the white tiles, bending their shadows and listening in.

"And what's that?" Riley asked in a breathless whisper.

Ella was all too aware of her heart drumming against her ribcage, of the notion of laying herself bare in the arms of someone she cared so deeply for. And what doing that would mean.

But it didn't seem the right moment to say it. Not after the emotional day that Riley had had. She wanted it to be perfect, not tainted by the anniversary or Riley's ex-girlfriend.

But just like people, life could never be perfect, either. She couldn't wait for the perfect moment because a perfect moment didn't exist.

"I don't want to scare you," she started, brushing Riley's knuckles. "I know you've had a rough few days, and I don't want to add to that. And I'm leaving soon. I know how crazy it all seems, and I know it's complicated, but..." She blew out a breath, rippling the water around them. "What I want, is you."

There. She'd said it. She exhaled again, feeling a weight lifted.

Riley kissed her neck, and Ella melted into a fit of giggles, splashing the water. She turned her face to meet her lips in a soft kiss, but Riley pulled back, her finger tracing Ella's mouth.

"Even after everything I've told you?" she asked.

"What do you mean?"

"I'm a hypocrite, Ella. All the talk about letting go and forging new paths, yet here I am, crumbling every year over something I should've probably got over by now." Her arms tensed. "All this talk about going after what we want, about what will make us happy, and yet I'm terrified of it. That doesn't bother you?"

"The fact you're not a perfect, mistake-free human? Of course not. Riley, we all have a past. We all have weaknesses. I'm not going to judge you for that." She swivelled in the tub so she could face her, their limbs slipping together. Riley caught her arms to stop Ella's head from going under the water, and they shared a laugh. "I want to know all of the things that make you *you*. Even the ugly parts. Especially those. And it's actually comforting to hear you're also scared, because I am, too. I want you, Riley. Even though it's messy and complicated, my heart just wants you. Do you know how scary *that* is?"

"I do." Her eyes studied Ella's face, and she moved a loose strand of hair behind her ear.

Ella released a breath, flopping her head forward and pressing her hands against Riley's chest, feeling the strong thumping of her heart. Riley adjusted her legs, so Ella was lying on top of her, those blue eyes dark and dreamy pools in the candlelight.

She made circles over Riley's freckled skin. "The pressing question is, what are we going to do once this week is over?"

Riley's face fell, and Ella's heart along with it.

"I've always struggled to think about the future." She moved her hands to Ella's back. "After what happened with Elodie, I never wanted to get my heart broken like that again, so I just…stopped. What was the point in planning for something, when it could all be ripped away in one instant? It was better to focus on the present. Take it day by day. That's all I've been doing ever since, really."

Ella's throat tightened. If Riley didn't see a future, then…what did that mean?

"I used to be fine with that," Riley continued. "Fine with all of it. But ever since I met you, Ella…that blurry, pixelated image of the future has started to get clearer. I want you too—"

Ella kissed her, and Riley pulled them closer together. Sparks erupted in Ella's belly as those soft lips melted into hers, wet hands gripping her neck. The water sloshed all around them, and they broke apart, laughing. She couldn't believe they'd had this conversation in the bath.

But Riley's next words were the most surprising.

"At the end of the week, I'm going to tell Senhor Arenoso."

Ella's mouth fell open. "What? But…won't you lose your job?"

Riley nodded. "Yes. But it's okay. I'm going to leave Sandy Springs."

"Leave? What? Why?" Out of all the things they'd said tonight, Riley leaving the island was one thing Ella couldn't comprehend. "You love it here."

"I know, but it's time."

"I can't ask you to do that."

Riley brushed her cheek. "You're not. It's my decision."

This time, Riley was the one to press her lips to Ella's. They fell into the water, creating a big splash and extinguishing a few of the candles. Ella didn't care. Had she really heard Riley right?

She broke the kiss. "Are you sure? I don't want you to rush into anything."

Riley's gaze held hers. "I want you, Ella. You're my future."

That hit her like a ton of bricks. Dizzying her in the best way possible. *Fuck's sake.* She blinked back tears, but the warmth swelling in her heart continued to get bigger and bigger.

Luckily, Riley kissed her again, and the movement of her fingers over Ella's thighs was more than enough of a distraction. In no time, they were making out, their hands wandering over each other's slippery bodies. Riley hauled Ella on top of her, so that one leg was straddling Riley's torso. The water, lukewarm now, swirled around them as they pushed and pulled, trying to eliminate any spaces between them.

"Really?" Ella asked, breaking the kiss. "You want me?"

Riley pressed her lips to her neck, her tongue collecting the water droplets and sending a shiver down her spine. "Yes, Ella. I want you."

Heat spread between her legs. Who knew those

words were such a turn-on? *Fuck.* She found Riley's lips again, and Riley's hot tongue slipped into her mouth, slow and silky. Her stomach flip-flopped, her senses sparking to life.

Ella was suddenly very aware she was naked and pressed up against a wet and also *very* naked Riley.

The kisses built, growing harder and more forceful, until they were both slipping around the tub. A dull ache grew inside her, and she gasped as Riley hooked her leg up and spread her folds. Riley sunk a finger into her easily, and Ella moaned against her lips as she glided in and out of her.

"Oh…god…Riley." She clawed her nails into her back, sliding them over her wet skin. But Riley continued her slow pace, her playful tongue sending throbs right where Ella needed it. "Fuck."

Arousal flooded her, drowning out anything other than Riley. *Riley.* Riley, who wanted Ella as much as she wanted her.

Riley added another finger, and Ella hummed, needing her to fuck her right here, right now. But their bodies slipped in the tub again, and they both let out a short laugh.

Riley hooked her fingers upwards, and Ella bucked. She planted a kiss on Ella's breast, her tongue flicking over her nipple.

"Shall we get out of the bath now?"

CHAPTER TWENTY-ONE

Riley

Riley pulled a towel from the hook and wrapped it around Ella's shoulders. A slow, seductive smile spread across her face, the moment elongating. A few lone candles continued to flicker by the side of the bath, but the real heat charged in the air between them.

She admired every curve of Ella's body. Her thick

thighs, soft stomach, and Riley's favourite—her magnificent full breasts. A low pulsing grew between Riley's legs. She'd be an absolute idiot not to follow this woman to the ends of the earth. It was funny—if someone had said this to her a month ago, she'd have thought they were a few sandwiches short of a picnic. But looking at the beautiful redhead in front of her, everything had changed. Everything.

Grasping the ends of the towel, she tugged Ella closer, planting the softest of kisses on her lips.

Ella groaned as she brushed her mouth across her jaw, kissing her neck. She traced her tongue over her pulse point, soaking up the water droplets. Ella grabbed her waist, tilting her head to the side to give her more room.

But Riley was torn. She wanted to give in to her primal urges, to kiss, bite, and suck Ella's skin. To mark her so deeply that nothing, not even the gods or the guides, would ever dare to think about taking her away from her. To have her unravelling at her fingertips, the evidence marking Riley's cheeks and tongue, to drown in her.

But she also wanted to cherish every single thing about this moment. Her heart had never felt so full. Ella was an amalgamation of qualities Riley didn't even know she needed. Open and patient. Hot and fiery. Beautiful, unfiltered chaos.

If Ella could be all those things, Riley could too. So she let go of her reservations, kissed a little harder, sucked a little longer, and demanded Ella's attention with every movement of her mouth over her skin.

And it was working.

"Fuck…Riley." Ella's nails raked across her back, encouraging her.

She followed the trail of droplets down her neck, over her collarbone, and into the dip of her cleavage, then cupped her breasts, mixing the hard and soft together, a gentle squeeze paired with the nibble of teeth. She swirled her tongue around Ella's nipple and lowered herself to look up at her. Her cheeks were flushed, those plump lips parted as her chest heaved.

Time to step it up a notch.

She gripped her waist and pushed her back against the bathroom door with a thud, and began to kiss her all over, hands exploring every inch as Ella grasped back at her.

"You're so fucking perfect, Ella," she murmured as she took her other nipple into her mouth. She bit gently, causing a rumble in Ella's throat, and then dropped to her knees, placing herself between Ella's thighs. She lapped at the water marks, sucking and moving closer to her pussy, where she hovered, letting her breath dust against her clit, already glistening and begging for a taste. Ella's dark eyes pinned her there, demanding the same. But they knew how the other worked by now.

God, she loved this. The freedom of giving herself to someone so completely. She hadn't felt this much like herself in years. Of course, the future still scared her. But with Ella there, it didn't seem such an impossible mountain to climb.

She pressed another kiss to the inside of Ella's thigh, then brushed her tongue over the length of her.

"Shit." Ella's hand found Riley's shoulder, her nails digging in as Riley swiped over her again. "Why do you love…teasing me?"

Riley's gaze met hers, and she let her tongue swirl around her clit, ever so gently. "I just wanna…" Ella shuddered at the contact as she planted kisses over her. "…give…" Kiss. "…attention…" Kiss. "…to every last part of you." She sucked Ella's clit into her mouth, rolling her tongue. "Is that okay?"

"Absolutely no…complaints." Ella threaded her fingers around Riley's messy bun, and Riley slipped her tongue deeper inside, finding an area that was even wetter than before, indulging in her sweet taste.

She positioned her hands under Ella's thighs and pulled her tighter to her mouth, pushing her tongue deeper. It wasn't long before Ella was panting above her, moving her hips and thrusting against her face.

"There. There. Just like that." Ella groaned, her legs trembling beneath Riley's hands. "Ah, god, fuck…" She came, her legs giving way, her grip tightening in Riley's hair.

Riley stayed buried inside her, tasting her pleasure as it coated her tongue, feeding the primal urge as the sounds of her orgasm echoed against the tiles. The woman's weight slumped against her, but she held her up, pressing her against the door.

When Ella exhaled a shaky breath, she pushed herself up to her feet. Their eyes locked, Ella's pupils blown so wide they were almost all black.

"My legs." She laughed as tremors wobbled her thighs.

"Here. Let me help." Riley scooped her up, wrapping her legs around her torso. Her own thighs were a little shaky from kneeling on the tiles, but the adrenaline firing through her easily overpowered the quivering. She slammed Ella back against the wall, kissing her hard, before pulling back to open the door and carry her into the bedroom.

Ella squealed as they tumbled down onto the mattress. Riley hooked her under her thighs, moving her higher, placing kisses over her stomach and breasts. Ella's mouth marked her too, hungry and desperate, their bodies humming for more.

"I love fucking you," Ella murmured, sinking her teeth into Riley's shoulder just hard enough to make her wince and her muscles tense. Ella's hands grasped her bum. "I want to feel how wet you are." Her chest heaved, her eyes taking in Riley as she towered over her. "Ride me."

Riley didn't need to be asked twice.

Already throbbing and overpowered by desire, she parted Ella's legs and glided their hot centres together. A stream of curses left their lips, and Riley didn't waste any time thrusting against her. *Oh...Jesus.*

The sensation was almost too much. Waves of

pleasure rippled through her, making it extremely difficult to concentrate. But she wanted to come, and mixing their combined wetness together like this was such an incredible turn-on…

"Fucking hell…Riley…yes."

…As was hearing Ella's voice.

A bolt of arousal fired between Riley's legs, and she let out a groan, grabbing the headboard for better support. Ella's hands guided her, while she lifted her pelvis to meet and brush their slippery clits together.

Riley whimpered as Ella caressed her breasts, rubbing her thumbs over her nipples, bringing her closer and closer to bursting, until she couldn't take anymore and spilt over the edge, slapping the headboard and letting out a cry of pleasure. Her orgasm engulfed her, and everything went white. Their heavy breathing filled the room, and her lungs felt like they were going to explode.

She hummed as she slid off her, still high in a post-orgasm haze. Rolling onto her side, she planted a fleeting kiss on Ella's lips, her head still dizzy.

"I don't think that'll ever get old," Ella whispered, and Riley tilted her head to face her. "Seeing you come like that. *Feeling* it."

Flutters gathered in Riley's belly. "I know. I can't get enough of you."

Ella smiled and then hid her face in her hands, which was so freaking adorable.

"What?" Riley chuckled and peeled them back, kissing her fingertips.

She giggled, batting those thick black lashes at her. "I like hearing you saying these things. I like it. I uh, really like it."

"You do? Do you want to hear about everything I want to do to you?" Their eyes locked as Riley took one of Ella's fingers into her mouth. She groaned as she sucked harder then kissed the inside of her palm. Her wrist. She brushed her lips along Ella's forearm and soft bicep. Her sun-kissed shoulder, collarbone, and chest. She kissed her large pink nipple then flicked her tongue over the hardened nub. "I wanna tease you. Push you. Have you begging for me to touch you." She grazed her with her teeth, biting, and then smoothed over the mark with another lap of her tongue. She inched higher up her body, Ella's breathing heavier with every movement.

She held herself above her, pressing their hot bodies together and gauging Ella's reaction. Her mouth quirked, knowing the woman was hanging on her every word. Riley's own heart pulsed hard in her chest, arousal coiling in her stomach. It felt so unbelievably good to say these things out loud. To have no more restrictions.

She held Ella's gaze. The darkening of her irises, how they pulled her in, made her feel safe. Getting lost in the moment, she leaned in and kissed her, scattering her train of thought. Soft, soft kisses curled her toes and deepened the ache in her clit.

"Fuck," they both said at the same time and laughed.

Riley wet her lips, her throat suddenly dry. Then she kissed the corner of Ella's mouth, her jaw, her neck. "I want you in all the ways," she whispered against her neck, eliciting a groan from the woman underneath her. "All the gentle and the teasing…but the hard too." She sucked at the sensitive skin, hard enough to bruise, and then matched it with her teeth. "The messy and the desperate. I want it all." She sucked at her again, and Ella clawed her nails into her back, stinging. "I want to mark you. Selfishly. Body and soul. I want you to be mine, Ella. Mine."

Ella's voice came out in a hoarse demand. "Fuck me, Riley."

Riley's hand fell between Ella's legs, and her eyes rolled backwards. "Holy crap. You really do love this. You're soaked."

"Well, yeah—"

Ella didn't have time to finish her sentence because Riley was already pumping her fingers inside of her.

"Oh god, *yes*, fuck."

"You like that?"

Ella pierced her with her stare, eyelids fluttering. "I fucking love it."

Riley pushed herself up to her knees and hooked under Ella's legs. She fucked her harder, using her body weight to hold her down. Her thumb traced Ella's mouth, and Ella kissed it, wrapping her tongue around the end. The coil inside Riley's stomach tightened, and she leaned down to capture Ella's lips with hers. To feel that tongue against her own.

Ella licked into her mouth, and Riley groaned, the

ache in her clit multiplying tenfold and almost crippling her. They found their rhythm, desperate hands exploring the other with an impatient need, while their tongues and kisses did the opposite. The soft and the hard, coming together in a perfect balance of beautiful chaos.

Riley felt Ella tighten around her fingers, and she pulled back, breaking their kisses.

Ella scowled at her, her plump lips open in a beg.

Riley slowed the pace of her fingers but hooked them upward, gaining a gasp and a moan from deep in Ella's throat. She leaned down to whisper in her ear, "Do you know what else I'd like to do to you?" She continued to glide her fingers in and out of her.

"W–what?"

Riley pressed her lips to her pulse point, tasting the salty skin. "How about I show you?"

She removed her fingers, despite Ella's protests, and slid off the mattress. Her core throbbed with need, but the image forming in her head overpowered it. She pulled out her box from under the bed and glanced up at Ella.

"Close your eyes."

Ella's eyebrows furrowed. "You can't be serious."

Riley's focus snapped to her hand, which was circling her glistening clit with three fingers. Words stuck in her throat, but when she didn't say anything more, Ella closed her eyes anyway.

Riley slipped on the harness, tightening the restraints around her hips and waist. Truthfully, it'd been a long time since she'd used it, and she didn't want to lose this new confidence roaring through her veins.

Once everything was secured, she stood at the end of the bed, a lump forming in her throat at the woman lying in front of her. Ella continued to touch herself, and Riley wanted to burn the image into her eyelids forever: her damp hair falling loose from the bun on her head; flushed cheeks; large, perfect breasts and nipples; and the expert way her hand moved over herself, making her quiver.

She's perfect.

The urge to paint her washed over her like a wave. To immortalise this moment in time. She could always take a photo, she supposed, but nothing would capture the whirlpool of emotions swirling between them like the markings of a brush.

A short, sharp laugh escaped Riley's lips, imagining Ella's reaction to that imaginary scenario. *Just pause the sex for a few hours, Ells. Let me paint you.*

Ella frowned. "What're you laughing at?"

"I was just thinking how much I'd love to paint you right now."

"Like fuck you are." Ella's brows pinched together, a smile teasing at her mouth. "Get over here."

"That's what I thought."

She shook her head, her grin growing wider. "Can I open my eyes now?"

Riley sucked in a deep breath. "Yes," she said on the exhale.

Ella's eyes flicked open and focused on the strap attached around Riley's hips. "Oh my god…yes." Her gaze moved over the length, up Riley's abs, her small breasts, and then landed back on her eyes. The corners of her mouth curled, and she uttered one word that undid Riley completely—"Please."

Riley flung herself back on the bed, and Ella giggled. Her laughter was soon washed away by kisses and groans and fast, deliberate hands pulling them closer together. Their lips met, bruising, hard, nipping, tongues swiping and sucking at any bit of skin they could find. Riley grabbed Ella's hips and rolled them both over so that Ella was on top.

"Do you remember what you said to me that first time?" she asked, locking Ella's gaze.

Ella shook her head, breathing heavily.

"You told me to ride you. To use you to make me feel good." A slow grin spread across Riley's face as she took her in. "Now, I want you to do the same."

Ella's brown irises regarded her, and she gulped. "That's so hot."

They wasted no time in slicking the toy with lube, and Riley backed herself up against the headboard. She held the dildo and swallowed, her mouth going dry at the sight of Ella hovering above it. *Sweet Mary and Joseph.* She felt she was going to burst.

Ella lowered herself, easing onto the shaft as it disappeared inside her. She let out a breath, and her eyes flicked open and landed on Riley's. Everything inside her pulled taut, threatening to snap or break or come—or all three at once. She'd never had so many feelings circling around her. *Our energies must be insane right now.*

Ella's eyes crinkled before turning serious and sultry, and then she started to move. Riley let her dictate the pace, and then, once she found a rhythm, she rose her hips up to meet her. Ella whimpered, and it took all of Riley's composure not to start fucking her hard and fast like she wanted.

She dug her fingers into Ella's hips. "You tell me exactly what you want, okay, Ells. I'm all yours."

"Fuck," Ella breathed. "It feels so good."

Their heavy breathing filled the room as their bodies slapped together. The sounds of Ella's pleasure made Riley's core ache, and she bit her lip, tightening her hold on Ella's waist. It was a beautiful kind of torture, letting Ella take control in this way, but also sensual on a whole other level Riley didn't even know existed.

"I love how loud you are," she said.

"G–good." Ella quickened the pace, another loud moan leaving her lips. Her eyes rolled back, fluttering before landing on Riley's. "Harder…Riley."

Riley increased her thrusts, and Ella cried out, gripping the headboard. She tightened her hold, squeezing as she brought Ella closer and closer, pounding the toy inside her. Sweat beaded her forehead and the back of her neck, but she only went harder. The force pushed against Riley's clit, and she couldn't contain her own groans as they came together. Hard and rough, their bodies gave in to their urges, louder, faster, more, more, more. Riley licked and sucked and lapped at any skin she could reach, and it wasn't long until Ella reached her crescendo.

She let out a stream of curses as Riley continued to bury the toy inside her, her muscles contracting underneath Riley's hands. Riley came to a stop, and Ella collapsed forward, breathing ragged.

"Fuck. That…was so…good." She let out a happy sigh and then leaned down to kiss her.

Riley rocked her hips, still incredibly turned on, and Ella whimpered, the dildo still snug inside her. Wet and soft kisses only amplified the feeling. And when Ella's tongue brushed against Riley's, she thrust her hips again, breaking the kiss. Their eyes locked, and need swelled between Riley's legs, overpowering everything else. She wasn't finished yet.

Ella's flushed face seemed to study hers, and then she leaned forward, albeit shakily, giving her consent to fuck her again.

"Have you got another for me?" Riley asked in a hoarse whisper.

Ella's mouth curved upwards, and she shrugged. "I'll give it a go."

They laughed, coming together for more kisses that fanned the flames surging in Riley's centre. She wound her arms around Ella and rolled her, dragging her to the edge of the bed. Holding Ella's legs up, Riley leaned over her, pushing the dildo deeper inside. She watched Ella's mouth open, kissed her, and then sucked hard on her neck. Ella let out a gasp, and Riley went harder.

She'd never tire of this.

Soaking up every sound, every feeling, every movement of their bodies. This connection was all she wanted. She knew she'd made the right decision to leave. Separating herself from Ella now would be like tearing her body in half. She'd follow her anywhere.

She caressed Ella's curves and then gripped her hips, pulling her deeper onto the shaft.

"Mmm…god." Ella's focus drifted over Riley's body, her hands reaching out to trace her abs.

Riley adjusted the angle so the motion would hit against her own clit, and then she started to slide in and out of her, slowly. It didn't take long for Riley to pick up the pace, gliding into Ella while they panted, hands and mouths exploring the other like it was the first time. Each hard thrust sent pleasure rippling through Riley's clit. Her heart drummed in her chest as her orgasm built.

Sensing Ella was close to the edge as well, Riley circled her clit with her thumb. Ella reacted immediately, and the sound almost made Riley combust. She fucked her harder, rubbing Ella in circles, the pressure against her centre making her eyes roll backwards.

"Riley, yes, like that. Oh shit—" A gasping moan left Ella's throat, and Riley fell right over the edge with her. Pleasure exploded inwards in waves, stars floating behind her eyelids.

With an exhausted grunt, she pulled out and collapsed beside Ella, both of their sweaty bodies heaving for breath.

"Well," Ella breathed. "I think I might be pregnant."

Riley shook her head, a chuckle rising in her throat. She kissed Ella's forehead, and they snuggled together, muscles trembling, hearts pounding, their bodies moulding against each other's.

As the beautiful woman curled into her side and fell into a peaceful sleep, Riley vowed that today was no longer the mark of everything she once lost. It was the mark of a new start. And she couldn't wait for it to begin.

CHAPTER TWENTY-TWO

Ella

"And…open your eyes."

Ella squinted as she adjusted to the warm light streaming in through Senhor Arenoso's windows.

"Release a final breath and ground yourself back in the room," he said, opening his eyes and doing the same.

She exhaled, tuning into the sounds, the caress of the

breeze in her hair, the softness of the mat beneath her fingers. The blue sky stretched out across the sea, the chatter of the birds filtering in through the open air.

"How do you feel?" he asked.

"Great," she answered honestly. She stretched her arms and back but froze when she remembered the chiffon scarf wrapped around her neck. She styled it out, bringing her hands back to check it was still securely in place.

Phew. She released another breath and pretended to look out at the view.

"I'm very pleased with your growth." He nodded, and she turned back to him. "You should be proud of yourself."

"You know what? I am."

His eyes crinkled at the edges, but Ella didn't miss how his gaze wandered to the scarf.

The pink-and-purple garment wasn't something she'd usually opt to wear—unless she was being held at gunpoint or it was for some high-paid dare. She'd borrowed it from Pauline, with a no-questions-asked agreement, but under Senhor's steely gaze, sweat beaded beneath the material.

"It's not that bad," Riley had commented earlier.

She'd observed herself in the mirror, the collection of purple and yellow bruises marking her neck. Ella had twirled the fabric. "I look like my mum. Tragic."

"Do you think anyone will notice?" Riley thumbed her own singular bruise before pulling up the collar of her shirt to hide it.

"That we're both acting strange and wearing different clothes…? Nah, I'm sure it'll be fine."

Riley groaned and slinked towards her. "I know. I'm sorry." She dipped to plant kisses along her neck. "I might have got a little carried away."

Ella turned to putty in Riley's arms as her mouth explored the delicate skin. They'd quickly fallen into bed again, making Ella late for her last session with Marco Marcos. Everything at Sandy Springs was coming to an end—except for one thing, her relationship with Riley.

She couldn't stop the stupid smile from erupting across her face. Senhor Arenoso glanced at her, and she bit her lip to hide it.

"I'm sorry," she said, when he continued to watch her expectantly. "Did you say something?"

He rose to collect the empty mugs in front of them. "I asked how you felt about the fire ceremony tomorrow."

Ah, yes. The fire ceremony was a key event for the course. It marked the end of their old life and gave them a chance to cleanse and make way for the journey ahead of them once they left Sandy Springs. They would also receive their animal totems, something to carry and guide them through the next stages. Ella didn't really know what to expect.

From the ceremony or her new *old* life back home.

Was Riley going to come back with her? And both of them make the token lesbian move and start living together after a few weeks? She could just imagine Winnie's face when she showed up with Riley on her arm.

Or did Riley's idea of leaving mean something different?

Ella doubted Riley would want to go back to Ireland after everything she'd mentioned about her dad, but if life had taught her anything, it was to never be too sure. She needed to bite the bullet and talk to her about it tonight.

"Something on your mind?" Senhor Arenoso asked.

Oh, shit. She *still* hadn't answered him. She forced a laugh and shook her head. "Sorry. Just thinking about the end of all of this."

He filled the cups with water and set them in the sink before turning around. "There's a lot to think about." He regarded her in that all-seeing way that made Ella itch at her stupid scarf again. "The fire ceremony will help you steer your path. And, of course, the discovery of your familiar also."

"Any chance you can let me know now?"

"*De grão a grão, enche a galinha o papo.*" When Ella looked back at him blankly, he beamed. "Grain by grain, the chicken fills its crop. You can't rush these things."

A simple "No" would've sufficed.

Ella should've known to expect something cryptic from him. She smiled back; one more day wasn't long to wait. And she wasn't looking for quick fixes anymore. That was something she hoped to leave behind here. She was still finding her purpose in life; she was still jobless and unsure about her next steps, but truthfully, she was okay with that. Who really knew anything? Just because

Devin and Clarice had *seemingly* got their shit together, didn't mean Ella was a disappointment. Just because they were set on achieving every medical award ever created, and their two little perfect twins were already more talented than she was at playing piano—especially considering all Ella's years of lessons—that didn't mean she was failing. She was more in touch with life than she'd ever been. She had to stop comparing herself to others.

She nodded and rose to her feet. "Thank you."

Senhor Arenoso opened his palms to her. "You did all the work."

Not quite. She bit her tongue. If it'd been up to her, she'd have happily catnapped on the comfy chaise-longue in the corner until the sessions were up. But Senhor and Marco Marcos had pushed her to look past the barriers she constructed around herself. Removing them had helped her see where she'd been standing in her own way, and where she'd been blaming other people—her mother, for one. Over the last few years, their relationship had faded in parts. Ella was too busy or, more likely, too embarrassed to turn up when she'd got nothing to show. But she realised she'd piled that pressure on herself. It was enough to just turn up.

She considered the man in front of her. His kind eyes and patient demeanour. She understood why Riley held him in such high regard. A small fleck of guilt peeled away when she thought about how he might feel about Riley leaving. She glanced at the floor, swallowed, and then forced herself to speak. "No, really. Thank you for everything. This whole experience has changed my life."

"I'm happy you're finding yourself again. That's all we can ask for." He placed a hand on her shoulder, those dark eyes peering into hers. "I'll see you tomorrow at the fire ceremony." The corners of his mouth quirked, and then he removed his hand.

What was that smile about?

Ella uttered another thanks, grabbed her bag, and stepped out into the hot Portuguese sun. Ah, she was going to miss this. She let the light warm her skin and then checked her watch. Riley should be done with her classes for the day.

The thought of seeing her sparked something hot in her stomach, and she started walking faster. Ever since the anniversary of Riley's accident, their relationship had shifted. The fear had dispersed, making room for more openness and touching. Riley especially had seemed to get a new lease of life. Ella was almost too afraid to say it out into the universe, but…she was…excited about the future.

God, I even make myself wanna puke.

But the shit-eating grin stayed on her face as she hiked up the steps and drifted through the courtyard. People were milling about, carrying logs, firewood, and decorations, readying themselves for the ceremony tomorrow. Ella's gaze combed the space, finding the familiar mane of blonde hair as Riley carried her surfboard out of the hire shop. Her blue eyes immediately landed on Ella.

"Hey, you." She smirked, her focus drifting to the scarf wrapped around Ella's neck.

"Hey, yourself."

They stood watching each other for a moment, and butterflies multiplied in Ella's belly.

"You wanna walk?" Riley asked, and the two of them started making their way up the path to their cabins, narrowly avoiding a young girl pulling a cart full of wood. "How was your last session with Senhor Arenoso?"

"Good." Ella nodded as their steps fell into sync. "He's happy with my progress."

"That's great. How you feeling about the ceremony tomorrow?"

Ella glanced at Riley as she readjusted the board under her arm. She admired the curve of her bicep, briefly thinking about tracing the outline with her tongue. She cleared her throat, raising her eyes to greet a passer-by. "I'm a bit apprehensive. Nervous. I don't really know what to expect."

"The fire ceremony is a guest favourite for a reason. The fire cleanses and marks our new start, clearing the past and guiding us forward." Riley grazed Ella's shoulder with hers, and the fuzzy feeling in her stomach grew. "Though I admit I'm nervous about this one too."

"You are?" They rounded the corner, the tree with the creepy fingers waving its greeting from the top of the hill. "How come?"

"It's also my last. Leaving all of this behind…saying

goodbye…it's going to be difficult."

Ella's heart sank. "You can still change your mind. If it's not what you want."

They reached the creepy tree and stopped outside Ella's door. Riley rested her surfboard against the wall and turned to face her. She took her hands and brought them to her lips, planting kisses on her fingers. "I've made my decision, Ella. When our path starts to merge with another and change direction, we have to listen." Her steady blue irises held Ella's. Tingles spread down her arms and spine. "I'm scared, but I have faith in my path. I know Senhor Arenoso will understand that too. I hope." She glanced over her shoulder before crushing Ella's lips in a kiss. "I want you," she breathed against her.

Ella's belly flip-flopped, and she kissed her back, heat flowing through her veins. Riley met her with just as much force. Something about being affectionate out in the open was really getting Ella's motor running. They'd fucked in about every place possible in Riley's cabin…but they'd yet to explore hers.

"I want you too," she whispered against Riley's lips, desire coiling in her abdomen. "Right now."

She guided Riley back against her door, her heartbeat racing in her chest. With a shaky hand, she produced the key from her pocket and unlocked it, and they stumbled into her apartment. Riley pressed her up against the wall, her mouth nipping at hers and drawing a groan from her throat as she wrapped her arms around her shoulders. Her hands swept Ella's body, already pulling at her dress and sliding it up over her hips. Ella's lips parted to welcome her tongue, and everything pulled taut, hot, burning heat slipping between her thighs.

Riley's palm pressed her clit through her underwear, and Ella gasped. "God, yes, Riley. Take me right here."

An ear-shattering wolf-whistle pierced the air, and the two of them jumped apart.

"I really wish you wouldn't," a familiar voice said.

No. It couldn't be. Ella peered at the figure lying on her bed and let out a loud squeal. "Winnie! What the hell are you doing here?"

Winnie jumped up, blonde hair in disarray like she'd been caught in a hurricane, wearing a white tank top that was at least two sizes too small. "Bitch, I'm here for your graduation thingy. Surprise!" A moment later, Ella was crushed between her best friend's boobs, suffocating on a mix of her expensive perfume and a lingering whiff of plane alcohol.

"Oh my god! I can't believe you're here." A swell of emotion rose in Ella's throat, and she squeezed Winnie a little tighter.

"Want me to pinch you to check you're not having a wet dream?" Winnie pulled back and looked at Riley, who was turning red at an increasing rate. "Oh, hello." Winnie let out a low whistle as she took her in, peering over her glasses. "And this must be the lovely Riley, I assume. Good job, Ella. Really good job."

Ella nudged her. "Stop looking at her like that!"

Winnie raised her palms and shrugged. "What? I

have good eyesight. A girl can appreciate."

Unbelievable.

Ella readjusted her damp underwear and sucked in a breath to calm her racing heart. She took Riley's clammy hand in hers and gave it a squeeze. "Riley, this is my best friend and favourite worst nightmare, Winnie."

"So nice to meet you." Riley offered her free hand. "Ella's told me a lot about you."

"The pleasure's all mine." Winnie looked between them and raised her eyebrows. "Now, where's the tequila?"

***

Winnie took a sip from her glass and grimaced. "It tastes funky."

"That's probably because it hasn't got any vodka in it."

Riley had left the two of them to catch up, so Ella had taken Winnie on a quick tour around Sandy Springs. They'd only got as far as the food hall, where Winnie had been sure she could find some booze to celebrate. Now, her pouting mouth said it all.

She raised her glass to Ella's. "Well, you look fucking fantastic. Maybe they're onto something with the no alcohol." She nodded. "Apart from that awful scarf, though. What is that?" She reached out, but Ella knocked her hand away.

"It's good to see you too, Winn." Ella gave her friend a squeeze, ignored the raised eyebrow at her scarf, and they both took a seat on the bench overlooking the cliffs. Birds were ferrying back and forth, and the late afternoon sun was still warm above their heads. "I can't believe you're here."

Winnie laughed. "Between me and Chezza, I thought you'd prefer my surprise arrival. I hope so anyway."

"Of course. Though I do need to speak to her and thank her for all of this." Ella felt Winnie's gaze on her. "What?"

"Holy mother of moly. Have they spiked the water? Chopped up some funny mushrooms in your food?" She made a show of checking Ella's pulse and temperature, and Ella batted her away. "Or did you really just ignore the Chezza comment *and* say you wanted to *thank* your mum?"

Ella bit the inside of her cheek. "Fuck off. I've got a thank you for you too."

"Oh, boy, this should be good."

"You're the worst."

"That's an unusual thank you."

Ella jostled her, and they both broke into a grin.

"Really, Ella. How's it been?"

Ella noted the concern in her eyes. "It's been…challenging, but necessary, I think. As much as it pains me to admit it, you and Mum were right."

To Ella's surprise, Winnie didn't remove her shirt to run a victory lap around her as she fist-pumped the air.

She just bobbed her head and took another swig from her bottle of fruit juice. "What about Riley?"

Ella told her Riley's plan to speak to Senhor Arenoso the day after the ceremony and their plans to leave together, though her vague answers to Winnie's questions were obvious.

"Wow. Are you sure you're ready for all of this? Things are moving very quickly."

Riley's face popped into Ella's head. Those kind blue eyes, her gentle heart. The dolphin tattoo between her shoulder blades. The way she made Ella feel more like herself than she had…ever.

"Yeah, Winn. I am."

Winnie smiled, her eyes crinkling, then tugged at the scarf wound around Ella's neck, letting out a happy cackle. "I knew you would be sure, with marks like that!" She let out another whistle and wiggled her eyebrows. "Damn, girl. Has Riley got any siblings?"

CHAPTER TWENTY-THREE

Ella

Under the deep indigo sky, Riley wrapped her strong, warm arms around Ella. The clear night had a slight bite to it, but the comfort seeping from Riley's body chased it away as they lay together in the hammock. They swayed gently from side to side, Ella's head against Riley's chest, Riley's legs snug around Ella's torso, wrapped tight in their own cocoon.

The moonlight reflected off Ziggy's collar as he curled into a ball on Ella's legs. He'd tucked his head under himself, making him appear headless. His gentle snores said otherwise. Endless stars pierced the sky, white lights twinkling, glowing brighter with every glance. Ella's gaze passed over the million dots, more appearing with every breath. She'd never seen so many.

She sunk further into the heat of Riley's body and let out a sigh.

"I told you," Riley whispered, her breath tickling Ella's cheek. "There's nothing quite like the stars out here."

Ella yawned, catching the movement with the back of her hand. "If I'm a walking zombie at the fire ceremony later, though, I'm blaming you."

Riley's chuckle vibrated through her, and Ella smiled, wiggling so she could lay her ear against Riley's chest and listen to the soft thrum of her heartbeat. Ziggy flopped over, so Ella scooped him with her arm to stop him from falling out of the hammock.

"Are you nervous?" Riley asked, her voice a low rumble.

"Yeah." Ella chased the muscle of Riley's shoulder with her free hand, her fingertips grazing down to where Riley's own hand rested across her waist. She *was* anxious about the fire ceremony, the end of all of this...receiving her totem. But she was most nervous about her next steps with Riley. What if Senhor Arenoso made her change her mind? Winnie's surprise arrival had put her conversation with Riley on the back burner, but now it pushed to the front, demanding attention.

"Wanna talk about it?" Riley's breath danced away into the night, and Ella turned back to the sky, noting the faint orange light peering over the horizon. The light bled upwards, hiding the stars beneath the blur of colour. Ella's focus was caught somewhere above them, and Riley leaned forward to nuzzle her lips into her neck, rocking the hammock. "Talk to me."

Ella squirmed under her touch and let out a giggle that was loud in the quiet night. She sucked in a breath and exhaled, steadying herself. "What if you change your mind?"

"Ella." Her voice was stern, possessive, strong enough to lift the hairs over Ella's arms. "I want you. I'd follow you anywhere. Unless you didn't want me to." There was a heavy silence. "Do you want me to?"

"Of course I do." She threaded her fingers through Riley's. "It's just a little hard to believe sometimes."

"Do you need me to show you just how badly I want you, right here in this hammock?" Her warm lips found Ella's neck, and she squealed. "We might scar Ziggy for life, but I'll do it. Try me."

Ella laughed and bit her lip, unable to stop the grin spreading across her face. "But what are we going to do? What about the big baby?" She looked down at Ziggy, sleeping peacefully in the crook of her arm.

"He's my son. He comes with me."

She traced over Riley's knuckles. "And where will you both go?"

"I'm sure there are hotels in England while I find my feet. I've got my savings." She squeezed her arms around her tighter, planting a kiss on her temple. "We've got time to figure it out. There's no rush."

Ella pressed back into her, feeling her skin, grounding herself. Then she spoke the words she'd been afraid to air. "What if it all changes?"

"It will change."

Oh.

"Nothing can stay the same forever, Ells. It's not how the world works. We're always changing, evolving, growing, regenerating. The earth never stops turning. The sun always rises. No matter what." Her smooth hand found Ella's cheek, and she turned it towards her. "Time is a funny thing. I've felt more myself these few weeks with you than I have in three years. If we didn't embrace change, we'd just be stuck. We'd never see the starry skies or the beautiful sunrises." She grinned, dimples forming in her cheeks, and lifted Ella's chin. "We'd never fall for the fiery redhead."

Ella's heart squeezed. "You've fallen for me?"

"Of course I have, you eejit." She kissed her, soft and slow, pulling a moan from deep in Ella's throat. When they parted, both breathless and panting, she cupped her face. "I think I fell for you when I pulled you out of that bramble bush the first time I saw you. You stepped onto the island, and my whole world shifted. Bam."

Ella kissed her again, struggling to find the words to explain how she was feeling. The hammock rocked with their movement, and Ziggy meowed, swatting Ella's cheek with his paw.

They laughed, and Riley tightened her grip around Ella, keeping them warm and safe in their own little world. The sun burned bright ahead of them, deep orange and pink hues painting the sky with the promise of new possibilities. The promise of change.

Ella blew out a breath, finding a new sense of determination as she witnessed the stars fade into the awakening dawn. She could do this. She was ready.

***

Nerves coiled in Ella's belly as she took in her reflection. The same brown eyes observed her, but so much about her felt changed. Her long red hair, which she'd dressed half up, half down, in a way that elongated her neck and showed off her cheekbones, shone under the bright lights of her cabin. The marks from Riley were barely visible underneath the makeup, but she traced them with her fingertips anyway. She smiled, watching the lines form in her sun-kissed skin.

She swivelled, making sure there was no toilet paper or any ugly big knickers attached somewhere they shouldn't be, and then there was a knock at the door.

"Come in," she called, openly admiring the long

forest-green dress that, to quote Winnie, fit her *like a motherfucking glove.* Winnie had trashed her original choice of outfits, deeming none of them worthy of her graduation, and so they'd visited the market, finding this long-sleeved dress that caressed her curves and exposed just enough of her chest. The material was embroidered with red, orange, and yellow flowers, reminding her of the wildflowers on the island, and she beamed as it glided across her thighs and hips.

She couldn't wait for Riley to see it.

"Wowsers!" Pauline gasped, standing in the doorway in a red-and-white strappy dress and a red fascinator. "If only I were a few years younger, I'd be over you like a rash."

Ella snorted, laughter bubbling in her chest. "A few years? More like a few decades." She turned to Pauline with a wink, noting her soft but not-quite-matching eyeshadow and lipstick. She let out a whistle. "You on the prowl tonight?"

Pauline giggled. "Who knows what might happen if Marco Marcos is willing?"

The image of the hairiest man in existence and her favourite divorcee in a compromising position on his office chair flashed before Ella's eyelids. She blinked it away. "Whatever tickles your pickle, bestie. You ready?"

Pauline nodded, holding out her arm, and Ella linked it, pulling the door shut behind them.

They walked to the courtyard as the sun sank. The sky was pulled into a deep purple hue, and streaks of white cast heavenly glows around the clouds. Ella squeezed Pauline's arm tighter as they descended the path, anticipation building with every step. A weight pressed on her, all the expectations and fears and promises making her drag her feet.

Acoustic music carried its way up the hillside, the strings and clapping matching the rhythm of Ella's heartbeat. Then she saw the courtyard, and her face lit up.

Huge garlands with pink, orange, and blue flowers decorated the entryway, covering the buildings and dangling from the wooden beams. Torches brightened the stone floor, casting warm light and shadows over the people gathered, who were clapping their hands to the lively beat.

A large stone firepit took centre stage, its two rocks curling around the firewood like a pair of grey snakes. The seating was formed from beautifully carved logs ringed around the fire, each one with a basket stacked on either side, filled with bundles of plants, herbs, and flowers.

Strangers congratulated Ella and Pauline as they passed, encouraging them to go stand at the front by the fountain, where the other people on their course waited. Ella scanned the crowd for Riley or Winnie, but the faces were hard to make out in the sparse light of the flickering flames.

Senhor Arenoso stood with his arms wide, the moonlight bright behind him. A large, red-and-black beaded headpiece sat atop his head, white and grey feathers covering the front, with two tufts on either side that Ella realised were the ears of an owl.

He slowly brought his palms together, and the music and clapping fell into a silence that echoed in the space. Pauline and Ella were the last to arrive. It was time to begin.

"Welcome," he boomed, his gaze falling across the group. He gave them a wide, gleaming smile. "And thank you for joining us as we celebrate the crossing of our latest group on the Sandy Springs course and award them with their totems.

"Life is a powerful, precious gift. It can be easy to forget this as we're swept up in the everyday, but we must reconnect with our roots, with nature—smell the fresh air, listen to the earth, feel the textures, taste the rain. We need to give thanks for what has been, let go of what no longer serves us, and ask for blessing for what is to come." His grin grew wider, flames flickering in his dark brown eyes. "So join me as we light the ceremonial fire."

He led the way through the parted crowd, and they followed, circling around the firepit. Ella's heart raced, searching for Riley in a gap in the crowd, but she couldn't see her among all the commotion.

Senhor Arenoso bowed as he was handed a flaming torch from one of the teenage boys.

"Fire is cleansing," he announced, his voice carrying over the courtyard. "It clears the old and makes way for the new." He commanded each of them with his gaze, his words echoing in Ella's chest. "When the fire is alight, I invite each of you to give a gift to the flames. A symbol of your new regeneration as you take the next steps on your path. Some people make a wish. Others state what they'd like to leave behind. Ultimately, you can take and create your own meanings, forge your own purpose, and embrace the night for all that it is. Celebrate your journey with family and friends." He raised the torch high above his head and let out a joyful laugh. "Celebrate life!"

He lowered the torch to the base of the fire, and bright flames burst skywards, drawing a collective gasp from the crowd. Enthusiastic applause followed, cheers and whoops rising above the sound of the growing fire.

Ella's eye was drawn to one particularly loud voice, and she smiled when she recognised Winnie. She'd cupped her mouth, tilting her head back to shout a high-pitched "woo" that turned more heads. Ella's heart swelled with love for her. Even though her decision to come out here probably had a little to do with the lovely weather and the promise of sea, sand, and sex, Ella was so grateful to have a best friend like her. Without her, none of this would've happened.

Her group lined up to give their offerings to the flames, each admission bringing another round of applause as they each took their seat by the fire. As they shuffled closer, the orange and yellow light coating every wall and making the shadows dance around them, Ella's brain short-circuited. What should she wish for? What should she leave behind?

There were too many things. They were piled on top of one another, fighting for space and overcrowding her thoughts like demanding toddlers. She could wish for Maeve's sleek suit collection to catch fire or Annabelle's hair to fall out, but she no longer felt the tangle of sadness in her stomach at the thought of them. In stark contrast, she actually—*maybe*—wanted them to be happy. What was the point in all the suffering otherwise?

Hmm. Maybe Winnie's right, and they are spiking the water here.

It'd taken her a little bit of time, but she'd done as Senhor Arenoso asked and surrendered to the course. It had meant hearing things she didn't want to listen to. Not only facing them but digging deeper into why she held these beliefs so close. It had been difficult to learn that the biggest obstacle standing in Ella's way was, in fact, herself—and not her mother—and that her fears were overpowering her desires. But she wasn't staying stuck in her loop anymore.

She lifted her gaze, searching for that particular person who embodied all of her fears and desires in one. When she landed on Riley, already seated by the fire, a surge of love passed through the connection between them, coating all of her body with the intensity of the dancing flames in front of her.

Riley's eyes captured hers, buoying her heart with a soul-defying ache in the best way possible, lifting her and carrying her above the crowd, higher than the pillowing smoke, cradling her in a softness that made her feel she could do anything and be anyone.

As the two of them watched each other, lost in the

haze of their energies, saying a thousand things without words, Ella's mouth curved into a smile.

Being with Riley, she'd learnt a whole new meaning of the word surrender.

She might not have found her purpose yet or her "soul key" or whatever, but she'd found her happiness again. As Pauline threw her bundle of sage into the fire and Ella moved to the front, the realisation struck her like a flash of lightning.

Of course. Her purpose was so simple. She'd expected it to be rooted deep within her, to spring forth and fill her with a life-changing epiphany that would sweep her off her feet, perhaps render her unconscious at its weight. But as she stared into the flames, the heat warming her face, another ripple of joy crested in her chest, and she knew she'd found it.

Ella's purpose was to be happy.

She wasn't intent on winning every award, like Devin and Clarice, or on building a hefty nest egg, like her parents. Ella's focus was on the simple things: sharing the sunrise with someone who appreciated it just as much as she did; picking fresh oranges and kissing under the trees; painting badly because it was better than not painting anything at all. Even trying to surf, because you might surprise yourself and actually be good at it.

She couldn't stop a bubble of laughter from leaving her throat as she stepped forward and took a bundle of something green to offer to the fire. The bark was rough under her fingertips. Sucking in a lungful of burning wood, she cast the bundle into the flames, squeezing her eyes shut and sending her thought to whoever was listening.

I just want to be me.

Applause rippled around her, and another whoop from Winnie brought her eyelids fluttering open to take in the scene. The happy faces, the smoke, the all-consuming feeling that Ella's life was about to change for the better.

After exchanging thumbs-ups and waves with her best friend, and then a lingering smile at Riley, Ella took her seat beside her new bestie, Pauline, joining in the celebrations as the last of their group gave their offerings.

Some time passed while the fire grew and climbed with ferocity, spitting and sparking, specks of ash drifting around them like snowflakes. The crowd lost themselves in the hypnotic burning as they waited until it stopped pluming smoke to continue their celebration. A calmness possessed Ella as she watched the dancing flames, feeling the stone under her feet and the collective quiet as the fire sparked and popped. Smoke curled and spiralled upwards, and she breathed in the scent, embracing the moment as everything passed through her. The past. The present. The future.

She wondered if everyone else was feeling this, too.

She peered at Pauline from the corner of her eye, hoping she felt as much love as Ella did in this moment. Just to be sure, she took the woman's warm hand in hers and gave it a squeeze, before returning her gaze to the flames.

When the burning steadied, Senhor Arenoso retook his place at the front, ready to award the totems.

"Our familiars are not new to us. They may live in the shadows for some time, shut out from our hearts when we close ourselves off. But being here, reconnecting with nature, is the perfect opportunity to build on your relationship with your guide. When you nurture that relationship and tune into the energy, life flows easier. When you take a moment and listen, you'll be amazed at all the things you've been missing that were right there all along." He flashed his practised smile and called the first person to the front.

Ella expected to feel nervous at this point of the night. For weeks, the familiars had been a constant topic of conversation between the guests and the staff alike. She thought about the dolphin marked between Riley's shoulder blades. How the dolphin represented a beautiful balance between playfulness and protection, and how that fit Riley so well.

Ella loved all the variations of Riley; she was excited to see what other sides of herself she could unlock with her guide's influence.

When Senhor Arenoso called her name, she wiped the stickiness from Pauline's clammy hand on her dress and blew out a breath. The heat of the fire warmed her as she circled it, and then she waited opposite Senhor Arenoso, her palm facing upward.

His knowing gaze combed over her, and she swallowed, intimidated by the owl headpiece that was also staring into her soul. "Passionate, fiery, fierce, loyal. Your energies lie on the strong tip of the scale. A key focus for you, Ella, is to remember the spiritual connection with the earth and how this feeds and restores balance to yourself. This connection is just as important. Don't lose that. Balance is key." He touched her palm, closed his eyes, and a deep rumble came from his throat. "Ella, your guide has come to me, in all their light and mightiness." He dipped his head, producing a wooden totem wrapped tightly in his hand. He hung the string over her head, and Ella held her breath, waiting for the next words to leave his lips. "The turkey."

A...turkey?

Raucous applause engulfed her, and he spun her to face the cheering crowd. She caught Winnie's hooting laughter, not even trying to hide it as she echoed Senhor's announcement to the people seated next to her.

Ella thumbed the totem in her hand, feeling the smooth edges and the carved feathers. A turkey. A *turkey*? Then, a giant grin broke across her face. Sure, why the hell not?

"Woo!" she cheered, lifting the totem high and earning another surge of appreciation from the crowd. Happiness coated her head-to-toe, and when her gaze fell on Riley once again, it multiplied tenfold. Ella was exactly where she needed to be.

***

Once the last of the totems had been handed out, the real party began. Riley and the other staff moved the log seating to the side, making room around the burning fire. The band sprang to life, encouraging people to dance to the lively beat in the new space on the stone paving. The locals took to it immediately, the guests needing a bit more encouragement—apart from Winnie, who had first made sure to congratulate Ella on her graduation *and* also to give her best impression of a turkey, *gobble gobble,* before spying a handsome man in her peripheral vision and quickly making her move.

Ella smiled as she watched the people twirl around, stepping this way and that, while the well-rehearsed ones clicked fingers and stomped their feet to the tune of the piano accordion and drum. Winnie tried her best to keep up with the tree trunk of a man wheeling her around, but the sight made Ella's sides ache from laughing. Pauline, newly equipped with the cougar totem hanging around her neck—*who knew?*—threw her head back in a fit of giggles too, as she spun her sister in clumsy circles. The two were like twins, separated only by a different colour fascinator. Ella hoped Pauline would get to have a shot at dancing with Marco Marcos later in the evening.

Her cougar guide could surely only benefit her.

"I did have the feeling you'd be a bird." A warm, silky voice sounded in Ella's ear as Riley nestled in the space beside her.

Ella let out another laugh—she'd been doing that a lot tonight—and squeezed her new totem between her fingers. "Does this mean I can't eat them anymore?"

"Probably not. Cannibalism is frowned upon in most countries."

Ella snorted, shifting her body so that she pressed her shoulder to Riley's. Heat burned through the touch, and Riley leaned into it. As much as the dynamic between the two of them was fun, Ella couldn't wait to be in the open with her. To be able to touch her, and hold her, and kiss her without consequence.

Just one more day.

She exhaled, catching the whiff of food being served at the other end of the courtyard.

"Anyway, what're you doing over here?" Riley asked, a teasing lilt to her voice. "Tonight's about celebrating." She took a step forward and held out her hand.

Ella hesitated. What about all the watchful eyes?

"A dance isn't going to get us thrown into jail, Ells. Come on."

Ella took her hand, and Riley pulled her right into the centre of the dancing bodies. She shrieked, unable to help it, as Riley guided her side to side, dropping her hands to clap to the beat and picking them up again as they glided across the floor. How was this woman so good at everything?

"I thought you weren't supposed to have favourite guests," Ella said, as Riley tugged her into a spin.

"Well, I do." She ducked in close to whisper in her ear. "And this dress is also a new favourite of mine. You look incredible."

New heat prickled the back of Ella's neck and chest, and she bit her lip, suddenly hyperaware of Riley's strong hands commanding her body.

A small woman playing the *cavaquinho*, which Ella understood to be a small Portuguese guitar, stood from her stool and dived into an enthusiastic solo. The crowd roared, hungry for more, and the other band members brought their hands above their heads to encourage the clapping.

But Ella wasn't focused on the music anymore—just the fire that Riley ignited in the places the other couldn't touch. Adrenaline fired through her veins, and she slid her arm around Riley's waist. "Just how much do you love this dress?"

Riley took in Ella's cleavage and her exposed neck with hungry eyes. "So much."

Ella wet her lips, and Riley caught the movement. A throbbing need grew between her legs, stirring up an intoxicating ache. "Show me."

The rhythmic clapping continued around them, building, echoing, beating along with Ella's heart as she watched the realisation wash over Riley's gorgeous face. Her lips parted slightly, mouth pulling into a sexy grin that brought out those dimples. Then Ella was being pulled away, out of the crowd and the heat of the fire, away from the upbeat music.

They giggled like teenagers, hand in hand, running deeper into the night, the moonlight guiding them along the darkened paths. Ella had no idea where they were going, but with her fingers threaded through Riley's, she didn't care.

Riley lifted Ella over a gate just off the main path, and she squealed, legs kicking the air. Riley's mouth covered Ella's as she landed, her strong hands steadying her as their kisses quickly became frenzied. She guided Ella into a wooden shack in the field, kicking open the door and pushing her inside. A lone window cast moonlight into the space, and the earthy scent of straw filled her senses.

"Is this…a barn?" Ella asked, glancing around but not seeing much.

"Sort of. It's only used for the goats in winter. More just for storage now."

Goats. Of course. Ella laughed, and Riley pulled her back, keeping her hands firmly planted on Ella's hips, gripping the creases of her dress.

"Is that a problem?" she asked, tightening hold of the fabric. Her voice lowered, reaching new, deep, sexy levels. "Because I *really* do love this dress."

Ella shook her head, her heart stuttering at the dreamy look swirling in Riley's irises, which were deep midnight pools in the lack of light. Her stomach pulled, heat spreading between her thighs with an all-consuming longing. "Only a problem if you don't make me come, 'cos I fucking need you right now."

Wasting no time, Riley lifted her dress, bunching it behind her back while sliding her other hand into her damp underwear.

Ella let out a groan as their hands and mouths came together desperately, their cries of pleasure lost to the crowd of guests as they partied in the courtyard.

When they came apart, gasping, sweaty, and satisfied—even with a little bit of straw-burn on Ella's thighs—they ran back to the party, finding it still in full swing.

They rejoined the festivities, laughing and dancing under the moonlight until the very last ember in the fire burnt out.

Their new journey had begun.

CHAPTER TWENTY-FOUR

Riley

"You're pathetic." The gruff voice scoffed from the armchair nestled in the corner. Riley didn't need to look at her dad to know he'd been drinking. She could hear the slur to his words, smell the open bottle of whisky that no doubt rested on the side table next to him.

She'd closed the bathroom door as quietly as she

could before sneaking into the dark hallway, but he must've heard her crying. She hated that. She lingered for a moment, unsure whether the statement was directed at her or one of his horse bets gone wrong.

"Thought ye were leavin', so why're ye still here?"

But of course his scorn was directed at her. She'd be stupid to ever think otherwise.

She'd only been home for a week—not *home*, but Ireland, anyway. Since she'd packed up and moved out of Elodie's place, she'd been in such a state, she'd actually thought things might have been different. But things never changed here. Her dad never changed.

She inhaled a shaky breath, squeezed and relaxed her fists, then stepped into the doorway. "I am leavin', Da."

He scoffed again from the corner, the chair creaking with his weight as he emptied his glass and refilled it from the bottle on the table. The TV lit his face as it flickered whatever rubbish they played at two in the morning. A mix of black-and-white reruns, teleshopping, and gambling, no doubt. His grey hair was thinner than she was used to, but the sneering lip and the red, bulbous nose were the same as her memories.

He shook his head, eyes dazed and sluggish as they took in her small form. "Sure, but ye still standin' there."

"I'm leavin' in the mornin'."

"It's the mornin' now." His voice hardened, his body stilling as his fingers tightened around the glass.

Riley tensed, adrenaline licking up her spine and shaking her tiredness away. She knew that voice; things could get ugly. She sniffed and took a step back, her heart beating loudly against the quiet mumble of the TV. Quick steps led her back down the hallway and into her bedroom. The books she'd left here, along with her favourite poster of Keira Knightley, were long gone. The pile of unopened mail, dirty laundry, and random crap resembled more of a dumping ground for her dad's unwanted things than her childhood room—which was fitting, she supposed. Her dad had never wanted her, either.

She scooped up her damp clothes, which were drying on the radiator, and stuffed them into her suitcase, fighting the tears forming. *What was I thinking, coming here?* One ear listened for movement down the hallway, but her thumping heart made that difficult.

Finally, with another quick glance over the jumbled mess and a double-check of her pockets for her Irish documents, she was ready. Well, that was a lie. She wasn't ready to leave the only slither of normality she had left, now that her girlfriend and future had burst into flames—but what choice did she have?

Sucking in a shaky breath, she triple-checked her pocket. At least now she had her passport and Irish savings, she could go anywhere. But the prospect was much less exciting when standing completely alone.

A smash of glass snapped her spine straight, the grumbling groan down the hallway rolling through her bones like thunder.

Mum had left. Elodie had left. But Riley was

determined to build something from the ashes. She couldn't be like her dad.

Another crash from the living room swivelled her head. She had to go. Shrugging on her coat and pulling her beanie over her hair, she tugged her suitcase down the hallway, wheels clunking on the uneven carpet.

"Leavin', are ye?" Her dad's looming form stumbled into the hallway, swallowing her in a tall shadow. "Just like ye bleedin' mother."

Her pulse quickened, and she swallowed the bile rising in her throat. "I'd rather be like her than like you, you feckin' waste of space." The scowl on her dad's face deepened, but the words felt too good to stop. "You couldn't control her, and you can't control me. You're just a lonely, bitter old man, and I hope you spend the rest of your days in that battered armchair, wondering where your life went wrong. You're no father to me."

He lunged for her, his drunken feet tripping over the peeling carpet, and crashed against the wall with a groan.

Riley shook her head, pity and shame curling into a ball in her gut. "Goodbye, Michael." And she shut the door behind her, heading out into the cold, knowing she'd never see her dad again.

The memory rearranged itself before her eyelids, melting away into the present space of her cabin. This was the first place that was ever *hers*. She'd never had so much freedom or control over her life. She'd found herself here.

Doubt tiptoed into her mind. Would she lose that, leaving the island with Ella?

The woman beside her stirred, nuzzling into her shoulder. Warmth spread into her chest, curling and squeezing around her heart. As much as the island had shown her parts of herself, Ella had too. Parts of herself she'd thought were dead or lost to the world.

In the same way she'd known she had to leave her childhood home four years ago, she knew she couldn't let Ella go. What they had was special, mind-bending, soul-affirming. A searing, possessive, heated connection that she'd never even thought possible. For the first time in a long time, Riley could think about the future.

That told her everything she needed to know.

She ran her hand over Ella's sleeping form, and she groaned, batting her away.

"What time is it?" she mumbled, looping her leg over Riley.

Riley planted a kiss on her forehead, breathing in her scent. "It's still early." But Riley knew…it was time to talk to Senhor Arenoso.

***

Leaving Ella dozing with Ziggy curled up between her legs, Riley snuck out into the morning air. They'd had such a wonderful night celebrating with the others on the course and with Ella's friend Winnie—who might have also had a rendezvous in the old barn, judging by her reappearance with straw tangled in her hair and her glasses steamed up. Riley didn't want to dampen Ella's spirits. She'd go, speak to Danilo, and then come back ready to move on.

The sun's orange glow hung in the sky, coating her skin like fresh paint. She filled her lungs and started down the steps, her gaze finding the sea waves as they crashed against the cliffs. She walked the path she'd walked a thousand times before, brushing her fingers through the green leaves and kicking up the dusty stones underfoot. A peaceful quiet had descended over the island this morning. The courtyard still stood decorated with garlands, the firepit still covered in ashes. People celebrated hard every time the end of the course rolled around; the locals looked forward to it every month, and it had become a healing ritual of their own.

Riley would miss it here, there was no denying that, but like the ceremonial fire last night, she had to let go to make way for the new.

Nerves bubbled in her belly as Senhor Arenoso's hut came into view. It'd been a place of refuge for her over the years, but now, every step closer made the heavy stone in her stomach sink lower and lower. Was she really doing this?

She grasped the obsidian necklace Danilo had gifted her between her fingers, hoping to channel some of the healing energies. The smooth rock grounded her a little, and she forced her feet to move.

He was sitting cross-legged on his cushion like he normally was, a deep green kaftan covering his dark skin.

He tilted his head as she approached, his ears pricking at her movement.

"Riley," he hummed. "I thought I might see you this morning."

She resisted the urge to laugh. The man had a sixth sense for this kind of thing.

"*Bom dia*, Danilo." She hovered in the open doorway, the sea breeze tickling her face. She tried to force her gaze to meet his, but she couldn't shift her focus from the large fern in the corner. "Great ceremony last night. You outdid yourself."

He smiled, then with a sigh, brushed himself off and stood, finally turning to her. "You're too kind. Now, come on. Sit. Tea?"

She sank into the faux-leather chair in the corner while Danilo boiled the kettle. She wiped her hands on her shorts, but they still felt clammy. What did she usually do with her hands? Did they just…hang there? She suddenly felt like a teenager sitting in the headmaster's office, waiting for a scolding.

The early birdsong mingled with the hum of the kettle. Riley watched Danilo glide around the space, browsing his drawer stocked full of incense and pulling out a stick of bergamot. *For releasing stress and anxiety. Why does this man know everything?*

The citrus scent filled the room, and he handed her a steaming cup of green tea. She thanked him, and he took the seat next to her, turning to look out the window and the rolling sea below.

"So," he began, keeping his focus outside. "What's got you all nervous this morning?"

This time, the panicky laugh passed her lips. She shook her head, attempting to sip from her mug, but it was still far too hot. "I can't hide anything from you, can I?"

His moustache twitched. "You can talk to me, Riley. Unload a little."

The memory of her dad ghosted around her. His ability to wilt her with his sneering lip and steely glare. She forced herself to meet Danilo's dark gaze, soft and patient and full of concern, and she had to look away, unable to stand it. She didn't deserve his understanding after letting him down the way she had.

She swallowed the lump rising in her throat. Leaving her dad had been easy, upon reflection. The title was meaningless and empty, their relationship dead and buried as soon as her mother had walked out the door when she was small. Disappointing Senhor Arenoso, the man who'd helped Riley find her feet when she didn't have anything, that was going to cripple her.

"Is it the anniversary?" he asked.

Her lip wobbled, tears filling her eyes. She looked to the sea again and imagined the waves parting as she slipped through, washing away her worries and fears. The water would glide over her back, propelling her forward, building and building until she could leap up into the sky, just like a dolphin.

She exhaled, forcing herself to meet Danilo's eyes again.

He eyed her knowingly. "It's about her, isn't it?"

She caught a falling tear with the back of her hand, but more spilt down her cheeks, the floodgates officially open. "I'm so sorry, Danilo. I'm very grateful for everything you've done for me, and I love my job. The last thing I wanted to do was let you down or disappoint you and—"

He held up a hand, an assortment of gold ringers on his fingers. "You could never disappoint me, Riley."

She shook her head, tears blurring her vision. "I've broken your trust. I knew I shouldn't have relations with a client, but this isn't just a fling. I hope you know I wouldn't throw all this away for something temporary. I…I…" The words caught in her throat. "I had no idea I could feel this way again. She's everything, Danilo. Everything." She shook her head, but her mouth couldn't stop moving. Her chest heaved as more words poured out of her. "That's why I have to resign. Don't worry. I'll leave. I wouldn't want anything bad to come from my actions, and I'm sorry. I'm sorry to let you down, but—"

A cool hand covered hers, and she realised she was shaking. "Breathe with me, Riley. It's okay. You're safe here."

Senhor Arenoso's words grounded her, and she closed her eyes while he counted the beats. When her chest lost its tightness, she dared look at him again.

"Hear me when I say this, Riley. You haven't let me down."

She opened her mouth to protest, but he silenced her

with a stern glare.

"I'd only be disappointed if you didn't follow your heart. It would go against everything we teach here. Life works in these mysterious ways... The guides, the energies, they're always working to try and help us on our path. If you deny that, when you know it to be true in your bones? Well, that would mean that *I* would have let *you* down. All these years would've been a waste."

Riley's eyebrows furrowed as she tried to make sense of his words. "But...I don't understand. António and the triplets... The scandal. It wrecked you. I remember it."

"António couldn't keep his snake in the cage. That is completely different." He touched his hand to his chest. "I know you feel with this. And with everything you've been through, I'm relieved that it can still experience these things so deeply." A warm smile spread across his face. "I might be an old man now, but I still know love when I see it. You've been different these last few weeks. It's wonderful to see you happy."

He tapped her hand and then moved away to drink from his mug, as though the things he'd just said were completely everyday and not a healing medicine to Riley's soul. She followed suit, savouring the warm tea as it slid down her throat.

He set his mug down. "If you still want to leave the island, that is your decision. You know I would never stand in the way of your path, wherever that leads." A sparkle returned to his eyes. "However, I may have another proposition for you."

Riley's stomach clenched, her grip tightening on the mug. "What is it?"

"I've been running the course for twenty years now. You're not the only one who can feel change pulling at their windsails."

Riley's spine shot straight. "No, Danilo! You can't leave."

He chuckled, the sound reverberating in his throat. "I'm not leaving. Sandy Springs is my beating heart. I'll just take a step back and enjoy some more of the quiet."

Relief flooded her for a moment. But his steady gaze refused to give anything away. "What are you saying?" she asked.

"You know the island inside out, love her like I do. There's no one I would trust more to lead the course, inject some fresh life into it."

"You…you want me to be the manager?" She could hardly string the sentence together.

"If that's the way you want to phrase it." He grinned. "Yes."

She rubbed her hands over her face. Danilo trusted her? Wanted her to run things? *What?* She'd just come to terms with her time at Sandy Springs coming to an end. This news sent everything back into a spin. Maybe the fumes from the fire had propelled her into a long, deep sleep? Or did Romeo pick the wrong type of berries for the punch again?

"Should I take your extended silence as an

acceptance or a refusal?" he teased.

"No. No. This is great. Amazing. I just…What about Ella?"

Riley couldn't do this without her. More than that, she didn't want to. She didn't want a future without Ella.

He eyed her and arched an eyebrow. "I'm sure someone as outgoing as Ella wouldn't have any trouble finding a suitable role here on the course."

Riley's jaw almost fell off its hinges. "You mean you're okay with this?"

"All I've ever wanted for you is to find your happiness again. To break the cycle that chains you to the past." He nodded, his hand tapping hers. "She has a big heart."

"She does." She smiled, thinking about the way she'd left her. Curled up in Riley's sheets with Ziggy between her legs. Could that be her new normal? For her place to become *their* place? She finished her drink and stood, feeling a little uneasy on her feet. "I need to speak to Ella first. But wow. Thank you, Danilo. For believing in me. For understanding."

"It's my pleasure." He collected their mugs and set them in the sink before joining her by the door. He placed a hand on her shoulder, those gentle eyes studying hers.

Without overthinking it, Riley wrapped her arms around him. His scent mingled with the citrus smell of the bergamot, and she breathed out a sigh of relief when he hugged her back. Tears welled in her eyes again, but this time for a different reason.

She was accepted; she was loved.

When they parted, Riley caught the glimmer of emotion shining in his eyes, too. Before she started bawling completely, she said goodbye and stepped out into the sunshine. Now, she needed to talk to Ella.

Riley had never even given it half a thought. The two of them staying on the island had been such an impossibility. Would Ella feel the same? Would she leave England behind for good?

And what if the answer was no? What then?

EPILOGUE

Ella – Eight months later

"Okay, Zigs, cross your little cat toes." Ella eyed her adopted son as he observed her from the safety of the garden wall. "This time, it's going to work."

His green eyes betrayed his indifference as he turned away to begin cleaning himself.

Ella blew out a focused breath, peeking back inside the window to check everything was still dark. She didn't want to wake Riley on the first day of her new job. She'd been such a jitty ball of nerves, Ella wanted to make sure she had the best possible start to the morning.

She plucked at her wet pyjama top, the sticky citrus scent of the oranges filling her nostrils. *This shouldn't be this hard.* With a silent prayer to her turkey guide, she turned the dials, and the blender started to whir. *Easy...easy.* She inched it higher, and it let out a whooshing noise, firing juice up into the brightening sky.

"No, no, no." She slapped her hand on top of the fountain, and Ziggy jumped down to sniff at the juice covering the patio. "Fuck's sake." She should've paid more attention to Riley when she'd shown her how to use it, but, well, Ella was easily distracted by her strong arms.

The door to the patio swung open, and Ella's stomach dropped.

"No!" Ella flailed her arms, and more juice shot up, hitting her in the face. "You're not supposed to be up yet."

Riley pulled the door open fully, her eyes following the extension lead through the window, then the stains on the patio, before landing back on Ella. "What are you doing?" Her mouth curled with amusement as she turned off the machine and pulled a strand of orange peel out of Ella's hair.

"I wanted to make you fresh juice, but I didn't wanna wake you, so I moved it out here." She huffed, shaking her head. "But the juice won't stay in the damn thing."

"You're adorable." She grabbed her hands, tugging her upright so she could plant a kiss on her mouth. Ella swooned, and Riley licked her lips. "You really have got oranges...everywhere."

"I think it's broken."

"You're missing an important piece that goes in the top. Which stops it from looking like you've massacred a grove of innocent oranges."

"Where? I wanted to surprise you."

Riley grinned. "Well, mission accomplished." She ducked inside to fetch the missing piece that must've been hiding from Ella and slotted it in the top.

Ella rolled her eyes, and Riley leaned in to kiss the corner, making her giggle.

"Try it now."

Ella switched the machine on, and the blender whirred, keeping all the contents inside. "Show off," she muttered.

After they'd shared fresh orange juice, watching the sun rise higher over the gentle sea, Ella jumped in the shower to wash the fruit remnants out of her hair. Her own belly tingled with nerves. As much as this was a monumental day for Riley, it was for her, too.

The eight months since their agreement to stay on the island had flown by. Truthfully, the decision to swap England for the beautiful shores of Portugal wasn't a hard one for Ella, and she'd practically leapt at Riley to kiss her face off. Sure, she missed Winnie and her family, but video calls helped lessen the distance—she'd even seen her mother *more* since living abroad. The time apart from Riley in the beginning was difficult too, but the space just affirmed everything she already knew. She was hopelessly in love with her.

They'd worked tirelessly updating the island in the quieter winter months, working with the locals to fix some of the abandoned structures on the cliffs into usable areas and giving them a new burst of life. This was Ella's biggest work project ever, and Riley's support and unwavering trust gave her the confidence to push herself. Her marketing and design experience came in handy when updating the course materials, and her new advertising strategy had them already sold out for the year. To say Senhor Arenoso was pleased with Ella would be an understatement.

She was pretty damn pleased with herself too.

She towel-dried her hair, letting the natural humidity shape it into waves over her shoulders, then slipped on the dress she'd been saving—a red knee-length floaty number that hugged her curves and pushed up her breasts. Matching red lipstick coated her lips, and she gave herself a smile in the mirror before stepping out of the bathroom.

Riley pulled her brand-new uniform over her head—another part of Ella's rebranding process—and ran her fingers through her hair. Ella had suggested they switch to blue for the uniform, Riley's favourite colour, and the fresh look seemed to give her a shot of confidence.

"Ready to go, boss?"

The teasing lilt to Ella's voice made Riley turn her head, and her mouth dropped.

That was exactly the reaction she'd been hoping for.

Ella twirled her hips, the dress swaying around her thighs. Riley's eyes roamed her hungrily, and she raised an eyebrow. "You keep looking at me like that, and we're gonna be late."

"I'm sure they'll wait five minutes," Riley said,

closing the distance between them and roaming her hands over Ella's waist. "Maybe ten."

"Cheeky."

Riley kissed her, and they melted together, her mouth soft and inviting. Ella would never tire of that first brush of their lips. The soft curve of Riley's mouth and how it fit so perfectly against hers. She pulled away, breaking the kiss, but Riley held her firmly by the hips.

Ella brushed a thumb over Riley's mouth. "You're getting my lipstick all over you."

"I don't mind."

Her eyes flicked over her with amusement. "What will people think?"

"That I can't keep my hands off you? And they'd be right. I love you. I don't care what people think." She kissed her again, slipping her tongue into her mouth. Just a little tease that made Ella groan.

Ella pulled away once more. "I love you too. But we can't be late. You can do whatever you want to me afterwards." She traced a fingertip up Riley's sternum, watching her inhale. "How about that…boss?"

Riley grinned, dimples forming in her cheeks. "You've got yourself a deal."

Hand in hand, they walked down the steps and onto the dusty pathway leading to the courtyard. They passed friendly faces, each offering their congratulations. With every one, Ella's anticipation grew.

"You've got this," she said, feeling the same energy buzzing around Riley. She pressed a kiss to her knuckles as they rounded the top of the hill.

Riley tilted her head back, letting the sun's warm rays on her face, and Ella mirrored her. Sporadic cirrus clouds swirled in the blue sky above them, dissipating as they drifted along the breeze. Riley's favourites.

"Look." Ella bumped Riley's shoulder, and she followed the tip of her finger to a cloud above their heads. "That one looks like Cher. See the long hair down her back?"

Riley chuckled, squinting to try and see Ella's vision. "Mm. I don't know. I'm getting more of a horse than Cher."

"Do you think the cloud believes in life after love?" Ella bit her cheek.

Riley nudged her with her elbow. "Shut up, you eejit."

Below them, some of the locals had gathered on the stone flags, chatting among themselves. Once they spotted Riley and Ella walking towards them, cheers erupted from the courtyard. Senhor Arenoso stood among the group, and when he laid eyes on them, the biggest grin spread across his face.

"*Bom dia.*" He embraced Riley and gave Ella a kiss on the cheek. "You ready?"

The group descended the steps towards Senhor Arenoso's hut and the cliffs, winding down the hillside. The flora bloomed, dotting the greenery with purple and blue flowers. The light breeze tousled Ella's hair, and she threaded her fingers through Riley's, inhaling the salty sea air.

When they arrived at the renovated cabin nestled in the rockface, freshly painted white, the view stretched for miles ahead of them. Birds ferried between the cliff faces, the sun casting white reflections across the gentle waves.

Ella turned to Riley, noticing the moisture gathering in her eyes. "You deserve this."

"Thanks, Ells." She returned her smile and gave her a small nod, and Ella joined the small group of locals excited about the grand opening, leaving Riley with Senhor Arenoso.

Ella greeted everyone in her broken Portuguese. She was getting progressively better, but somehow, she didn't mind so much that it took time.

Her gaze fell on the cabin. They'd spent the last few months fixing the old storage space, fitting new windows and clearing out the debris, repairing the roof and ordering the new stock. Ella was actually pretty decent with a hammer; who knew? It'd been a busy but quiet few weeks without any guests, finalising everything for the new course, but they were more than ready for the fresh wave of people due on a plane tomorrow. Ella's family were also due to visit soon, and she couldn't wait to see them. But for now, it was time to put their hard work into practice.

Senhor Arenoso clapped his hands together, quieting the group. Without a word, he rested his hand on Riley's shoulder, passed her the scissors and bowed out of the way to stand with the others.

Ella's attention landed on Riley, and her heart squeezed.

A year ago, Riley had never dreamed of sharing her paintings with anyone. Now, as part of some of their changes to the course, she had her very own studio. Her very own studio for teaching classes.

Tears pricked Ella's eyelids, while pride burst in her chest.

Riley's gaze moved over the friendly faces before finding Ella's. Ever since they'd shared that terrible first kiss—if you can even count giving someone mouth-to-mouth as a first kiss—Riley had left a mark on her. They'd tried, pointlessly, to fight their connection, but it was clear that the guides had other plans. She'd challenged her, opened her eyes, helped her to heal and move forward. Ella knew she could do anything as long as the two of them were together.

The dolphin and the turkey. What an unlikely, perfectly imperfect pair.

Riley grinned and slipped the ribbon between the scissors. Lifting her gaze, she blew out a breath before snipping the silk in two. Applause thundered around her, and Ella ran to wrap her arms around her neck, planting a soft kiss on her mouth.

Sandy Springs was officially under new management.

THE END

If you enjoyed this story, please do leave a review and let me know. Reviews and sharing/engaging on social media really make such a huge difference to indie authors like myself. The more support we get, the more novels we can write, and the more books there will be to read! If you got this far, I'm so humbled by your support, thank you.

ACKNOWLEDGEMENTS

Thank you so much for reading! I hope you enjoyed Ella and Riley's story. I truly loved dreaming this up, and I'm so excited for the Sandy Springs adventures to continue. The idea was sparked by the Arctic Monkey's song 'Piledriver Waltz', and I couldn't get the image of this poor woman (#poorella), constantly getting hit back, and facing disaster after disaster, out of my head. Ultimately, I wanted to write a story reflecting on self-love and accepting yourself for who you are. As much as I adore romance—as I hope is obvious from my job hahaha—I think finding peace with yourself is so important for other areas of your life to flourish. It's not something that comes easy, and is a constant work in progress, but if you take anything from this story, I hope that you know that who you are is, and always will be, enough <3

I'm always a little sad when a story comes to an end, but this time, there's another book on the way! Ella and Riley won't be the main characters, but they will definitely cameo, which I'm looking forward to.

Now for the thank yous. This story wouldn't be where it is today without my wonderful beta readers, editor Helena, and proofreader Imogen—thank you so much for all your input and hard work. You're true superstars. Another big thank you to my ARC team! I love getting to know you all with each release, and your excitement and enthusiasm helps squash the anxiety around release day. I hope you know how much I appreciate you.

Another huge thank you to all the lovely people for supporting me on Patreon. I love being able to share my WIPs with you. An extra special mention to Adrienne, Andy, Amanda, Christiane, Chance, Josh, Nix, Shannon, Tammy, and Tun for being Sapphic champions of the world! Thank you for all your support and encouragement. It humbles me every day that you want to read my work (even it its uglier forms) and accompany me through this journey, book-to-book. There aren't enough words to express how much I value you. Thank you, thank you, thank you.

My next release is book two of the Sandy Springs series, and I'm aiming to release on the back end of summer. My WIPs are uploaded to Patreon weekly, along with some other fun benefits. If you're interested in checking it out and joining the club, my username is @emilywrightwriter.

Thank you to my girlfriend, Laura, for putting up with all my blabbering and panics and late-night stresses. I couldn't do this without you.

Last but not least, thank *you*, lovely reader, for taking the time to check out my story. Writing Sapphic romance books is all I've ever wanted to do. Thank you so much for your support, you're making dreams come true (and hey, that rhymed!)

Em x

ABOUT THE AUTHOR

Emily Wright is a dog-loving, book-sniffing, ukulele-playing author who lives in Barnsley in the UK. When she isn't attached to her computer writing, she loves the outdoors, especially the crash of the ocean and starry night skies that make her feel obsolete. She drinks far too much tea and eats an unthinkable amount of Bourbon biscuits but burns it off chasing her two naughty Spaniels around the house.